Notes for a Memoir

Janet Jeppson Asimov

Notes for a Memoir

on

Isaac Asimov,

Life,

and Writing

 **Prometheus Books**

59 John Glenn Drive
Amherst, New York 14228-2197

Published 2006 by Prometheus Books

Inquiries should be addressed to
Prometheus Books
59 John Glenn Drive
Amherst, New York 14228–2197
VOICE: 716–691–0133, ext. 207
FAX: 716–564–2711
WWW.PROMETHEUSBOOKS.COM

10 09 08 07 06   5 4 3 2 1

Library of Congress Cataloging-in-Publication Data

Asimov, Janet Jeppson.
    Notes for a memoir : on Isaac Asimov, life, and writing / by Janet Jeppson Asimov.
        p. cm.
    Includes bibliographical references.
    ISBN 1–59102–405–6 (alk. paper)
    1. Asimov, Isaac, 1920– 2. Asimov, Janet. 3. Authors, American—20th
century—Biography. 4. Science fiction—Authorship. I. Title.

PS3551.S5Z519 2006
813'.54—dc22

                                                                      2006003368

Printed in the United States on acid-free paper

DEDICATED TO MY FRIENDS, IN-LAWS, AND RELATIVES—
with much gratitude for what you've meant to me over
the years, and with many apologies for leaving almost all
of you out of these notes.

CONTENTS

INTRODUCTION

This book is a series of notes, mainly about the human imagination, the sense of identity, the compulsion to write, and Isaac Asimov, who was good at all of them.

There's a lot of Isaac here, and not merely because that's what publishers want. His life and mine overlapped for only a few years, but I'm grateful for that happiness.

The book is also about me, and includes a few of my published but uncollected stories and articles.

I've quoted from a few books—please see the bibliography for the neatly alphabetized origins of quoted material.

I have tried to avoid verbal diarrhea about the crap of life. This will undoubtedly disappoint readers who enjoy wallowing in the unpleasantness of their own or other people's lives, hoping that a focus on the worst will magically render it impotent.

I've also tried to keep in mind the words of the sage, Russell Baker: *the computer, enabling a writer effortlessly to include absolutely everything, is a priceless tool for writers to pride themselves on showing the reader no mercy.*

Not to worry. I can't and don't want to remember everything or to write about all that I do remember.

1
IMAGINATION

Most young children love to be told stories that end with that imaginative lie—"they lived happily ever after." I was one of those children, and so was Isaac.

We belonged to the generation that grew up in the Great Depression and were teenagers or young adults during World War II. That generation had good evidence for knowing that there are no permanently happy endings, but we hoped and worked for happy lives.

I firmly believe that imagination, when not giving us idiotic ideas and fears, adds to the happiness of life. It even enables us to shuttle in and out of what could be called a private virtual reality.

This is important to most humans because, as Stephen Jay Gould said (and I've forgotten where), we *organize the world as a set of tales.*

Whether the tales are classified as poetry, fiction, or nonfiction, they usually touch on the uniquely human capacity for knowing and worrying about the past and the future. As the poet Robert Burns expressed it in *To a Mouse*, "But Och! I backward cast me e'e, On prospects drear! An' forward, tho' I canna see, I guess an' fear!"

Isaac had this to say about it [in a letter]:

"Burns laments that the mouse whose nest he turned up with his plow is concerned only with present sorrow while he himself can look back with grief and forward with dread.

"*Homo sapiens* alone of all the known objects in the universe can look forward to inevitable death; he alone can sigh for the might-have-beens. It is the penalty of humanity. Shall we accept the gifts of humanity;

the consciousness of beauty; the exaltation of abstractions; the knowledge that makes gods of us;—and not accept the penalty, too?

"To refuse the penalty is to refuse the gifts; to live in a false world of our own making (whether . . . of the saints and prophets [Isaac first typed 'profits,' crossed it out, wrote 'prophets' and in the margin wrote 'Freudian slip'], or . . . of day-dreaming) is to deprive ourselves of the real world—and the real world, with all its faults, has a grandeur and glory for which there is no substitute.

"No vision of God and heaven ever experienced by the most exalted prophet can, in my opinion, match the vision of the universe as seen by Newton or Einstein—and I would not exchange the vision of the Galaxy as I have seen it in writing my novels for the vision of the Virgin. It is only by abandoning the false that we can achieve the true, but oh, how hard it must be—

"In fact, how hard it *is*, for I have had my illusions from which I have labored to disengage myself."

We labor (well, we ought to labor) to see through our illusions, for otherwise the human imagination has a miserable time trying to cope with the problems inherent in being human. Some of these are:

a) The biological and psychological need for relatedness, which is accompanied by the distressing question: but just how do I relate to this puzzling universe and all these strange beings in it?

b) Those horrible intimations of mortality. I'm really going to end? Everything will end? A young female fan of Isaac's once sobbed on the phone because she'd read his article about the Earth being fried when the Sun becomes a red giant. She said she couldn't stand the idea that everything she knew would end some day. Isaac tried to console her by saying it would be billions of years from now but she went on crying.

c) The (usually repressed) fear of meaninglessness. What does it all mean? Who thought it up and why? What is my function, my place in the universe, and what in hell am I supposed to do about it?

Please don't remind me that there are zillions of other problems stemming from the human ability to think, remember, and dread. For instance: Does the meat I'm eating suffer when being killed and should I eat it? Will

I get on the hit list of a fundamentalist if I mention that I'm an agnostic? Is the toilet about to explode or is it just leaking? Are there a set number of potholes in Manhattan streets and do they move them around at night?

But back to the short list. During my thirty-odd (often quite odd) years as a psychiatrist and psychoanalyst, it seemed to me that under all the trivia, most people tend to use their imaginations to worry about relatedness—problem (a).

I happen to think that the problem of meaninglessness is ultimately more pertinent to the human condition. After all, animals relate to each other. They don't imagine anything about their own mortality, much less sit down and ponder about the meaning of it all.

I will therefore state right off the bat that I imagine that although the universe is basically meaningless, it acquires meaning when intelligent beings evolve and use their imaginations to think up purposes (small p) for life.

I stole this from the physiologist Sir Charles Sherrington (see Endnotes), who said that while the purpose of all life has always been to get more life, humans can decide to achieve not more but better life. I also agree with Sherringon that humans are (so far!) the one part of nature that's trying hard to understand itself. This does not comfort most people as much as a belief in an omnipotent deity who presumably knows what he or she is doing.

The imagination can make patterns—most often in words—that seem to give connection, security, meaning, and immortality. Techniques for making patterns differ from one human being to the next, and what suits one talent does not suit another.

I once asked my husband what sort of pictures came into his head when he was creating a story. Isaac frowned.

"No pictures. I have problems describing my characters because I have only a vague notion of what they look like. I hear them talking and I record the conversation."

"You only hear them talking? You don't see them?"

Isaac was always impressed by my ability to remember faces, read a map, and locate things in the apartment.

He said, "No. You're the one with a talent for visualization."

"True—I can just close my eyes and a movie of what I'm imagining rolls inside my head. But it's so hard to put the damn thing into words, which are such a bother."

"Janet! Words are *everything!*"

Words did mean everything to Isaac, and while he used words (and I favored pictures) to travel in a private virtual reality, there are drawbacks, especially when your imagination goes into overdrive.

Isaac once called me after he'd driven somewhere to give a talk. He sounded shaken.

"What's the matter!"

"I'm fine."

"But what's the *matter?*"

"Well, I obviously drove here safely, which means that my reflexes were working just fine, but I was busy thinking about the plot for my new novel and I arrived with absolutely no memory of how I got here."

Such immersion does feel like another life, yet if a relatively sane person is interrupted while in the throes of imagination, he-she usually knows the difference between what's real and what's imagined.

It pays to remember, however, that "reality" is usually perceived through a haze of cultural and personal distortions which often makes it almost as fictional as that which the imagination creates.

In childhood, some of the haze surrounding me was produced by the WASP family penchant for euphemisms and careful concealment of Personal Matters. It's probably no accident that I became a psychiatrist and psychoanalyst, trying to help patients clarify their inner and outer experiences so that they could become more skilled at helping themselves, and get rid of me.

Cultural distortions have a long history. When the cave paintings were being created (probably by women who hoped that their men were out hunting dinner and not females of neighboring tribes), the artists no doubt chanted spells. Even now, creativity often comes with the sensation of a spell being cast.

During one of the early years after Isaac died, I was asked to contribute to an anthology of modern fantasies based on Lewis Carroll's *Alice* books. Stuck for a plot, I looked at Tenniel's illustrations and realized that the garb of the White Queen reminded me of the down coat I'd been wearing for many winters. So I wrote about the coat, expecting it to be a humorous story. But I was a new widow and it wasn't.

It's hard to explain the intensity of immersion in imagination to people who don't use it much. There are two types of immersion:

a) Unplanned: Your mind just lets itself go into some aspect of a private virtual reality without any conscious effort on your part. This can be the ordinary sort of daydreaming almost everyone does, full of primitive wishes, hostility, and desires.

For instance, a large female much younger than you are steps on your toe in the supermarket and a vivid image appears in your mind that she has just been totally obliterated by that pyramid of soup cans collapsing upon her. You try not to implement this imagined scenario by pushing said pyramid in her direction, and feel very guilty about having such aggressively uncharitable thoughts.

Or you're in a taxi, stuck in traffic, and feeling frantic because you're supposed to meet people at a specific time at a posh restaurant. Suddenly you notice that you've imagined that a powerful alien from outer space is beaming all the other cars—especially the ones that are honking—to a planet without any roads. And at the same time, you notice that your stomach is rumbling with hunger and your brain has conjured up a seven-course meal of incredible deliciousness that is just out of reach because said superalien is eating it in order to get energy for all those beam-outs . . .

Isaac was usually immersed in his imagination—which was not always practical. He would arrange to meet me somewhere and, after his usual difficulty in finding the geographical location even if it was on the next block, he would stand there working out his latest plot while imagining that he saw me coming from every direction, a technique which made him anxious because by then he wasn't sure he remembered what I looked like.

b) Planned: This is conscious, deliberate use of imagination for many purposes, such as an effort to structure life, map out the future, escape unpleasant reality, or work on the next book which you must finish because you've already signed a contract and if you don't sit down at the computer you'll have nightmares about it instead of just fooling around with daydreams.

I admit that no matter how good one's imagination is, it's still hard to put the lid, even temporarily, on serious worries and/or grief. All too many people use drugs or drink to accomplish this, but with mere imagination you can often accomplish mental escape for a while. It certainly is better to avoid drugs and drink by just messing around in some plot other than the one you're living. Preferably on some other planet.

Or you can suspend (perhaps transcend is a better word) conscious thinking, including the imagination, and try one of the various techniques so much in the news these days.

I took two courses in biofeedback and have studied Zen and meditation techniques. I know how to meditate and can mentally warm up my hands so that my autonomic nervous system calms down, but I frequently find that imaginary plots work better.

I've managed all these various techniques, including the retreat to a planned private virtual reality, when under rather severe physical or emotional stress, but for some reason they all fail (for me) at certain times.

I will NOT list the times, except to mention that one of them is when the phone rings, which explains why I turn the phone off at night or during calming techniques. As a doctor's daughter, I was trained to hear and answer the phone no matter what.

Once some relatives came late to the house when my parents and young brother were away and I—a teenager—was taking care of the cat, the dog, and the garden. The relatives shouted beneath my window (this was way before medical school, when I became addicted to sleeping with earplugs) and finally drove back to an all-night gasoline station to use the phone (this was WAY before cell phones). The phone rang softly, down the hall in my parents' bedroom, and through my closed door I heard it and woke up instantly.

Those of us with an overenergetic imagination don't understand how other people get along without it, and we tend to ignore the fact that it can fill life with fears about the worst happening. The rewards, however, outweigh the pain. Isaac wrote in a letter:

"I have a diseased imagination. It is hypertrophied in the first place and over-sensitive and beyond my control. I once wrote a story called *Dreaming is a Private Thing* in which I tried to express the complete helplessness of the overimaginative person in the face of his imagination. . . .

"I would not abandon my imagination. It makes it possible for me to write (and my straight science is as much dependent on imaginative development as was my science-fiction) and it gives me an added richness of dimension to life."

Children who enjoy using imagination in planned daydreams (often complete with plots) are usually just entertaining themselves and perhaps their friends, without any plan to be professional writers. Nevertheless, a good many people who write for publication, whether they make a living at it or not, started out with a childhood full of planned daydreams, the kind that's deliberately created as if one were writing a story.

When I was eleven, I read L. M. Montgomery's somewhat autobiographical novels about a young writer named Emily, who also made up stories in her planned daydreams, so I knew I was not so weird after all. I told stories to my friends, and we acted them out, sometimes in costume.

Isaac also told himself stories when he was a child, and he also started telling them to other people. But he started to write them down. In *It's Been a Good Life* he recounts how—when he was eleven—he wrote a story and told it to another boy. When he stopped talking, the other boy said, "Can I borrow the book when you've finished reading it?"

That (I say enviously) is the most galvanizing praise a would-be young writer can get.

Isaac continued: "I was astonished. I had either neglected to make it clear to him, or he had failed to understand, that I was *writing* the book. . . . The implied compliment staggered me, and from that day on, I secretly took myself seriously as a writer."

Isaac was already a writer who responded to praise with determination to continue. The imagination became a tool he would stick to no matter what.

2
IMAGINATION AND READING

Isaac and I both believed that the imaginary beings invented by other people not only enrich one's life, but feel like old friends to whom one can return from time to time to say hello, to reexperience their adventures, and to see what new things one's own continued life experiences bring to the reading.

Some of my favorite imaginary beings are Kabumpo, Eeyore, Mr. Mole, the Psammead, Marco Loristan, Emily of New Moon, Mehitabel, Miss Marple, Jeeves, Lord Emsworth, Oliver J. Dragon, Frodo, R. Daneel, Snoopy, Mr. Spock, Data, and our own Norby.

And then, of course—as Isaac was fond of saying—rereading one's own stuff is often pleasurable because it "fits into the grooves of your brain" from which it emerged. It's too embarrassing to reread one's own stuff in public, so Isaac and I always carried reading matter with us, just in case.

During our years of writing science (Isaac all of his writing life) it was important to carry around the latest science articles in order to keep up with the world of science. Now that I'm retired I still do it, or take with me a paperback novel. When standing in a post office line, for instance, it raises blood pressure less to enter a private virtual world (anybody's) than to grind one's teeth while staring at the woman ahead, who's sending ten packages return receipt requested.

I told Isaac how mystifying it is to me that most people just wait in line, without reading anything, even the posters on the walls.

He said, "Most people stand still and look at space because the engine of their minds idles at such low speeds that they are not very conscious." As far as I could tell, Isaac's mind never idled at low speed.

History and science—in his own books or those of other writers—were tremendous escapes for him. He had a genuine passion for history, but science meant more, for he felt that an imagination devoted to science could help save the world.

We were once discussing realms of fantasy, like those we'd known in childhood (our own or those in the Buck Rogers and Flash Gordon comic strips, or the Jules Verne stories in books borrowed from the library).

I said that as a child I preferred fantasy to the stories and cartoons about so-called reality, even when the author-illustrator was trying to be funny. It seemed to me that Dale Arden was better off adventuring with Flash Gordon than Blondie was in coping with Dagwood.

Isaac agreed absentmindedly, but when I said that nowadays lucky kids have the romance of fantasy blended with real science, like the thrill of a rocket soft-landing on the moon, his eyes lit up.

Isaac said, "Yes! Science, as the great fantasy of our time—the first fantasy made real! I must use that some day."

That's the idea—enjoying the imagination (one's own or that of others) and USING it.

You'll notice that many of my favorite imaginary beings are from the books I read when young and from the children's novels I ended up writing. Isaac also wrote many books for children and told stories to his own children when they were very young. Here's one of them (from a letter):

"For the last few weeks I have been conned into telling Robyn a long, rambling, incoherent, senseless story in order to con *her* into eating her breakfast without a daily fist-fight in which she is always the winner.

"The basic plot of this story involves the trek to the big city on the part of Cyril the Squirrel, who has been elected by the animals of the forest to take their life savings in order to purchase ears for Bun Rabbit (who unfortunately lacks ears, and who plays no part in the story).

"On his way Cyril the Squirrel picks up an ally in the form of Sherm the Worm, who is now rapidly taking over as the real hero of the story, for Robyn is wide-eyed at all his great feats of derring-do. Most recently, Cyril the Squirrel in attempting to pile up his wealth played the pin-ball machines against Sherm's advice and lost all his money. In the disorders that ensued the police arrived and swore Sherm the Worm in as a special deputy because they needed someone to creep through a keyhole and spy on some gangsters.

"This Sherm the Worm did, and a recent episode ended suddenly with a gangster throwing open the door, pointing a big gun at Sherm the Worm and saying 'So!!!! A spy!!!' and poor Robyn was very perturbed and reassured herself by saying that Sherm the Worm was very small and that if the gangster shot he would miss.

"The only thing that bothers me in all this is that I can't stand the thought of worms. The kids may be interested but every morning I sit there revolted at my own story—like the time Cyril the Squirrel disguised himself as a furpiece so as to keep from being trampled on in the subway, and someone said to the woman wearing the make-believe furpiece, 'Yech, you've got a worm on it.' The kids laughed and I sat very still, fighting nausea.

"Oh, what we artists won't do for a story.

"Anyway, Sherm the Worm has just received a medal for his part in the spying activity but had to give it back because when they pinned it on him, it was so heavy it pinned him to the ground.

"It occurs to me I will have to bring in some love interest; Sue the Gnu, perhaps."

Alas, for most of the generations younger than mine, the virtual realities of television are more popular than those found in reading.

Incidentally, the virtual realities from reading are *private*. Each person brings something different to the experience, and although you can talk about it with each other, you can't possibly describe *exactly* what a character looks and sounds like to you.

Sometimes the first illustrations you see in a book are much closer to the author's descriptions than later ones, and it's rare that movies made from books show what you conjured up in your head.

I was dismayed by the fact that the movie *Wizard of Oz*, which came out years after Baum's book, had a dark-haired Dorothy instead of a blonde—but "Over the Rainbow" (words written by Isaac's friend E. Y. Harburg) reconciled me to Judy Garland.

In retrospect, it seems to me that imagination and reading came easier to my and Isaac's generation. Although we were too poor to buy books, we both frequented the public libraries. Our imaginations were also stimulated by movies, stories on radio, and comic books (which Isaac could read because his father's candy store sold them, but which I seldom saw). And of course we also had make-believe—which many kids used in games. I'm told that for youngsters nowadays, computer games do stimulate the imagination. I hope that's true.

My childhood was full of imagination (about the only thing the Great Depression didn't stifle). In 1931, after my family settled in New Rochelle, New York, we lived in a walk-up apartment in a neighborhood with lots of children (all of them poor like us), near Hudson Park on Long Island Sound.

In those days, a suburban apartment was not much like city living. In addition to the park, children could play in plenty of vacant lots, some containing foundations of houses unfinished due to the Great D, and also on the uncrowded sidewalks and streets.

Most of our playing (and reading) was unsupervised by adults. Isaac and I certainly were unsupervised, although I do remember my father pretending to read a book on the front porch (of the house we rented when I was ten) while I learned to ride my bicycle, going up and down the sidewalk, falling off and trying again.

Although I envy the modern child's easy access to knowledge via television and the Internet, I look at all the expensive gadgets they have and wonder what happens inside their heads.

I pity their harassed parents who must take them to and from school and every appointment, including "play dates." It's sad that the world is so crowded and dangerous that many modern parents feel driven to supervise every facet of their children's lives. Nevertheless, research has shown that children, even infants, need to be alone at times. They must have the chance to integrate emotions and experience; to complete actions on their own; to explore their bodies and to daydream; to create and sing sad little songs that help them accept the complexity of life.

I not only told myself stories, especially at bedtime when I couldn't get to sleep, I played in the make-believe games of other children and made up some of my own.

At Trinity School (where I stayed until I was ten), I spent recess telling stories to schoolmates and drawing maps of the story action on the graveled yard. I was always making maps for stories; and now when I reread Tolkien, I follow everything on the wonderful maps that have been made to go with the books.

In my neighborhood, the children also put on what could be called plays (without stage or scenery) from stories that were heavily influenced by the movies and comic strips. The following is an example—which I probably don't remember with crystalline accuracy, but does it matter?— of what we were like:

He was a neighbor in the apartment building, an older man of six. While our parents played bridge, he and I retreated to his bedroom because he wanted to play the game of showing and not telling. It was winter.

"We'll pretend we're married. I'll get undressed first," he said, removing shirt and knickers and starting on his long underwear, buttoned up to the neck. At this point his mother entered to get a handkerchief.

"The landlord's saving on coal and you'll catch cold," was all she said. That generation was born in Victorian times, but they'd been through the Roaring Twenties.

After she returned to bridge, he resumed work on his buttons. "Aren't you going to take off your clothes?"

At five, I may have been oblivious to the possibility of sin, but I knew when an apartment was freezing. "It's too cold."

He sighed and dressed. "Well, it's Saturday tomorrow and we'll be playing The Game in the morning before we go to the movies. The Good Boys rescue the girls . . ."

"Who are the Good Boys?"

"The ones not being the Bad Boys that day."

The next morning boys leapt over the rusty chain strung across the entrance to our building's feeble excuse for a courtyard, pranced into the street (there was little auto traffic and the milkman's horse was kindly), and chased the girls who, dutifully captured, sat on a wide ledge near the top of a fence owned by an old man who, it was said, made soda pop— or something (Prohibition ended only in 1933)—in his cellar.

The leader of the Good Boys (sometimes referred to as Dick Tracy) was dark-haired, strong-jawed, and incredibly handsome, like my father. To get near him, I tried to pass myself off as the maid of the girl who played Tess (I knew about maids—rich people in the movies had them), but was told I was too little.

Whatever, the Good Boys did rescue the girls from the Bad Boys. I was only in that neighborhood for about two years, but I remember the fun of The Game. The fun of using the imagination.

It was also comforting to know that under the ongoing misery of the Great D, the world was comprehensible, neatly divided into the Good and the Bad.

When World War II started, it seemed to us that there were no shades of gray. Hitler was evil, an evil that was not in anyone's imagination. Is it any wonder why so many of us senior citizens have a modicum of nostalgia about those vanished times?

Isaac—six years older than I—was a chemist in a war research facility during World War II, and wrote about it in his autobiographies, but he remembered and wrote with deep affection about his childhood in Brooklyn, where he made good use of imagination, his own and that of others.

Although Brooklyn is part of New York City, in Isaac's childhood it was more like my part of New Rochelle. He read books and thought thoughts in the green sanctuary of the nearby cemetery, or sat in a chair outside the wall of the candy store (from *It's Been a Good Life*):

". . . life is glorious when it is happy; days are carefree when they are happy; the interplay of thought and imagination is far superior to that of muscle and sinew. Let me tell you, if you don't know it from your own experience, that reading a good book, losing yourself in the interest of words and thoughts, is for some people (me, for instance) an incredible intensity of happiness.

"If I want to recall peace, serenity, pleasure, I think of myself on those lazy summer afternoons, with my chair tipped back against the wall, the book on my lap, and the pages softly turning. There may have been, at certain times in my life, higher pitches of ecstasy, vast moments of relief and triumph, but for quiet, peaceful happiness, there has never been anything to compare to it."

Isaac's love of reading started as soon as he taught himself to read, long before he went to school. In the first volume of his autobiography— *In Memory Yet Green*—he said:

"I read omnivorously and without guidance [all the classics]. Unaware that they were classics I was *supposed* to read and should therefore avoid, I enjoyed them and read and reread them, often beginning again as soon as I had finished, until I had almost memorized them (I was so ignorant that it was years before I discovered that Achilles was not pronounced ATCH-illz.) . . .

"I had to read nonfiction too, because at least one of the two books I was allowed [by the public library in the thirties] had to be nonfiction, and I would read *anything* rather than nothing. I found, by experimentation, that history and science fascinated me, so I picked out every book I could get on those subjects.

"And, because I had (and still have) a retentive memory and instant recall, everything I read remained with me and was at my service and made schoolwork all the easier. It was to be many, many years before I learned anything in school that I did not already know."

Some authors moved Isaac no matter how many times he read them. For instance, he always cried when he got to Enobarbus's last speech (in *Antony and Cleopatra*). He cried reading Robert Burns, and said (in *How to Enjoy Writing*), "his poetry always makes me cry. That's my definition of art. If it makes you cry, it must be what the critics say is bad. If it makes you throw up, the critics say it's good."

3
ISAAC

Isaac died at age 72, of the tragic consequences of a blood transfusion. Before that he lived life happily, with imagination, humanism, skepticism, humor, courage, and love. He was unique, and although he's gone, his books keep him alive. In a sense, this is another one of those books.

First as the author of books I loved, then as the friend whose letters added so much to my life, and then as my beloved husband—Isaac filled most of my so-called mature years and made them full of happiness.

He was always interesting, with a sense of humor that hardly ever failed—something I consider vital in friendship and love. We were both rather pleased that people laughingly referred to us as "Darby and Joan"—the happily married elderly couple in an eighteenth-century song. Although we were past middle age, we nevertheless seemed pleased with each other, given to walking with our arms around each other (someone took a photo of us from the back, in Central Park, and it appeared in a newspaper).

The following conversation (which I put in our *How to Enjoy Writing*) exemplifies our marital situation: It's a true story. While laughing, I wrote it down.

JANET: I absolutely adore you.
ISAAC: As well you should.
JANET: Narcissist!
ISAAC: In my case I don't consider narcissism a disease but an expression of good taste.

Isaac's cheerful appreciation of himself, and me, helped me get over my shyness, but I think I will be permanently afraid of being well known (Lindberg's murdered baby has haunted me all my life), so I go around saying that I have a natural bent (i.e., neurotic desire) for cultivating a low profile (I even bought a book on how to do this).

Isaac did not cultivate a low profile. He wrote three very detailed autobiographies, plus very personal essays, headnotes, comments, etc., that reveal him in astonishingly complete ways. And he was a sometimes highly personal speaker on the lecture platform, or anywhere.

A fellow author asked Isaac, "Do you have an interest in the lives of other authors?"

Isaac said, "My main fear in meeting another author is that he'll talk about his writing before I have a chance to talk about mine."

I wrote down a typical Isaac remark made during a lifeboat drill on a cruise ship. We were on the ship because Isaac was one of the speakers. (It's also in *How to Enjoy Writing*.)

OFFICER: Remember that it's women and children first.
ISAAC: And geniuses.
YOUTH: *Young* geniuses.
Isaac laughed, too.

Although Isaac was somewhat old-fashioned in his criteria for the behavior of a wife in the kitchen, he was very Pro-Women's Lib. The following is from a letter:

"I attended a small gathering to meet a woman who's running for state representative from a newly formed district that includes my section of town. She's a liberal Democrat and this newly formed district is 3 to 1 Republican, so she has little chance. . . . I pointed out that she might be hampered by belonging to a minority group.

"She looked surprised and I amplified. 'You're a woman.'

"She smiled and said, 'But women are in the majority.'

"'Yes,' I answered, 'but almost all of them are in the enemy camp. The woman who tries to get somewhere is an oppressed minority, and the worst oppressors are women who are content to be nowhere.'

"Everyone looked uncomfortable (me and my peculiar views!). . . . Anyway, I'm forever preaching women's rights."

That didn't stop him from writing ribald and heavily chauvinistic limericks. Isaac and his friend, the poet John Ciardi, even did some books of ribald limericks. This annoyed me at the time, not because the limericks were lecherous but because I wanted Isaac to spend the time writing another book about his marvelous character, the android robot R. Daneel.

On my birthday, Isaac would often write a funny ribald poem, but occasionally it was clean and serious. He said I shouldn't show these poems to anyone because he was definitely not a poet. But he's been dead for a long time now and I want to share this one:

Love Is a Three-Letter Word

Love does have ecstatic days
    And yet when all is done
Our passion most deserves our praise
    Because our love is *fun*.

Love is good and warm and kind.
    True love will never pall.
In fact I'll say, if you don't mind,
    That love, for me, is *all*.

Our love is just my sort of speed—
    It's fond and sweet and true
But three letter words are all I'll need
    For love is simply *you*.

I admired Isaac's liberal intelligence. He said, "Every nation in the world should agree that in any battle fought, the losing general would be instantly executed. In the event of a threatened war, the military services of either side will claim they're not ready—because the generals can't risk losing a battle."

His good friend Arthur C. Clarke wrote Clarke's Law: "When a distinguished but elderly scientist states that something is possible, he is almost certainly right. When he states that something is impossible, he is very probably wrong."

Isaac added that "when the lay public rallies around an idea that is denounced by the distinguished but elderly scientist and supports that idea with great fervor and emotion—the distinguished but elderly scientist is then, after all, probably right."

He added that "human beings have the habit of being human; which is to say that they believe in that which comforts them."

While comforted by his own uniqueness and brains, Isaac was secretly quite humble. He said:

"When I was a little boy I knew some people who had the 'Book of Knowledge' but my family was far too poor ever to buy me one. Occasionally, I would be in the house of the lucky people who had it and invariably I would sneak over to the book case and—if no one were looking—I would take out one of the volumes and leaf through it. As I think back on it now, I realize that nobody would possibly have minded and that I could probably have received permission to come there and read through it at leisure if I had only asked. Unfortunately it never occurred to me to ask, because it seemed patent . . . that these wonderful books were not meant to be touched by little children. . . .

"So when I was first asked to do a couple of articles for the 'Book of Knowledge,' my first impulse was to refuse because they gave me a very short deadline and God knows I have enough work as is. However, the thought of myself at the age of ten came sharply back to me as though the little boy were someone else with whom I could maintain contact. I was overwhelmed with the thought that somewhere the little boy existed and somehow he would know that the man he grew into was going to write articles for the 'Book of Knowledge' and that he would be very pleased and excited by it. So I agreed to do it."

I can't resist putting in one of my favorite Isaac anecdotes, from a letter and published in *It's Been a Good Life*:

"There is no orgastic pleasure whatever in reading galley proof on a bus . . . the galleys kept slipping this way and that and the motion of the bus kept lulling me to sleep.

"The worst moment I had was when I went to the rear to visit the rest room. I took my galleys with me being too paranoid to leave them on my seat. There is a handhold on the side of the restroom so that you don't get killed while the bus careens. I grabbed hold of it with the same hand that held the galleys.

"Then I waited for something to happen (the mad swaying of the bus back and forth and the certainty of imminent death inhibited the natural urinary process). As I waited, I noticed that my galleys were swinging back and forth with the bus's motion as I held them with two fingers and that if they shook loose they would go *right into the hopper.*

"It took me a tenth of a second to put the galleys down in a safe place, but during that tenth of a second, the vision of those galleys in the hopper seared my soul. I still haven't quite recovered."

With his brain, memory, and verbal skills, Isaac usually did not suffer fools gladly and—especially in his younger days—could be merciless in outwitting people.

Here's Isaac describing to me in a letter how he handled a verbally aggressive male at a party:

"[He was] one of these loud fellows used to dominating all conversations with his coarse wit (very much like myself, you understand). [He] hammered away at me . . . and wanted to know why I wore sideburns; did I think they were aesthetic; did I feel they attracted the opposite sex; was I merely a 'follower' (a supposition he repeated about half a dozen times) who would do anything that was in style. I smiled, answered gently, evaded the issue, did everything in order not to fight back because I have tried to get over my habit of striking back at every attack, real or fancied. But, you know, it didn't look as if he would ever stop and the trouble is with our modern sexual permissiveness that middle-aged people have taken to the casual use of coarse words in mixed company. And this guy was coarse. So I sighed again. I put my right hand on my right sideburn, gently pulled the hair out at right angles so they stretched a full inch or more away from my face and said—

"'Actually, the hair of the sideburns grows to a length proportional to that of the prick. I notice you have a trace of sideburns with very short hairs while mine, you see, are quite long.'

"After that, he remained under control. I *wish* people didn't feel it necessary to prove their intellectual manhood by engaging me in a battle of wits. I am perfectly content to not-fight."

Whatever talent he had for the sharp retort, he was capable of good humor when someone defeated him, as in this example (from *It's Been a Good Life*):

"I was with a group of people . . . and one of them said, 'I saw you on the *David Frost Show.*'

"A young man of nineteen was part of the group and he said, with genial insolence, 'And what did you do, Dr. Asimov? Read commercials?'

"With a haughty determination to squelch the young cockerel at once by a thrust too outrageous to parry, I said, 'Not at all! I was demonstrating sexual techniques.'

"'Oh,' he said, smiling sweetly, 'you remembered?'

"I was wiped out completely."

Isaac was reasonably kind about my various foolishnesses. For instance, when we were still apart and writing letters, I became preoccupied with going to the entire *Ring Cycle* at the Metropolitan Opera, and wrote him the following (please keep in mind that this was before I'd heard Anna Russell's masterful and hilarious song that recounts the entire plot of the *Ring*):

"The whole thing *could* be blamed on women, if you realize that poor old Alberich started the damn thing by reacting badly to his rejection by the Rhine maidens, and poor old Wotan got enmeshed by trying to appease his jealous wife by building Valhalla, which he had to pay for by stealing the ring that Alberich stole, if I make myself clear. Actually, Fricka wanted Wotan to build Valhalla as a way of keeping him home nights. All she accomplished was the whole nasty business of the giants, which led to Alberich's curse. Then, to try to forestall doom, Wotan had to leave home anyway and go procreate—begetting the Valkyries to collect heroes for him, and the Walsung (the incestuous siblings) to produce the biggest hero, his grandson. The whole thing is so ridiculous, so why do I cry at the end?"

Isaac wrote back, "Well, I guess no one is perfect. I'm egocentric, oblivious, loud-mouthed, fat, rude, and libidinous. And you like Wagner. About even, I should say."

We were more kindred souls when it came to Shakespeare, and after listening to a radio version of *Henry IV*, Part One, I wrote to him that "you're supposed to fall in love with Hotspur but I can't—he's played as such a bloody extrovert in this version. Maybe he's supposed to be. I don't know."

Isaac answered (this was before he did his masterwork, *Asimov's Annotated Shakespeare*), "Hotspur *is* an extrovert. He is Prince Hal's foil. Prince Hal is a whole man without *at first* the superficial skin of 'honor.' Hotspur is that skin and *nothing else*. Touch him and he reverberates hollowly. Shakespeare lets you admire Hotspur and be depressed over Prince Hal, then lets Prince Hal put on the skin to show you how much superior is the man to the skin. For when Prince Hal gains honor and reveals himself like the glorious sun, putting the clouds to flight, you suddenly see how worthless and empty the show was without the *substance*. *That's* why you can't fall in love with Hotspur. Only fools can."

Isaac (not I) enjoyed being slightly (he emphasized that) famous but he was—rumor to the contrary—modest about it. I was walking with him on Columbus Avenue when someone stopped us to ask for his autograph. Isaac said, "Am I really who you thought I was?"

When he said to me, "It's so puzzling. In writing, I went from a promising beginner to a grand old man, with little in between. How did it happen?"

I said, "It helps to be a talented genius who works harder than most people."

Isaac smiled.

Fame did have its moments (see his autobiographies or my condensation—*It's Been a Good Life*). I think the following is not in those books.

When coming home on a rainy night from one of the stag dinners he often attended, he and two male buddies tried and failed to get a taxi. They eventually took the subway uptown, Isaac getting out first. The other two men went on to the next stop, but, in between these stops, three huge hulking youths walked up to them, with apparently sinister faces and large powerful hands. Just as Isaac's (elderly) friends were sure they were about to be assaulted and robbed, one of the youths bent forward and said, "Hey, was that *really* Isaac Asimov?"

Even secondhand fame bothered me, but I was pleased when Isaac rushed home to tell me a boy had leaned from a taxi and shouted, "Dr. Asimov, *loved* your wife's book!"

Isaac, naturally, said, "Janet, this nonsense has got to stop!"

People often said to Isaac that they loved his book, and then he'd wonder which book they meant.

Becoming recognizable has its problems. One night we were stuck in an open-air production at the Delacorte Theater, hating it but afraid to leave because Isaac was one of the sponsors of Shakespeare in the Park. Not that this was Shakespeare. It was *The Golem*, which I hope I never have to see again.

As the monster lurched back and forth on the stage, a small bat, apparently confused by the bright lights, fluttered out of Olmsted's masterpiece, over the heads of the actors, to land on the shoulder of the woman sitting in front of us. She screamed.

The befuddled bat took off and fluttered back into the sheltering darkness of Central Park's trees while I looked on enviously. It had escaped.

And Isaac, in his usual carrying voice, said, "That's the best thing that's happened all evening."

Isaac's voice was distinctive, his accent varying from pure Brooklynese (especially when lecturing in a synagogue) to perfect King's English. He loved to give lectures, and in a letter to me during our years of long-distance friendship wrote about that joy.

At that time, he had won his fight for tenure at Boston University Medical School (fully described in his various autobiographies) and his right to keep lecturing to the medical school at least once a year although he received no salary. He was finally supporting himself solely through his writing and public lecturing.

"I gave my lecture at school this morning.

"I slept poorly last night, rather dreading the ordeal, and left at 7:30 so that I could get there well before the 9 A.M. deadline and look over my notes one last time. Before I knew it, it was almost time and I went downstairs.

"I began my lecture by saying 'Once a year the department carefully selects a strategic moment when it is considered safe to entrust me with a lecture. Yesterday, you had a biochemistry examination; this afternoon you will have a physiology examination. Outside it is a dull, gray, miserably rainy day, and to top it off it is Friday the thirteenth—and here I am.'

"There was a roar of laughter and everyone relaxed and I did, too, and was off. With that encouragement I was near the top of my form. At one point, when I mentioned the fact that cattle and sheep afflicted with anemia in the trace-metal deserts of Australia were relieved by administration of impure iron but not of pure iron, because the impurity (cobalt) was what turned the trick, I paused and said, 'And the moral of that is that a little impurity never hurt anyone.' At another point, I mentioned the fact that it was no longer necessary to isolate B_{12} from liver once it was discovered that fecal bacteria could manufacture it in quantity. 'This,' I said, 'proves there is good in everything and allowed the fecal bacteria to earn their fee.'

"Anyway, when I finished there was tremendous applause that continued through a couple of my embarrassed waves of the hand and lasted without interruption until I had left the room and for some time thereafter. So I guess . . . that I have not lost my touch.

"Of course, though, it annoyed me. Before the lecture, I was wishing I were not assigned any. But about half-way through, when I realized that I was enjoying myself tremendously I grew resentful of the fact that I was being prevented from lecturing—especially now that even if they were to offer to let me lecture as once I had, I could not accept. . . ."

The following is from my comments in *Foundation's Friends.*

Isaac has a point of view that makes me glad I know him. For instance, he woke up once with his legs making running motions in the bed. He said, "I dreamt someone told me I was making a good living out of writing, and I said yes I was. Then the person said, 'It's amazing to see someone make all that money out of beaten swords.' I was running to tell you because it instantly struck me that the phrase meant I made my money out of the instruments of peace—the pen is mightier than the sword and thou shalt beat thy swords into plowshares."

A professor of chemistry once wrote Isaac a fan letter praising his books and Isaac answered, "Every author should be judged by his readers and I am proud of mine."

After writing this, Isaac showed it to me, saying, "I'm happy about this." I was, too. It was perfect Isaac.

One more anecdote from *How to Enjoy Writing*:

> ISAAC (on the train): To avoid thinking bad thoughts on trips I can always amuse myself by planning what I'm going to write when I get back to my typewriter. Shall I continue writing my history of the world where Columbus just discovered America on page 750 or shall I work some more on my Bible book where Noah's ark is floating on the flood? Or shall I put the most recent Black Widowers into final copy?
>
> JANET: But your novel . . .
>
> ISAAC: Or should I write my next *F and SF* article or my next editorial for *Asimov's* or should I do the intelligent thing and write my energy piece at a buck a word with only two weeks to deadline?
>
> JANET: Isaac, we're on a trip. Life is a journey, you know.
>
> ISAAC: Life is a journey, but don't worry, you'll find a parking place at the end.

4
JOURNEYS

Yeah, life is a journey and, until that final parking place, there are shorter journeys, some real and many of them virtual. Whether or not they are happy is up to luck and the traveler and imagination.

Come to think of it, are any journeys absolutely real? I agree with Jerre Mangione, who wrote in *The Ship and the Flame*, that aboard a ship "time compresses itself into a single tense; the present . . . he [the traveler] builds a barrier between his past and his future, a green veil of sea water on which the moon, the sun, and the sky casually drop their etchings."

Isaac and I enjoyed the unreality of ship travel in spite of Isaac's not being able to swim and having come to America from Russia at the age of three in distinctly untouristy steerage. Not that Isaac and I were ever simply tourists. All his journeys involved speaking engagements (and as I said, Isaac *loved* to give speeches).

We were fond of the *QE2* (Isaac did several trips as one of her lecturers) and were always reduced to quivering colonial jelly by the strains of "Pomp and Circumstance" issuing from the loudspeakers as we sailed under the Verrazano Bridge into the Atlantic. Although we met various celebrities, many of them interesting people, we were most smitten with the food. Years later we'd still talk about the assortment of individual soufflés. I have never been able to make a soufflé. In my next incarnation, if I can't marry a chef, I would like to be able to cook, perfectly, the chocolate soufflé from the *QE2*.

On our first *QE2* trip our cabin's bathroom had a bidet, which I experimentally turned on, causing a jet of water to hit the ceiling, and all of me.

The manager came, and got a face full. The plumber was summoned, but in the meanwhile, dinnertime was approaching and missing the food was unthinkable. I had to take a shower and was almost finished when the plumber arrived. Unable to leave the shower, I wrapped myself in the shower curtain while the plumber worked his mysterious ways.

Isaac said, "My wife frequently takes a shower and cries."

"Oh?" said the plumber.

"She always says, 'Why is there no plumber here?'"

The plumber said the expected words, "You're terrible, Dr. Asimov!"

Once home, I took to studying the shipping news in the *New York Times* so I'd know when which ships were arriving, but then the newspaper stopped printing this information. I was highly annoyed so Isaac wrote them:

". . . you have not considered the feelings of my wife, a respectable woman of Viking descent. From the window of our apartment we can see that portion of the Hudson River where the liners dock and many a morning my wife sits with her nose pressed against the pane watching the ships come in and leave, knowing each as though it were an article of household furniture.

"Without the information in our daily *Times,* however, she doesn't know when to expect what, or how to decide if some ship is late, or when and what new ship will arrive. Her pleasure is ruined and she sits in a corner quietly sobbing to herself. That means my life is ruined, too, since all my happiness is bound up in hers. Can't the shipping news be restored?"

It never was.

On another journey, by train, Isaac and I were in a supposedly posh Chicago hotel. He found a large cockroach under the bathroom sink and yelled for me to do something about it. Now I admire cockroaches, which were around millions of years before humans evolved, and which will undoubtedly be around long after we're gone, but I am willing to vanquish them as part of my job description as a wife, so I got the cockroach with a strong right smash.

I also got the sink, which came apart, gushing water over the floor. After the management and its plumber gave up, we had to trudge down the hall in our bathrobes to another room.

On our longest trip to England, Isaac nearly disrupted services in Christ Church Cathedral because he suddenly stopped and exclaimed,

"There's Soapy Sam!"—a bas relief plaque of Reverend Wilberforce, who was against evolution in the famous debate with Thomas H. Huxley.

Isaac loved visiting the Royal Institution to see the lab of his next-to-favorite scientist, Michael Faraday, the self-educated scientific genius (1791–1867) who, among other things, discovered electromagnetic induction.

And in Westminster Abbey, Isaac actually cried when he looked down at the words "Isaac Newton" (his favorite scientist).

In the seventies we drove to Evansville, Indiana, for one of those gathering of the greats, or whatever. On the way there we did a few tourist things like a visit to Mammoth Cave (too big to arouse much of my claustrophobia).

In Evansville we were introduced to various celebrities, and I was pleased to meet the real, adorable Colonel Sanders, who had started his successful business with his first Social Security check.

My main memory of that trip, however, was a stop in a National Park motel in West Virginia that looked into a deep wooded gorge with a river at the bottom. As Isaac and I gazed down, a freight train (very tiny from that distance) came around the bend of the river.

I said, fatuously, "Oh, isn't this amazing?"

Isaac said, "One hundred sixty-eight cars!"

When we were on another speaking trip, I read the AAA book and discovered that Newark, Ohio, has Indian mounds in it. I'd just read Robert Silverberg's *Moundbuilders of Ancient America*, and begged to see them. We drove around fruitlessly, gave up, and went to our motel. Then we looked out the back window of our room, and there they were! The mounds had been made into a golf course.

On another occasion, we were driving somewhere in Pennsylvania and went past a field full of what I thought were cattle until I suddenly realized they were bison. I pointed them out to Isaac, who seldom noticed the scenery.

"What are bison doing in Pennsylvania?" I asked.

"I don't know," Isaac said mournfully. "Do you realize that this is December second?"

"What's that got to do with bison?"

"Nothing. It's just that today is the 170th anniversary of the battle of Austerlitz and nobody cares."

Although fond of driving, and able to enjoy ship and train travel,

Isaac was famous for not flying. He also worried about people who did fly. He wrote to a friend, "I know you do take planes and I wouldn't want you to be affected by my neuroses, but sometimes I think that all the people I like ought to avoid all forms of travel and sit in the middle of their living rooms keeping a sharp eye on the ceiling."

He once agreed to do a short film for the BBC that required traveling to Kennedy Airport and sitting in a Concorde for a conversation with the actor Dudley Moore. Isaac kept glancing nervously out of the window to make sure the plane was still parked on the ground, so later I reminded him that in the three hours of his stay in the Concorde he could have flown to Europe.

"Darling, you may fly on the Concorde any time you want."

"Without you?"

"Certainly. I will collect your mail for you, slowly starve to death, and tell all your patients that you have abandoned your wifely duties."

The last trip Isaac took (he was already seriously ill) was for lunch at the Soviet Embassy in Washington, to join other much more famous people in talking with Mikhail Gorbachev. I was not allowed up to the banquet room, but because Isaac was ill and I was not only his wife but a doctor, the KGB let me stay downstairs to read assorted Soviet pamphlets and a *Star Trek* novel I'd bought in the train station.

Upstairs at the banquet, Isaac enjoyed himself, except when he had to take a pill and by mistake drank from the champagne glass instead of water. In case anyone has not read Isaac's autobiographies, I'll reveal that most alcohol made Isaac either instantly sick, or drunk, plus breaking out in purple blotches. After the Gorbachev banquet, he told me that the champagne probably made his eyes bulge a bit, but either nobody seemed to notice or everyone was being diplomatically polite.

Isaac's gifts to Gorbachev were *Asimov's Chronology of Science and Discovery* and our *Norby and Yobo's Great Adventure*, which has in it characters that are Russian, ancient and modern. In fact, the Norby novel is dedicated "to the Cosmonauts and Astronauts who keep the dream alive." It turned out that Gorbachev and his daughter were fans of Isaac's.

Another Soviet official said that a short documentary about Isaac, made a few years before, was popular in Russia.

After the tape was made in Central Park, Isaac thought it was finished and came running to me across the lawn. I ran toward him, both of us doing it in slow motion the way it was done in a TV ad we liked. We laughed and hugged each other, not realizing that the Soviet crew had taped us.

We left Gorbachev's party early because we had a train to catch and Isaac was tired. We walked down the cordoned-off block in search of a taxi, being the only guests who didn't have limousines waiting for them. At the end of the police barricades was a clot of eager journalists who stuck microphones at Isaac and barraged him with questions. They asked why Gorbachev wanted to eat with forty intellectuals.

Isaac said, "I think that Mr. Gorbachev may have felt that a politician should not talk only to other politicians."

Tired but pleased with the day, we took a taxi to the train station and went back to Manhattan.

I was always delighted that Isaac liked trains almost as much as I did. Once a big corporation wanted a TV interview with Isaac, but he said he had to go to Boston at that time.

"Ah," said the executive, "we'll be at the airport."

"I'm going by train."

"We'll take a couple of compartments . . ."

"There are none on the train to Boston."

"We'll take over the dining car . . ."

"There's only a snack bar, full of people."

People who fly don't appreciate trains the way Isaac and I did. Here's an article I wrote about our one cross-country trip. (This is the original. A shorter version appeared in the *New York Times*.)

ISAAC ASIMOV AND AMTRAK

by J. O. Jeppson

There are two Isaac Asimovs. One believes that he stays cloistered with his typewriters in the dark cave of steel called his office, linked to the outside world only by telephone and the taxis that take him to his nearby editors. The other is willing to travel hundreds of miles by car or train into the hinterlands, where he is mobbed at interviews, receptions, dinners, lectures, and question sessions—all without a typewriter in sight.

I am married to both of them, and neither will fly. While the public speaker is committing himself to yet another lecture, the first is pretending that he won't have to travel to get there, so before our major trip on Amtrak, I worried.

"Isaac, don't you think we ought to allow a lot of time, getting there a couple of days before your first lecture, because in winter things will be difficult . . ."

"Nonsense. It'll only be December sixth when we leave."

"The Donner party was stranded by snow in October."

"We're not going over Donner Pass." He meditated. "Are we?"

"Yes."

"Now Janet, don't catastrophize."

The trouble is that I was raised on stories about pioneer ancestors who endured great hardships while pushing handcarts across the Rockies, and whose attitudes were handed down to my family, each of whom goes on any trip packed in preparation for all emergencies—medical crises, starvation, desert thirst, deep snow, hostile Indians—even when the traveling is only the eighty miles from New York to Philadelphia.

Having lived in Brooklyn, Philadelphia, Boston, and Manhattan, Isaac always assumes that civilization is within easy reach around the corner, and he has nothing but scorn for my preparedness. Furthermore, he was born in Russia and believes there aren't any real winters anyplace else.

Leaving out the snow shovel, thermal underwear, thermos bottle, and ear muffs, we packed everything for seventeen days into two suitcases, one garment bag, and one small canvas satchel; loaded these onto our two aluminum luggage carriers; and trundled ourselves out to Central Park West to hail a taxi. The only one that stopped had a broken trunk lid which the cabbie tied down on top of our possessions with an old rope. We were pleased that he did not complain because we were not going out to an airport.

One hour ahead of time as usual, we arrived at Penn Station to find the waiting room packed, so we went to the bookstore. I bought *Huckleberry Finn* to read again while crossing the Mississippi and Isaac bought a Ngaio Marsh and two *Wizards of Id* to supplement his anacrostics without which he does not travel. Bruce Catton's three volumes on the Civil War were already packed, waiting for Isaac to read them again. He is a history buff, which makes traveling with him anywhere a fascinating educational experience.

At 3 PM we boarded the Broadway Limited (silver, with patriotic trimmings), had the porter open up the dividing wall between our compartments (it was a business trip, after all), and relaxed on the comfortable couch. All Amtrak compartments seem to be decorated in an oddly tasteful color scheme of red, purple, and beige. After a nap across New Jersey and a glimpse of the Philadelphia Zoo, we got exercise walking through the swaying cars (walled with carpeting) to the diner, where smoking was mercifully forbidden and there were white carnations in blue bud vases to match the china and chairs and cloth napkins. The food was plain, good, and plentiful.

While Isaac was reading *The Coming Fury* and getting mad at Buchanan all over again, I asked the porter why there was a thirty-minute stop scheduled for Harrisburg. He said it waits there for a connecting train from Washington, and that today we'd wait longer because that train was going to be late.

"We have to go slowly in cold weather, you see, after that train in West Virginia went too fast and derailed. The roadbeds aren't in great shape—getting old."

I went back to tell Isaac that both the railroad and I can remember times when we were better put together, and that European trains are a lot faster.

"Of course they are faster," he said. "In addition to enlightened governments' railroads and prudent management, Europe had to rebuild its after the war and we didn't, so their railbeds are in better shape." He said he has a chapter in his new book, *A Choice of Catastrophes,* called "The Dangers of Victory."

By nighttime, I was going downriver with Huck, and Isaac was writing a story that he got well into during the long wait in Harrisburg, when the train was steady so he could write longhand. We went to sleep in our reasonably comfortable beds happy with the news eagerly given out by a passing conductor that sleet in Chicago had closed down the airport.

"Trains are more practical," said Isaac.

The next day we had lunch, nap, and shower in a Chicago hotel and returned four hours later to board the San Francisco Zephyr, whose apple pie was not quite up to the perfection of the Broadway Limited's, but whose diner napkins were red and whose dome car sat you high above the rest of the train to study the landscape of America going by.

Train travel is intensely personal. The land is seen not as a geologic pattern dotted with lights—the impersonal view from a plane—but with a sense of immediacy. It's full of homely, recognizable objects—that hill or that tree, this car waiting at the wooden barrier for the train to pass, or that house with the lighted Christmas wreath in a window facing the railroad tracks.

We woke to find ourselves stopped in Nebraska because there was a freight derailment ahead. The Zephyr waited until a Union Pacific crew could be found to take it on the old UP tracks through North Platte directly to Cheyenne, bypassing the blocked Burlington route to Denver, whose passengers had to be bused. Then it inched toward Cheyenne, three hours late, passing black Angus cattle, horses facing the sun, grain elevators built along the tracks, and lots of snow on the rolling land of Nebraska. Isaac ignored the snow, which he hadn't predicted.

"We seem to be going so slowly that maybe I'll get out and walk along the highway and let the train catch up to me," said Isaac, while I heroically refrained from mentioning the snow—and on only December eighth—and the logical alternative of traveling in the air.

Isaac fretted because he had almost finished all three Civil War volumes as we arrived at Cheyenne's pink and brown stone station exactly at the time we were originally supposed to. The station had no bookstall, not even a newspaper stand that I could see, and while the Denver passengers were left there, the Zephyr moved on into a blue horizon out of which the sun dropped behind a mountain ridge. The light changed slowly from saffron to rose and purple across land which seemed to have nothing in it but the train tracks and sagebrush sticking up out of the snow. All this and a strawberry shortcake with real biscuits.

"Terrific," I said, "and we're even on time again. If my pioneer ancestors could see me now."

Isaac was struggling with his longhand. "I thought you told me the railbed is better west of Chicago."

"It used to be. The conductor told me that the train is bouncing so much because excessive ice got on the roadbed before it had time to settle for winter."

We were enjoying twilight in the dome car when the train stopped at two red signal lights ahead. We could hear conductors talking on their intercoms (each carried one) and we gathered that the intense cold freezes switches and signals so the train has to wait until stations ahead give the go-ahead. We went on.

And stopped again—and again—and again. The wind moaned outside in the utter dark. Time passed. A lot of time.

"I think I should have believed you," said Isaac. "It's really winter here. And wilderness. We might as well be on an alien planet. We'll never get to California . . ."

"We'll be all right," I said, "my pioneer ancestors . . ."

"Did they travel in winter?"

They hadn't, I remembered. They also didn't go as far as the Donner Pass. I shoved the heat switch back to "on." In one of the empty roomettes, the conductor was sitting enveloped in his overcoat and earmuffs. I asked him what was going on.

"I don't know," he said mournfully. "And I don't know if we'll get moving again."

More time passed. I found out that there was another freight train ahead, its engine frozen on the only track. The Zephyr's engine was not strong enough to push the freight train, so we were waiting for an engine to be brought from farther up the line.

We sat in the wilds of Wyoming, padding the windows of our compartment with extra blankets and pillows, which promptly froze to the glass. The heat inside was getting feeble, the hot water was gone, and I would have welcomed a hostile Indian attack if they promised to take us to the nearest airfield.

Suddenly the train began to move, and proceeded along at what felt like a tearing hurry. Isaac sighed and went promptly to sleep. It was 2 AM.

The motion of a train, however rough, is ultimately soothing and seldom produces motion sickness in anyone, especially when you know you are moving out of a frozen wilderness with an engine alive enough to pump some heat back to you. I didn't know then that the engineers were also sighing with relief. Our engine had gone past the six-hour limit for rewatering or refueling, and any further delay would have been dangerous.

Relaxed, I was almost asleep when we pulled into a small station and I put on my glasses to read the sign. It was Rawlins, Wyoming. I worried much of the night about how I would tell Isaac, and in the morning I hoped outside would look like Nevada, indicating that the Zephyr had miraculously made up lost time, but I recognized the mountains. We were winding through the snow-covered Wasatch, going into the canyon that leads to Ogden, Utah.

"Isaac, I have some good news and some bad news."

He nodded cheerfully, for the sun was shining on the many cars zipping along the road next to us. Civilization was near. "Oh?"

"The good news is that we're moving. The bad news is that we're eight hours late." He took it very well. We had, after all, given ourselves those extra couple of days.

We had breakfast while crossing Great Salt Lake, pink on one side and gray on the other, Antelope Island sticking up ominously but the mountains lining the valley were beautiful. There was no coffee because the water pipes in the diner had frozen during the long night, but we drank concentrated orange juice diluted with ice cubes, and the corned beef hash was great.

By lunchtime the water pipes had been repaired. The Amtrak staff were apologetic, friendly, pleasant, and by now like a family. The young people in the dome car (going to a conference on Indian Education) recognized Isaac and we all talked as we passed both the mountains of Nevada and 4:30 PM, the time the Zephyr had been due in Oakland.

Time no longer mattered. The sun went down in folds of brilliant color punctuated by mountain peaks, while shaggy white-faced cattle wandered through the sagebrush. Overhead we could see the lights of planes. Dinner was at Amtrak's expense.

The Zephyr stopped at Reno in the dark, still eight hours late, but Reno looks better by neon. Then Isaac and I sat in our compartment with the lights off to watch as we went through Donner Pass. We forgot to think of cannibalism, because the moonlight cast such lovely shadows of the pine trees on the snow, and down in the valley, the lights of the resort reflected in Donner Lake. We even forgot to worry about whether our San Francisco hotel would save our room for us.

They had. We stood with our luggage carriers in the quietly elegant lobby, with an attentive bell captain, while Isaac (who believes the world should move on New York time) subtracted three hours from his watch.

"It's 1:30 AM," he announced with the pride of a survivor.

The next ten days in California were successful, but that's another story. [In addition to seeing relatives and friends everywhere, we also saw San Francisco and the redwoods in Muir Woods, Isaac gave a sell-out speech in San Jose, I had another glimpse of my alma mater (Stanford University), Isaac gave another speech in Pebble Beach, we drove to San

Diego for a special tour of the zoo, stopping at Disneyland on the way—
Isaac sang "It's a Small, Small World" all the time—and left our rented
car in Los Angeles.]

We still had to get back to New York by Amtrak. We took the Southwest Limited from a lovely Spanish building called Union Station in Los
Angeles, then at its best following a heavy rainstorm, with the snow-
capped mountains visible beyond the palm trees, the air breathable. There
were Indians—presumably not unduly hostile—taking the train to various
places in the Southwest, and many foreign interlopers like us, all trying
to get home for Christmas. It was December 19 and the train was full.

Our car had strange orange lights that gradually dimmed until we
couldn't read. When visibility was restored two hours later, we found that
the light circuits had been hooked up to the car in front, but electricity was
otherwise out in our car. Isaac had to use his electric shaver in the toilet
of the dome car to our rear.

There were some college girls waiting on tables when we had breakfast and lunch next day in Arizona, where sunlit snow and evergreens
changed gradually to red bluffs and mesas, and there was an occasional
snow-topped mountain in the background. In the evening we stayed in the
dome car with the lights out, the stars shining clearly all the way down to
the completely dark horizon.

By the time we crossed the Missouri the next day Isaac had finished
all his books and anacrostics and was at work on another story. The train
went beside the Mississippi for miles before crossing it—ducks and gulls
in the open water, ice along the edges.

The porter, a young college student working on his vacation, knew
Isaac and said that Ray Bradbury traveled on that train after coming back
from Paris last summer on the *QE2* (our favorite form of transportation).
Bradbury and Asimov do not fly.

We stayed overnight at the same Chicago hotel, watching a gorgeous
sunrise over Lake Michigan. Since Amtrak did not service us until 4 PM,
we visited the Field Museum and the Sears Tower, admired the Christmas
decorations along Michigan Boulevard, and bought more books at a
secondhand bookstore near the hotel.

Back in Union Station, Isaac was stopped by a young man who was
carrying a copy of *Isaac Asimov's Science-Fiction Magazine*. After a conversation, the young man turned to me and said, while Isaac turned aside

to get a newspaper, "Gee, I've just had an encounter with a celebrity! Then it's really true that he doesn't fly!"

The Broadway Limited now had a pretty, very helpful young woman as the porter for our car, was full of cordial Christmas vacationers, and crept across Indiana an hour late. We didn't mind. Train travel deepens the dimensions of the universe, one of those dimensions being time.

During the night I woke to see the blazing steel mills along the Ohio, and to recognize Pittsburgh when we came in, three hours late. At breakfast we were tootling along through the beautiful winter trees of Pennsylvania.

"This is my kind of country," said Isaac. "I like my hills furry."

Two little boys stopped at our open door, and in deference to their extreme youth, Isaac ceased singing the naughty verses he'd been inventing for familiar songs.

"Are you really a science-fiction writer? Are you Asimov? Can we have your autograph?"

When Isaac asked the younger boy for his name, he looked uncertain and whispered to his older brother, "How do I spell my name?" His brother told him.

"How old are you, Sean?" asked Isaac.

"Four," said Sean. "Are you famous?"

"A few people have heard of me."

Sean looked disappointed. "He's very famous," I assured him.

"Good," said Sean, moving onward.

Pennsylvania is a long state. At the Harrisburg station another train stopped beside ours, and we looked into a lounge car full of Pennsylvania Dutch men in beards, shirt sleeves, and black vests. Eventually we tore across New Jersey, shrieked with joy at the first glimpse of Manhattan skyscrapers, and plunged under the Hudson River. If you went by Pacific clocks we were right on time, and we adored Amtrak.

But you can't explain that to people. In California, at a symposium of very high-powered executives, one of our dinner companions was an influential businessman who asked when we'd flown in. Isaac said we'd arrived the day before by train. The man's face went blank.

"By what?"

"By train."

There was a long pause. "What'd you say?"

"By train from New York," said Isaac.

"But nobody takes the train."

"We did," said Isaac.

"My God!"

One of the wives present, a young woman of thirty-five from Southern California, said, "Do you know that I have never, in my whole life, ever been on a train?"

"My God!" we said.

5
QUIRKS

O r, as the psychoanalyst Harry Stack Sullivan said, all of us are simply more human than otherwise. The trouble is that "being human" is often taken to mean being at one's worst, while one's best is not "human" but something bestowed from above. I think it's better to accept full humanity, including one's own quirks.

My father taught me some of this. When I was approaching the testiness of the teenage years, I had to wait in his office while he examined the eyes of an old man who talked on and on about his family, his miseries, his escape from Mussolini's Italy. When the patient left, I said, "He was boring."

My father said, "Don't *ever* say that people are boring. Every person has a story they need to tell."

That's true, and I was almost never bored listening to patients, for I realized that most patients who seem boring can be seriously depressed, although a few are, of course, merely testing the listener's stamina.

When I was a psychiatric resident working at the Manhattan VA clinic, I had several patients, most of them with all-too-human quirks that made the sessions interesting and ultimately productive. All except one. He'd been last in a large more or less middle-class family, had had an uneventful stint in the army, and was in the clinic only because his wife told him he needed it and it was free. I tried to listen to his droning on and on about nothing, but it was right after my lunch and I was sleepy. After a couple of stultifying sessions, I told him about my reaction.

He burst into tears, and said he'd never been bright and go-getting, that he'd bored his parents and siblings and friends, and he'd come to believe that nothing he said or did would probably matter to anyone, so what was the point of trying to talk about what did matter?

I was about to pontificate about exploring this image of himself, and what to do about it, but instead I let him talk, and this time he really did. We worked for the rest of the year allotted to me, and I was never sleepy in his sessions again.

Isaac and I, like Russell Baker, had many habits and attitudes due to the permanent scars left by the Great D and by our parents' belief in hard work.

Isaac said (in a letter), "In general, I was brought up to believe that all money that is not earned by the sweat of your brow is *tainted*, which is why . . . it is only by working very hard that I can pile the money in without feeling guilty (I have a feeling that you suffer from the same neurotic tendency, complicated by the feeling that the only worthy object on which you can spend your money is other people)."

Some of our generation are excessively time-driven. Isaac and I (both afflicted) fretted at parties at which arrival at the table was preceded by what seemed like endless socializing (neither of us being good at small talk). Drinkers and smokers (which we were not) didn't seem to mind the slow passage of time as they twiddled glasses and (in the old days) cigarettes, while the Asimovs got hungrier.

Isaac and I also had the unpleasant habit of arriving everywhere on time, or too early. I still have it, but I know why, thanks to getting lost in the woods on the far side of Monhegan Island in Maine, when I was in my early thirties.

It's impossible to get completely lost on a small island, since you can walk around it to your destination, but I knew that in forty-five minutes the only boat would make its last trip to the mainland, where my friend and I were staying. I went slightly berserk, running around in circles, sliding on slippery pine needles, and shouting that we'd never make it to the dock in time, while my friend kept trying to quiet the chaos by reminding me that we could simply stay overnight at the island's famous inn.

We finally found the path, and by running hard (we were young and capable of it) we did make it to the boat, but that night I dreamt about taking a taxi through dark city streets in the rain, trying to get to an air terminal on time. When I arrived, at what looked like an old-fashioned railway station, the sign said that the plane had left. In a panic, I said to the ticket person, "What shall I do? I've missed the plane." Take another, I was told. Then I woke up.

I was then still in training analysis, aware of my chronic anxiety over "missing the boat" of conventional life. Still, when I returned to New York from Maine, I didn't call my analyst. I called my mother and asked if there had ever been a time in my childhood when I, or we, had been late for something that was very important.

Mother said, "In Oberammergau, when you were three, we nearly missed a train we had to take to get back to Vienna. We'd been told the incorrect time for the train, so it was moving when we arrived in the station. Daddy lifted me onto the train and then threw you into my arms. I was crying because I thought he wouldn't make it, but he did."

Time itself is often structured in the human mind in strange ways. When I think of time, it's structured so that the months of the year, or the years of history—or of my life—march on a clock-face pattern. I didn't realize how private this particular virtual reality was until I told my brother about it, saying that for me, summer was at the top of the clock.

He grimaced. "No! Summer is at the bottom!"

Perhaps children who learn time from digital clocks do not make a visual pattern of it. Or perhaps I'm just quirkier than most.

Another form of quirkiness shows up in efforts at criticism. When I was a reader of papers submitted to the journal of my analytic institute, I had to write opinions as to why a paper should be accepted or rejected. Here's one of them that amused the editor:

"Do not publish a paper like this or people will think we condone this sort of thinking and treatment of patients, which is only a step away from the pernicious garbage of Dianetics. I pity [the author's] patients. Judging from the way he talks to them, it's no wonder they feel paranoid and get 'addictive relation to a tyrant' [meaning their parents—or their analyst].

"While reading the paper, I observed two pigeons billing and cooing on my window sill, much in love, as they have been for two years (pigeons mate for life). The author says that the beginnings of love are formed by sadism—the death instinct—caused by the 'overwhelmingness of pain-to-extinction'—i.e., the trauma of birth.

"Maybe pigeons experience a bit of effort getting out of the egg, but there's no 'crushing, pounding which cannot be contained or integrated.'

"I'm glad my pigeons are able to love in spite of being deprived of the trauma of birth. I also envy them—they don't have to read crap."

Mating for life is one thing (pigeons have it over humans), but being sane and sensible about eating is another. New York pigeons apparently live mostly on handouts of bread, and I confess that I may have some peculiarities about food. At least, Isaac was sure that I did.

I don't relish huge helpings of cake, I hate the taste of coffee, and I don't clean my plate (I carry plastic bags so I can bring the leftovers home without the constant embarrassment of asking for a doggy bag).

I've also never been fond of sweet things—except fruit. I commiserate with A. A. Milne's Mary Jane, who obviously didn't like rice pudding either. In my, um, mature years, however, I have come to relish flan.

I've never had a real weight problem (I'd better not, since my blood pressure goes up if I gain five pounds). I attribute this—with much gratitude—to my father, who told my mother not to force me to eat what I didn't want, or to make me clean my plate, in spite of the fact that in childhood I was always underweight. Mother learned to give me small portions so I would not feel guilty about the millions who were starving for the food I was wasting. Years later I realized that Dad had helped me maintain a working "appestat," the ability to know when one is full and when one is hungry.

Isaac had a weight problem that eventually—through a series of medical disasters—killed him. The disasters are described in *It's Been a Good Life* so in this book I'm concentrating on Isaac's more lovable quirks, which some people equated with his genius.

Quirky or not, Isaac's genius gave him an amazing talent for productive creativity, the capacity for remembering everything he read, and an extraordinary ability to understand what he studied. His interest in and knowledge of history, for instance, seemed superhuman to me. He always read history, especially about Great Britain. In a letter he said:

"My own Anglophilia leads me to support the Britons against the Romans and the Saxons; then the Saxons against the Danes and the Normans; then the Normans against the French and the Germans. In other words, whoever is in occupation of England at the time is my people. . . . It shows what a strong force cultural assimilation can be, for I identify more strongly with the English than with either the Jews or the Americans on most occasions—entirely because of all the English books I read as a child. To be sure, there are exceptions. I am very anti-English in connection with the Revolutionary War and the War of 1812, and also in connection with the 19th Century Asia and Africa."

In my journal for 1971 (when I still wrote one), we were on a lecture trip in Ohio, trying to find the assigned motel that was on 1225 Church Street. I was driving, and kept asking Isaac for the address because I couldn't keep it in my mind. In all seriousness, Isaac said, "Well, 1225 is easy to remember. After all, that is ten years after the Magna Carta so it's impossible to forget."

"Oh, sure," I said.

One of Isaac's stranger traits (strange to me) was his claustrophilia. He loved enclosed rooms and always worked with the shades down. I'm just the opposite, although I don't panic in elevators. Yet. I did panic, however, when during a child's game of hide-and-seek I hid under a bed, looked up, and got out in a hurry.

Isaac majored in chemistry, something that to me is beyond quirkiness and borders on insanity, and I feel proud of having fallen in love with him in spite of it. The truth is that he even made chemistry interesting in his books, conversations, and lectures. Perhaps if I had gone to Boston University Medical School (as my brother did, in the last class Isaac taught full-time), I might not have suffered so much in my chemistry courses.

Isaac must have loved me. He managed to forgive me when I confessed that I had once asked my biochemistry lab instructor, "How do you make a one-to-one dilution?"

He also put up with my chemical stupidity over things I should have known but didn't use. Here's an example:

I laundered a down pillow, put it in the dryer, took it out, and it smelled *bad*. I thought that somehow it had become moldy and told Isaac so.

"It's not moldy," Isaac said. "The dryer was too hot so the disulfide linkages in the keratin broke up and formed smelly mercaptans. Nothing can be done about it."

I threw it away, pleased that Isaac assumed—correctly, as it happened—that I would understand his explanation (I had forgotten that I got better grades in organic chemistry than the others).

For a science-fiction convention (can't remember which) long before Isaac died, I wrote an appreciation of him that included the revelation that his famed memory had a few flaws:

"He has not memorized where anything is in the kitchen. He has been known to schedule two appointments for the same time on the same day. Sometimes it takes him two or three tries to recall my name. And he has actually forgotten one or two words from the lyrics written by William S. Gilbert, one of the members of our ménage à quatre."

His memory was indeed enviable. I woke up one night to find Isaac awake, with tears on his face.

"What's wrong!"

"Nothing. I just woke up thinking of a great plot that made me cry."

"Write it down!"

"Nonsense. I will remember it in the morning." He did.

In *How to Enjoy Writing* I also mentioned this:

ISAAC: I think that if I had any place on earth in any time in history up to now, I would choose to live here and now.

JANET: The only place to live is at the edge of the future.

ISAAC (who understood my memory problems): Write that down!

JANET: What did I say?

The sad truth is that I must write *everything* down—notes for stories, lists for the supermarket, etc.—and thanks to the privations of the Great D ("wear it out, use it up, make it do"), I usually use paper cut from blank portions of letters sent to me. (I also worry about the paper industry and trees, and am chagrined at the quantity of books that I read.) I do not use one of those tiny computers people carry around with them. Regardless of what I'm doing to trees, I still trust paper.

But as I said, my memory stinks. According to notes I made at the time (well, it was the only way to preserve some of the funnier aspects of living with Isaac), one night I was writing a Pshrinks Anonymous story about the King Jagiello statue in Central Park. I went into Isaac's office to use the encyclopedia, carefully memorized where and when King Jagiello fought a battle, and walked back to my own office.

I had already forgotten. I raced back to the encyclopedia, at which point Isaac stopped typing.

"*What* are you doing?"

"I've forgotten where King Jagiello fought . . ."

"Tannenburg, in 1410." And resumed typing.

6
RELIGION

Religion is one of the patterns created by the human imagination to cope with those uncomfortable problems of relatedness, mortality, and meaninglessness.

It's clear that I'm more than a bit prejudiced about religion, but I do think that most of it tends to disconnect and divide humanity, give false meanings and promises, and offer security only to the subscribers.

Isaac commented on his nonreligious upbringing in *In Memory Yet Green*:

"I was brought up myself without any religious training to speak of . . . and I was spared the great need of breaking with an Orthodox past and, after having done so, of playing the hypocrite for the benefit of pious parents, as so many of my generation had to. I was simply a freethinker from the start, a kind of second-generation atheist, and in that respect my life has always been a liberated one. I have been grateful for that always."

Much later in life, he wrote one of his favorite books, *Asimov's Guide to the Bible*, which he loved only a little less than his all-time favorite, *Asimov's Guide to Shakespeare*. At the time he was writing it, he said in a letter:

"I'm working on my Bible book. I've just reached the part where the Israelites have been seduced into apostasy by the Moabite women (in the book of Numbers) and Moses gets all self-righteous about the wickedness of the women who deliberately seduced the poor innocent Israelites (except that Moses ordered the slaughter of all the apostates without mercy). I think Moses was a most disgusting character and I am strongly suspicious of any God whose darling he was. Anyway, I had to keep from launching into an anti-Moses diatribe and denouncing the Israelite racists and saying that the Moabite women were probably all very nice girls and like that there.

"The strain of not doing this (the Bible book is written very unemotionally and with a calm, straight face—so the facts will more clearly speak for themselves) has been so wearing that I've decided to quit . . . and take a nice brisk walk for the exercise of it. If you suspect that my interest in the Bible is going to inspire me with sudden enthusiasm for Judaism and make me a convert of mountain-moving fervor and that I shall suddenly grow long earlocks and learn Hebrew and go about denouncing the heathen—you little know the effect of the Bible on me.

"Properly read, it is the most potent force for atheism ever conceived.

[And later] ". . . I wrote ten thousand words on the first three chapters of Luke. Do you know that Luke and Matthew both give material on the birth and childhood of Jesus and that they do not correspond AT A SINGLE POINT. Whatever one says the other doesn't say. Nobody but a dedicated Christian could possibly read the gospels and not see them as a tissue of nonsense—at least the legendary and miraculous material in them. . . ."

In public, in speeches, and in his published writing, Isaac tried to be kind to conventional believers, but he let himself go in his letters:

". . . Everyone who says that you cannot look at the sky (or at a leaf, or at a gazelle, or at a mountain) without realizing that God must exist, don't consider that the hypothesis *has already been put in their minds*. As children, they are taught that God exists and that they will go to Hell if they doubt it (I always capitalize Hell out of a natural reverence). . . .

". . . Talk about second-class citizenship. An atheist can't testify in court unless he violates his principles and swears by a god in which he (and probably the court, if the truth be known) does not believe. And no one in the U.S. could hold public office of even the smallest nature if he openly avowed himself to be atheist. . . ."

He was particularly vehement about religious contributions to the population problem that is currently ruining Earth. Only a few people (even atheists) will dare to admit in print that it won't do any good to try to clean up the environment and save animals from extinction if the human race continues on its merrily thoughtless and selfish way. Here's a letter from Isaac on the subject:

"I am to give a seminar at Harvard Medical School . . . and they want me to say something (if I can) about the future of biology.

"What future, for goodness sake? To patch up human beings with borrowed organs or metal-plastic prosthetic devices, to arrest all disease, to cure old age, to intensify the population problem with reckless abandon and feel uninvolved about it?

"I feel that any biologist, any practitioner in the medical sciences whose work is in any way likely to extend the life-span must consider it his duty, his *sacred* duty to fight desperately for birth control. It doesn't mean that there must be no babies, but we must simply see to it that there must be no more than two babies per couple on the average, however extended their lives, with an upward adjustment made if necessary, for deaths before maturity, for steriles and impotents, etc.

"Frankly, I wouldn't hurry to make the adjustment. If the world population sinks a bit, it will do us no harm. And even granted birth control, the next step is conservation of both the animate and inanimate environment, for even with a static population, pollution rate might increase, and probably will, from year to year."

May I remind everyone that during Isaac's lifetime the world population *doubled*! And here's more from Isaac:

"Shall I send the following to the Planned Parenthood League?

The Judeo-Christian cultural blight

Has wiped out the fertility rite.

Yet every Rose and Ann and Myrtle

Continues ruinously fertile."

The follies of humankind never ceased to amaze and appall Isaac. For instance: ". . . Creationists insist on *laws* defining what is scientifically valid and dictating what is to be taught. If the Supreme Court can be bullied . . . it would go a long way toward putting an end to pluralism in this country, and to free thought. Behind creationism are the old enemies bigotry and darkness, and we must not complain about this endless battle. The price of liberty, said Jefferson, is eternal vigilance."

Although Isaac was eternally vigilant about world problems that mattered, and was an outspoken atheist—or rationalist, as he preferred to call it—he also had his private superstitions. I can remember only the funnier ones.

When we left our apartment for a trip, wheeling our suitcases down the hall to the elevator, he always had to run back and try the doorknob to make sure he'd really locked the door, paying no attention to my remarks that it wouldn't open even if he HAD forgotten to lock the top lock because the bottom one locked the door automatically.

I suppose he was never sure that he had locked every lock because going on a trip was so emotionally traumatic for him that he'd be in some sort of fugue state while locking up.

He not only didn't trust the evidence of my eyes that he had truly and thoroughly locked up, but he also distrusted my statements that I had looked at the stove burners and they were turned off. Many a time he'd have to open the door and check the stove, not by looking at it, but by feeling the burner knobs. At the time, we had an old-fashioned stove with four pilot lights, which also had to be checked because if they were off, the apartment would be filled with gas when we returned. It sometimes was anyway because people renovating an apartment below us would turn off the gas lines, then turn them back on—but not our pilot lights.

Trips were emotionally traumatic for me, too, because he superstitiously would not look at the correspondence ahead of time. Perhaps he hoped that if he didn't see the words "Black Tie Obligatory," it wouldn't happen.

Then there was his spectacular law. Wearing clip-on dark glasses that flipped up from his regular glasses, he'd complain that it was a law of the universe that the sun would instantly go behind a cloud if the dark glasses were down, and come out if they were up.

Isaac did not abandon his "freethinking" and resort to any kind of superstitions when he was seriously ill, however—no turning back to an orthodoxy he'd never known, no turning on to some new aspect of religion that offered solace through the supernatural. He hated being ill but he wasn't afraid of dying, and he believed firmly in nothingness hereafter.

[From another letter] "I went out to Radio Station WEEI, where I was on a two-hour show. For the first hour, I discussed the origin of life, development through chance of nucleic acid molecules, of evolution by natural selection, etc., etc., etc. In the second hour, the listeners phoned in questions, and some of them were from Fundamentalists who were simply furious with me. They quoted from the Bible and denounced me as someone who would steal the beauty of the universe (as though the conceptions of evolution and the long history of the stars was not infinitely more beautiful than the story of a petulant God making and destroying a pint-sized basketball of a world).

"One questioner, her voice shaking, would refer to me only as *that man* and addressed her questions (or rather her denunciations) only to the announcer. You would have been proud of me, though. I was calm and polite and smooth and in answering these people, I kept saying, 'Science concerns itself only with the evidence of the senses. We neither back the Bible nor refute it. The Bible doesn't concern us one way or the other.' Of course, that reduced them to gibbering fury and the announcer would then cut them off.

"The trouble is that these people have a comfortable little world of miracles and literal-word-of-the-Bible and associate only with others who live in the same world and go to a Fundamentalist church on Sunday and (like the green peas in the pod who thought the whole universe was green) honestly think that all the world thinks as they do.

"They don't read books on the scientific view, or go to lectures, or attend courses—and then, they have the radio on and to their disbelief and horror, someone is spouting blasphemy at them and speaking of life originating by chance and mankind developing through the blind forces of natural selection and never mentioning God.

". . . [A]nyway, I think I brought some fresh air into the minds of a number who were not irrevocably wedded to ignorance. It was an interesting experience."

My own experiences with religion began in New Rochelle, where I attended various Sunday schools within walking distance of home because my parents thought it would be good for me to socialize, and good for their socialization in a new city if we seemed to Fit In. They had been born and raised Mormons in Utah, but there was (and is) no Mormon Church in New Rochelle. The nearest one was too far away to justify spending the gas to get there unless you were religious, which my parents were not.

When I was the obligatory age of seven, my parents did not have me baptized Mormon. I did, however, grow up feeling some affinity with the stories of Utah pioneers, loving the hymn "Come, Come, Ye Saints" (written by the ancestor of one of my uncles-in-law). I hoped to visit Utah someday—I'd been to my mother's home in Brigham City when I was six and remembered the good food, the mountains, the magnificent weeping willow on the front lawn, and the circle of nasturtiums in which I sat and ate the leaves.

At the last Sunday school I attended—Presbyterian—I was urged to become baptized into the church when I entered my teens, but I declined. By then, I did not want to join any organized religion. The Presbyterians, however, were open-minded. In spite of our peculiar religious history, we Jeppsons were put into a church pageant as "The Typical American Family." Walking down the aisle with my parents and young brother, I tried not to laugh.

Until I read Lin Yutang's *The Importance of Living* at age 13, I knew nothing about religious points of view that exclude the supernatural. (I also had no idea that Mr. Lin would eventually return to conventional Christianity.) Even before taking Wellesley's then required course in biblical history, and later studying books on Zen, I began to find it hard to take supernatural beliefs seriously.

In 1947 I traveled from Stanford University to meet my family in Salt Lake City, where most of my relatives lived. (I started out in life with fifteen blood aunts and uncles, plus fifty first cousins, and met only a few of them.)

I arrived at the home of Uncle Earl, my mother's only brother, to find that my father's brother Joe was there. Joe was the eldest, with children of his own older than my father (Dad was the tenth of eleven, and his father died when he was four).

Joe didn't say hello. He said, "Janet, why haven't you been baptized?"

When I said I didn't want it, he badgered my mother about baptizing my brother who, at eleven, was also overdue (my six-foot father, not there at the moment, would not have allowed shorter Joe inside, much less let him argue with me). I was pleased that my brother didn't give in either, in spite of mother retreating to the kitchen in tears and Aunt Topsy saying, "You both ought to be baptized to make peace in the family."

I didn't give a damn about peace in the family, at least peace with Joe, who had been behind the refusal of my father's family to lend him tuition money for medical school, insisting that Dad go on a Mormon mission.

Dad never went on a mission. He borrowed the money from the pharmacist for whom he worked after school, and paid it back within six months of entering Jefferson Medical School because my mother worked —with Grace Kelly's mother—on the Philadelphia playground projects, and he worked after school, collecting overdue books for the Philadelphia Free Library.

I'm still unbaptized, and grateful to my parents for not insisting. It seems that once you are baptized in any conventional Christian religion, the church never leaves you alone, and it's harder to develop a sense of identity that you know is all yours.

After my mother died, eighteen years after my father, a flurry of religious feelers emanated from the West, as if I were a lost soul ripe for saving. Feeling self-protective, I joined the New York Society for Ethical Culture, whose leader had married Isaac and me.

I had not made wedding plans because I did not believe it would happen or that I wanted it (at the time of Isaac's divorce I was forty-seven and had been independent for many years). When Isaac insisted that we be married, I said that if he wanted to be married by a rabbi, I would convert to Judaism.

Isaac raised his eyebrows and said, "If you do, I will convert to Mormonism."

Our wedding ceremony was totally nonreligious yet in its way reverent. I'm grateful to the Ethical Culture Society leader, Edward L. Ericson, for making it so, and to our friends Al and Phyllis Balk (who were our witnesses) for going along with it all.

I think of Ethical Culture as a religion, in the sense that humanism is. Although humanism doesn't subscribe to supernaturalism, it adds a religious dimension to life by celebrating reason and respect for all life.

I also think of science as celebrating reason and respect for all life. Some scientists do subscribe to a belief in a supernatural deity, and some think of the universe itself as a form of God, but others are matter-of-fact atheists.

Nowadays, religious fundamentalists fight nonreligous scientists by saying that their religion is scientific. But the point of view called "scientific creationism," although quite humorous in its own way, is nevertheless false and dangerous, promoting hatred, censorship, and ignorance. Isaac quit one publisher when he found out that his article on evolution, in the first edition, was expunged in the second edition.

When Isaac was first interviewed about creationism he told me there would be angry letters. If a fundamentalist, for instance, believed that the world was formed by God just as it is—full of dinosaur bones and things that scientists claim to be evidence of evolution, then, said Isaac, he could just as easily say that God had suddenly created the world only ten seconds ago, complete with Isaac holding the phone to his ear and with his library full of books about evolution. Then Isaac said that anyone who could believe in a God that would do such a thing must believe in a malevolent God who is trying to fool people. He did get angry letters.

I have some fundamentalist Mormon relatives (no longer part of the official Mormon church) who believe the nonsense Isaac attacked, but my nonfundamentalistic Mormon relatives are much more sophisticated. They are also appalled by the fact that my parents minimized their Mormon background. But the early thirties was a time when most Easterners thought of Mormons as strange people living way out west with several wives (well, my father's grandfather had two, and the first hated it).

My parents, newcomers to the East, were trying to survive the Great Depression. My three Eastern uncles (a stockbroker, a psychologist, and an architect) were out of work. My father's first job in New Rochelle was as an employee of two other doctors, with a salary of $3,000 a year, and he wanted to be able to have his own practice eventually. He made it, becoming a popular doctor in town.

Mainly due to the effects of the Great D, my brother and I suffered through the incessant need to avoid doing anything that would jeopardize my father's business. I was sent to the right churches, the right dancing school, the right whatever. No wonder my brother (a retired anesthesiologist) and I (a retired psychiatrist) chose professions that did not necessitate being socially acceptable.

I never call myself an ex-Mormon, because—having not been baptized—I never made it into the club. Isaac, however, called himself a Jew because he considered it an ethnic, not a religious label. Sometimes this got him into trouble:

"My mail today includes an item from the Encyclopaedia Judaica Research Foundation. They want a short biography and a photograph and included a mess of promotional matter about a fifteen-volume Enc. Judaica.

"In alarm, I wrote back to ask if they wanted to include me as an entry in the Encyclopaedia (get that 'ae') and warned them that the only thing that made me Jewish was the fact that when people said to me, 'Are you Jewish?' I answered 'Yes.'

"I told them that I didn't observe Judaism in any way, that my work didn't involve Jews or Judaism and that my presence in the Ency. might 'sully' (that was the word I used) the worthy people who would be in it with me.

"And they sent back a cool letter to the effect that they didn't care. (Apparently as long as I am a credit to anyone who claims me, they're going to claim me.) They also told me that I am included . . . in WHO'S WHO IN WORLD JEWRY, and they would use that biography if I didn't care to send one—only they wanted a photograph, too.

"So I gave up and sent them some biographical data and a photograph. I guess this is the Jewish version of that rite by which a Mormon can conjure all his [dead] non-Mormon relatives and ancestors into heaven.

"Gee, do you suppose that after we die you (kicking and screaming) will have to enter the Mormon heaven and I (kicking and screaming) the Jewish one, and we will have to spend eternity looking mournfully through the bars like the blessed damozel [of Dante Gabriel Rossetti]?

"Perhaps, though, there's only one hell and if there is justice all good friends can meet there. I rely on that. After all, the devil is a nice guy. When you think of how few people have killed and destroyed in the name of the devil; and how many have done so in the name of God; it makes you think."

Yes, Isaac. We are now in a large book called *Who's Who in Hell*, compiled by another atheist, Warren Allen Smith.

Speaking of Mormons, I must hastily say that they have many good qualities, and I like a lot of my relatives. Nevertheless, I'm more or less sorry for Mormons—their embarrassingly tardy official recognition of racial equality, their narrow-minded Republicanism, their really silly theology. I laughed heartily when a famous scientist (one of Isaac's friends) remarked that he'd thought the *Harvard Lampoon* had written the Book of Mormon.

As it happens, I now live on the same block as the NYC Church of Jesus Christ of Latter-Day Saints. Recently they erected a large gold statue of the Angel Moroni on top of their building. I have told everyone it's really a statue of Wynton Marsalis blowing his trumpet toward Lincoln Center.

I'm not totally against organized religion per se, because most people seem to need a sense of being part of a consoling support system that gives official hope that there's something beyond death.

I admit that it's cold shivering in the draft of an open mind while trying to be a decent human being without the prospect of supernaturally induced punishment or reward, facing nothingness with whatever courage it's possible to muster. In between shivers, I can respect people able to keep their minds open while enjoying whatever conventional, organized religion they need—providing they don't depend on their religious organization to do their thinking for them and tell them what to do.

I think patterns (living and otherwise) are an inevitable part of the development of any universe after its primordial gunk explodes in its own Big Bang. Nevertheless, if a part of said universe is a pattern that is terribly complicated, marvelously tuned, perhaps very beautiful—this does NOT mean that someone had to make it that way.

Furthermore, "free will" probably exists for humans thanks to the enormous multiplicity of determining factors that occur in the universe, especially at our level of organization. During the information processing of our brains we are not, and no doubt cannot be, consciously aware of each and every factor, or of the way we frequently and unconsciously tweak one or two factors, thus changing so much that we might as well say that we are operating with free will.

And finally, I believe, with Sir Charles Sherrington, that *we have, because human, an inalienable prerogative of responsibility which we cannot devolve, no, not as once was thought, even upon the stars. We can share it only with each other.*

I want to end this chapter on religion with Isaac's idea for a *New Yorker* cartoon:

". . . [A] conventional representation of God (flowing white beard, etc.) is hovering over the Earth, which has just been created, because you can see a little tree on it, with a naked man and woman near it and a serpent entwined in the branches. At the top of the picture is a still more majestic creature with an even longer flowing beard, an obvious super-God. He is speaking, and the caption reads: 'And for *this* you expect your PhD?'"

7
PHILOSOPHY

For keeping one's imagination on the saner tracks, and one's private virtual realities more useful than detrimental, I believe that one should make an effort to learn about all sorts of philosophical ideas, and to cultivate one's own.

I tended to pick up philosophical ideas as I went along doing other things. For instance, in November 1944, in my freshman year at Wellesley, the writer Christopher Morley gave two of the "Poets Reading" lectures.

As I listened, I learned two things—that middle age can be enjoyable and that "everything is made of the same stuff only the shape is different for a while." That quote (written in my journal) carried me through the many science courses I took from then on.

To Isaac and me, science has deep philosophical meaning. I've been studying and writing about science most of my life (my last job was twelve years of writing science columns every other week for a newspaper syndicate), and almost all of science interests me, but I don't pretend that I understand it or remember it well, the way Isaac did.

If I had not been able to form a visual image of Kreb's Cycle the many times I had to memorize it (starting over each time), I would not have passed the exams. (It's not just science. I've memorized the Wars of the Roses many times but I still have to run to my historical chart of English royalty to remember who was who.)

What does stick in my memory is the overall meaning brought home to me not only by Morley but by the Wellesley General Exam, given to seniors in each major. In my sophomore year, when World War II was over and I could transfer to Stanford the next year, the zoology seniors had only one question on their General Exam: "Discuss: Organization as the basis for life."

Hearing about this question was a eureka moment, for it dawned on me that the examiners had been incredibly clever. All the sciences necessary for a zoology major taught, in specialized ways, that organization is the basis for life. To pass the exam (I assume, not having taken it), you had to explain the organization of chemicals (biochemistry), of components of cells (cellular biology), etc.—all the various organizations of matter that are essential for life.

It seemed clear that energy is organized into fancier and fancier patterns, some of them living; and that living matter is organized and reorganized during embryology, evolution, and even human history—political, cultural, and technological.

At Wellesley, I came to think of death as disorganization of the patterns called living, with nothing supernatural left over, and began to develop a working philosophy of life which I've never been able to explain very well but which suits me. It was helped when I read a book of cartoons about college life (as it was in the forties) by Anne Cleveland and Jean Anderson. The title says it all: *Everything Correlates*.

I distinctly remember that the full import of the title came home to me while I was in comparative anatomy lab, dissecting something that had been dead a long time. I suddenly remembered the equally dead but freshly killed turtle that I'd dissected in freshman zoology the year before, when I couldn't help noticing that the heart was still beating and the legs twitching. The pertinent connections were gone that had once made the whole animal alive. Everything does correlate, you know.

I must digress, although the following history does have philosophical implications.

In my freshman year at Wellesley, there were hopes that Germany would be conquered soon, but it looked as if the end of the Pacific war would not happen for several years. Successful invasion of Japan seemed only distantly possible, with enormous casualties.

Every day I read the *New York Times*, listened to my roommate's radio, and worried. I had to go home periodically for adjustments to my dental braces and wrote in my journal that "at school I am deeply involved with learning and thinking . . . so it is quite odd to be suddenly transplanted to a suburban world where everyone is concerned with things that seem to me to be utterly petty . . . but one gets used to it."

Except that I never really have. I miss Isaac, who also suffered during social chitchat and tended to get up and examine whatever books were in the room.

When President Franklin D. Roosevelt died in April 1945, I listened to the radio constantly, crying and writing in my journal what people (also crying) were saying about FDR. One of our professors said, "We feel as if a mighty tree had been cut from our landscape." On the radio someone said that his death made millions of Americans feel *alone*.

Today's young people probably can't imagine how we reacted to the loss of FDR, the only president most of us could remember. One of the reactions was the desire for global unity, especially after Germany surrendered on May 7, 1945. My May 1945 journal records my garbled and—at that time—unoriginal thoughts:

"There isn't any real impossibility that the world can't become a united organization. Methods of transportation today have made possible anything . . . of course, the world is made up of strange and varied assortments of people, but they are getting to know each other. It is ignorance that keeps unity back—ignorance and closed minds, surrounded by a tight wall of nationalism."

Within a few days of the German surrender, nations were bickering about this and that. I still remember how angry I felt. I wrote, "Is it only in times of utmost peril that the world is ever united?"

Remember the few days immediately after 9/11?

Now, in this new century, we unphilosophical humans tend to be as parochial and quarrelsome as ever. I believe, however, that *Homo sapiens* is truly one people, and that Earth's ecosystem is a unity (and threatened). I'm glad for the consolations of science fiction, which often (at least in *Star Trek*) portray most future human beings as ecologically wise and genuinely united, minus prejudice about race, religion, or gender.

The war did end, and abruptly, thanks to the atom bomb which I was horrified to note was dropped on my nineteenth birthday. I thought, and still think, that the bomb was necessary to save lives—ours and theirs—and I'm ashamed that I had even one egotistical thought about it.

On V-J day I was in Jackson Hole, Wyoming. I will not digress long enough to tell how and why I got there, but I will tell the story about what happened, although it is (perhaps) totally unphilosophical (forgive me).

A movie called *The Bad Bascomb* was on location beside the Snake River. I had, briefly, a job as an extra, playing a Mormon pioneer for ten dollars a day and a box lunch. The job gave me more respect for the fortitude of my ancestors, since sitting long hours on the hard wooden seat of a covered wagon is painful (in spite of the fact that I was wearing blue jeans under the long dress of my costume).

The main concern of that day was not the war but whether the sun over the gray-blue Tetons would last until the crucial river-crossing scene could be shot. In the movie, Wallace Beery rescues Margaret O'Brien after her covered wagon overturns in the river. On location, Beery fiddled with the dials of his radio in his luxurious trailer and Margaret played with other seven-year-olds while a stuntman got ready to rescue a wigged very small stuntman given to smoking large cigars.

While most of us extras sat on prickly sagebrush, men on horses urged the cattle and the first wagon into the Snake River. The cattle protested and were driven again and again to the proper spot where the water was shallow enough to cross. Finally, they plunged into the icy river, which flowed at thirty miles per hour.

Suddenly one cowboy's horse bolted at the splashing of the cattle. Rearing up with a frenzied whinny, it leapt back to the riverbank. The cowboy stayed on, but the oxen pulling the lead wagon went out of control and, bellowing, stumbled into deep water. The wagon, caught in the surging water, turned over and the driver fell off. He could not swim, and the director screamed, "Save him!"

Cowboys (presumably also unable to swim) galloped up to lasso the drowning man, but failed. The wet cattle climbed back onto dry land and into the crowd, while Marjorie Main shook her skirts at them and yelled that there was too much hell breaking loose.

As the helpless wagon driver swirled down the river, a small young MGM hairdresser named Jane dove neatly into the water, hooked her hand under his jaw, and brought him back to the bank. Everyone survived, and at this point Wallace Beery came out of his trailer to announce that the war had been declared over. My friend and I went back to the then tiny village of Jackson Hole and stood on the board sidewalks while twelve town dignitaries solemnly rode on horseback around the town square. It was August 14, 1945.

In 1947 (back to the point of this chapter), when I took physics at Stanford, there was a short lecture course at the end on "atomic physics." Included was a modest account of Heisenberg's Uncertainty Principle (one capitalizes this automatically), the philosophical implications of which I wrote about extensively in my journal.

I will spare my readers except to report that the professor (the head of the department) seemed terribly bothered by the fact that "no matter how much we perfect our instruments we will not be able to achieve absolute precision of knowledge. . . ."

Maybe it was because I was young and nonreligious, but I easily accepted (and still do) this uncertainty about the very small and the very large (biology is in between, and Heisenberg's Uncertainty Principle doesn't affect it quite so much).

I even wrote a bad poem about cosmological uncertainty, which I'm including to prove that we oldsters were once young and Thought About Things:

WHICH SIDE OF $E=mc^2$ ARE *YOU* ON?

The universe
Catches infinity in a net of order
Where energy is moulded, and
Whirls in orbits (or oscillates
On the curve of probability)
With color and form.
Integration, correlation—
We, with ego proportional
To higher states of meaningless organization,
We, too, like to create order.

Well, I was growing up and getting cynical about the endless human efforts to insert meaning into everything.

In the last physics lecture of the year, the professor gave us the physics of the atom bomb. His voice shook as he said bombs were being produced that were one thousand times as powerful as that dropped on Nagasaki and "they don't really know what everyone's got."

We students walked out dazed, talking about the fact that some scientists were giving our civilization ten years. We wondered where to live in a world full of atomic weapons, since it would be living dangerously to settle in a major city. We joked about finding a nice lead mine as a home.

At the time (in 1948) it seemed foolhardy to go to medical school in New York City, but I had no choice, and once there, I was too busy to think about annihilation of the city or of me. I went on living in Manhattan for over half a century.

Then came 9/11. My reaction to that disaster, after crying, was such a deepening of love for my city that I hate to leave it even for a vacation. I tell people from elsewhere that I live (as the bumper stickers say) in The Center Of The Universe, so why should I go anywhere?

You have your philosophy. I have mine.

8
SEX

Isaac enjoyed the biological side of life, but he was, as I said in a speech I was asked to make (somewhere, sometime) about him, "possessive about his biologicality and fails to appreciate that primate sexuality is enjoyed by primates generally, in spite of his belief that he has a patent on it. He is positively huffy about the sins of pornography because it reveals to him that other people actually do have sex (badly, of course)."

Isaac told many jokes and anecdotes on the subject of sex, or on related subjects, including some things that happened to him.

For instance, a friend sent Isaac a strip-tease birthday card, for which an attractive young woman called upon Isaac seemingly to interview him on science or some intellectual topic. She had first called me to find out if I'd disapprove. I didn't, and sat next to Isaac on the couch while she attempted the interview. Then, suddenly, she turned on a tape recorder and began to take off her clothes, getting down to sexy underwear. While I laughed, Isaac sat with his mouth open in shock. I was afraid he'd have another heart attack, but he finally came to and congratulated her on a good performance. Afterward, he said he hoped I'd NEVER agree to such a thing again.

Isaac also listened in horror to my brother's tales of the cold in Alaska. John had been a doctor in the air force, stationed in Fairbanks, where in winter the temperature frequently stays under 20 below, made worse by the fact that the sun rises at 9:30 AM and sets at 2:30 PM. (I have been to Alaska—in the summer—and it is incredibly beautiful.)

John said that in winter, if you tried to walk three blocks without covering your ears, they might fall off. He also said that if you took off your gloves and your hand froze to something metal, the air force advice was to urinate on said hand because urine would probably be the only source of warm water you'd have with you.

Isaac said, "Think of what could happen if a *woman's* hand gets frozen onto metal. The solution is for women never to go anywhere without the company of some obliging male."

Most of Isaac's comments on the human body were considerably more ribald than that. And speaking of the human body, he wrote an entire book on the subject.

[From a letter] "I was at the Harvard Club today at a meeting of Houghton-Mifflin salesmen in connection with my book *The Human Body*, which, apparently, H-M means to promote hard and which they wanted me to impress upon the salesmen as something that had to be pushed. I had never done anything like this before and it was awfully difficult to sit there in front of dozens of people and tell them I was great (I managed it, somehow). They asked me questions to help them meet objections and one of the things they hopped on was what do they do if booksellers ask, 'But how can this book be any good when the author isn't an M.D.?'

"I had no answer for that. So one of the salesmen (there were saleswomen present, too) asked, perhaps in exasperation, 'Well, then, if anyone asks what is your connection with the human body, what do we say?'

"For a moment, the signs of strain were visible on my face, and then I said, mildly, 'Tell them I teach at a medical school.' The Houghton-Mifflin editor-in-chief heaved an audible sigh. He knew perfectly well what I might have said."

I must interject what happened when I was a medical student and really did study the human body, literally and figuratively (sorry, but this has nothing to do with sex).

All of us first-year students were in anatomy lab, assigned to a cadaver. My lab partners and I had a cadaver who was a very elderly man (when we got to the stomach we found that he'd died of a perforated ulcer).

He was also black. I remember turning back his skin, finding a body underneath that was like all the other bodies, whatever the color of skin that covered them. I remember thinking that all the opponents to civil rights should be forced to do an autopsy. It was 1948.

I was always interested in biology, and sex is merely part of biology unless you're in love, when—as I keep saying—it's considerably more.

When I was very young, I had a male playmate a year younger. He was walking, but, I think, still in diapers. His mother was changing him while I watched. I said, "May I touch that?" pointing to his penis. Notice that while I hadn't yet learned much about biology, I had been carefully taught to say "may" when the question involved permission.

"Go ahead," said his mother. My mother, who was also there, nodded in agreement. So I touched, thinking that boys seemed much more complicated than girls.

Some years later my two-year-older cousin told me "the facts of life" as we called them. (I asked my parents why they hadn't told me. They said they had.) Since I now thought I understood how sex was accomplished, I told a younger friend, who didn't believe me. She told her puritanical mother, who was furious.

When my brother was a kid, Dad explained the facts of life to him while they were sitting in the backyard. Mother told me, in exasperation, "Your father was explaining in a very loud voice." Poor Mother. She was ahead of her time in many ways, but never got over the small-town fear of "what will people think?" John later told me that he listened to Dad without telling him that all the boys his age already knew about sex.

When I wrote *Murder at the Galactic Writers' Society* a few years ago, I described the first sexual encounter of my heroine in such explicit terms that several critics were annoyed. They missed the point (or possibly I did as a writer). Said encounter is written in first person, and please keep in mind that my heroine has sappy ambitions about becoming a writer:

Everybody understands sex once they've done it well. As I was doing, moving in exquisitely gratifying rhythm. Kolix was happy. I was happy. I was sure the next sex scene I put into a story would make editors happy.

Then suddenly the intensity increased to a point I had not anticipated. . . . [W]aves of contractions took place within my fully functional vagina. I felt as if I'd been overcome by something I can only describe as a total physical and mental experience.

I counted thirty-four contractions. I hasten to state that I did not count them at the time they were occurring. My positronic brain automatically counts whatever is around to be counted. It was only later on that I noted the number.

There was more, including her pleasure at his pleasure, but the point is that I was trying to be funny (I mean, does *anyone* count the number of vaginal contractions?). The critics also ignored the fact that my heroine is an android (note the homage to *Star Trek*'s Data). Her sex partner is another robot brain in a highly alien but biological body. Perhaps trying to be funny about sex is a lost cause.

Sex as a subject for a book's chapter inevitably brings Freud to mind. He tended to be (I'm being charitable) a Victorian male chauvinist pig. To old-fashioned Freudians (and a lot of moderns), women are second-class human beings, deformed and forever longing for a penis—which is biologically "merely a hypertrophied and insensitive clitoris," to quote someone whose name I've forgotten.

When I was still learning to be a psychiatrist and psychoanalyst, I went to a Masters and Johnson lecture in which they presented some of the results of their extensive research on sex—movies of the female orgasm.

The scientific findings thereof were discussed, most vehemently by a bunch of orthodox Freudians who sat in the front row. They were the same ones who lectured at Bellevue when I was an NYU medical student, causing me to join the William Alanson White Psychoanalytic Institute, which was not only non-Freudian but made sense.

Anyway, those Freudians in the front row (all male) kept insisting that orgasm by vaginal penetration was different from that obtained through clitoral stimulation.

Masters and Johnson (whose sangfroid was remarkable) said calmly that orgasm is a total body response and, except for the psychological component, occurs the *same way* no matter how it is achieved. I expected the irate Freudians to have apoplexy but I've noticed in recent obituary columns that they are only now dying off—which just goes to show that stupidity and rigidity of mind may contribute to a long life span.

One further note about sex: I approve of learning about orgasms through masturbation, because it makes subsequent interpersonal sex much easier and better. Which reminds me of the following from one of Isaac's letters:

"When I first arrived at the Navy Yard, back in 1942, my immediate supervisor . . . had done research work in biochemistry—on the chemistry of sperm. Bull sperm, he added. My interest was instantly aroused . . . and I said, 'How did you get it?'

"'We placed a large condom over the bull's penis,' he explained, 'and masturbated it.'

"I was shocked. 'And the bull *let* you?'

"'*Let* us,' he cried. 'Why the damn animals would see us coming half a mile away and come running, bellowing with joyous anticipation.'"

9
IDENTITY

O ne's self-image grows from so many things that I shudder to think of the trees cut down to provide paper for psychoanalytic articles on the subject. I'm sticking to my belief that imagination plays a significant role.

Isaac, for instance, enjoyed being a minor celebrity with enough money to satisfy him, but said that in his imagination he was still a poor boy working in a Brooklyn candy store, with ambitions he doubted could be fulfilled.

He was proud of having achieved an identity as a writer while using his own name. In the book *The Tyrannosaurus Prescription,* he told about how an editor wanted him to change his name to something more Anglo-Saxon, and that he refused:

"I'm a strong believer in the value of name-recognition . . . the name *Isaac Asimov* attracts notice at once. People laugh and have long discussions over how it might be pronounced. When a second story appears with the same name, they see it again, and before long they can hardly wait for another story by me. Even if the story is no good, the name makes a terrific conversation piece. I would have sunk without a trace if I had not had the good sense to keep my name."

In a 1960 letter to me, when I did not know him well, Isaac revealed other aspects of his identity that made me realize how much he embodied and valued honesty, pacifism, and unpretentiousness:

"Thank you so much for the article from *Science.* By an odd coincidence when . . . I prepared a series of short biographies of famous scientists . . . I fell into a profound admiration of Michael Faraday, who became one of my heroes.

"Now I find out that he flatly refused to work on poison gas because it was inhumane and because he considered himself a human being before he was an Englishman. How refreshing. Lord Rutherford refused to engage in war work during World War I, too. This is a kind of intellectual pacifism that is much rarer than the moral pacifism. Or perhaps it isn't. There is perhaps the same percentage of pacifism among scientists as among ordinary people, but because there are fewer scientists, there are fewer absolute numbers of . . . pacifistic scientists.

"When I first applied for a chemistry-type job at an American Chemical Society convention, I placed at the bottom of my application: 'Not interested in any job that has any connection with atom bomb work in any fashion whatever.' You will perhaps not be surprised to learn that during the entire convention I was not interviewed by a single person. I wasn't. I considered it the inevitable fruits of virtue. (Virtue is its own reward, on account of because there is no other.)

"Not that I am a pacifist in the sense that I will go to jail for pacifism, you understand. When I was drafted into the army, I went quietly and without objection. (Although at the induction, when we were given our final instructions and just before we raised our hands to take the oath to place ourselves irrevocably subject to court martial if we tried to act like free men; and the sergeant in charge said, 'Any questions?'—it was little me who raised a voice in one final rebellious stroke and said, 'Yes. When do we get out?'

"In case you can't picture me as a soldier, let me state, unequivocally, that I was the worst soldier in the world. I never caused trouble; I followed orders;—but my God, was I incompetent. A pitying commanding officer told my platoon lieutenant (as I found out months later) 'Go easy on him. He's a big brain, but he doesn't know his right hand from his left.' Of course, I did show one quality that is excellent in a soldier—perseverence under difficulties. I persevered single-mindedly in applying for discharge. They laughed when I made out my discharge application blank but they didn't reckon with the eloquence of a professional writer. I was out of the army before the echoes had died away, on a thoroughly legitimate research discharge, and went back into civilian chemical research."

You'll notice that Isaac's self-image was unabashedly honest about his areas of incompetence, but, long before he became a full-time writer, he knew he was a professional one, and capable of eloquence.

My own imagined self-image seemed to jell when I finally finished medical school and became Janet Jeppson, MD, which I thought I would be for the rest of my life. After my marriage to Isaac, I tried to keep my own name (it's on four of my books), but in 1973 that brought problems.

The post office refused to give me a package registered to Isaac because I had no proof we were related. I got Isaac onto my medical insurance (obtained through MY medical society) only by agreeing to have it "in the man's name" (I think things are different now). After changing my name on all my medical records, and then agreeing to have our Norby books authored by "Janet and Isaac Asimov" (I wrote them and Isaac read them for errors, especially scientific ones), I gave up. I lost my name.

Which reminds me of the story—completely true—that Isaac loved to tell about the night before our wedding. I told him I was afraid of losing my identity.

"Don't think of it as losing your identity," said the love of my life. "Think of it as gaining subservience."

He was actually proud that I had an identity apart from him. I wasn't very subservient, either, although I never did persuade him to take over the cooking, except occasionally, when he'd make scrambled eggs, staring fiercely at the experiment on the stove while telling me that at least *he* knew how to make eye contact with food that was in the process of becoming edible.

While Isaac was growing up in the candy store, I grew up in a medical world. As a small child, sitting on my father's lap, I inhaled the faint aroma of ether mixed with that of his Old English Lavender shaving cream, and listened to the medical adventures he and his colleagues told.

After meeting Isaac, who taught biochemistry in a medical school, I discovered that medically oriented conversation, which I'd always thought to be quite normal in polite company, inevitably had Isaac saying "yech" and scuttling out of the room.

Incidentally, there was a candy store in my New Rochelle neighborhood in the thirties. To me it was a magical place, a small house with the store in the front. I had always lived in apartments and wanted desperately to live in a house.

The store itself contained a soda fountain and glass bins of colorful and remarkable eatables I could not afford. A family owned and operated it, just the way Isaac's family owned and operated their several Brooklyn candy stores. I told Isaac I'd envied that New Rochelle family. He laughed, but not heartily—to him it represented child labor.

Living through the Great D made both of us believe we should prepare for a practical career. Isaac's father wanted him to go to medical school, but when he graduated from high school he was only fifteen, he had no money, and he was Jewish. He was rejected by five local medical schools and went instead into a PhD program. He was relieved, because he'd never wanted to go to medical school, and, after teaching in one, he knew that he'd have hated *being* a doctor.

Nobody suggested that I go to medical school and, in fact, I did not think of it when I was in high school. I did want to learn something that would secure a way to earn a living. In those days it was easy to see that people (especially women) were out of luck if they had no training for a career that could genuinely support them. I'd also noted that during the Great D, when my uncles were out of work, my aunts had no skills like nursing or typing that would help them get jobs.

Although both Isaac and I were eleven when we wanted to be writers, neither of us could imagine earning a living that way. We went on—and on—in school, trying to find a pleasing occupation that would support us.

Isaac documented in his autobiographies how he wrote and published but doggedly continued to go to school, never thinking that some day he would be one of the few writers capable of earning a living through writing alone. He got a PhD in chemistry from Columbia University, followed by years of teaching in Boston University School of Medicine.

Nobody told me, as Isaac's parents told his sister, that because I was female I would not go to college. All of the females in my mother's family (not my father's) had gone to college, and by the time I was ready, my father could afford it. The war was on, and I worried that after college, especially if we were still at war, I might have to work as a secretary, so I took typing and shorthand in summer high school.

To get the college admission requirement for science out of the way, I also took biology in summer school, and fell in love with it. My mother told me it was to be expected.

When I was two, she and I were taking a walk after a heavy rain, trying not to step on the earthworms that had escaped the flood by crawling onto the sidewalk. Poor Mother did not like animals except canaries, which we usually had—the dog and cat came after I grew old enough to demand them. She was therefore horrified when her daughter said, "I don't want to go home. I want to be with my worms."

It's probably not a strange coincidence that when I was in high school I tried to write a children's story about a worm named Mudwinks (I still have the illustration I painted). Would that I'd come to know Isaac's Sherm the Worm! Think of the wormy best sellers we could have had through collaboration!

When I was accepted by Wellesley, I turned down Stanford because travel across the USA was difficult in 1944, and because I had to return home every six weeks of my freshman year to have my dental braces adjusted.

In wartime, at a girls' college, social life was rare, especially since I was a skinny eighteen wearing heavy and unremovable dental braces, with rubber bands from top to bottom. During one of the rare occasions when MIT and Harvard boys younger than we were (those our age had mostly been drafted) came to a dance, one of my partners—hot, sweaty, and erectile—left abruptly after one of my rubber bands snapped, shot out, and hit him on the ear.

A question on the Wellesley entrance form had said, "Are you premed?" I suppose it was clear to me that doctors like my father, his younger brother, and the fathers of my friends all worked throughout the Great D. Checking "yes" meant the rigorous program of a premed. But I enjoyed being a premed while taking as many liberal arts courses as I could.

College was much more difficult for those of us who came from high schools instead of prep schools. I had to learn how to study harder and how to write essay exams, the only kind we had back then. I also learned to take notes in class and from books, making outlines that sped up the process of studying for exams. I believe that memorization is faster and stuff gets into the brain easier through the act of writing down what you consider to be the essential points of what you are studying.

I often visited the small vivarium in the basement of the zoology building. I'd watch the sea turtle swimming in aimless diagonals through his tank, and talk to the person in charge—an elderly little man who resembled the turtle and assured me that "the first hundred years are the hardest."

Certainly the hardest subjects I took at Wellesley were two chemistry courses, Qualitative and Quantitative Analysis. I laugh, rather mordantly, when a lab technician on one of several popular television shows puts a test tube into a machine, waits, and lo—the results (qualitative and quantitative) of chemical analysis emerge from the computer neatly printed out. I suppose NO ONE now has to do the things I learned to do the hard way.

In 1946 I transferred to Stanford University, then crowded with older veterans. That junior year I took physics, not the course for physics and chemistry majors, but the one designed for stupid people like premeds.

Not having had physics in high school, and being mathematically deficient, I suffered and occasionally had nightmares, one of them waking me (as reported in my journal) "with the illuminating revelation that I'd left out spherical aberration as a source of error on my physics lab report." That was during optics lab. In electricity lab, the instructor always came over to my roommate and me first. We were the only females in the lab, and our electricity experiments always looked like spaghetti that some kid had unsuccessfully tried to twirl.

"Please, girls," he'd say. "Let me check your circuits before you throw the master switch."

The next year, premeds could not get into the overbooked organic chemistry lab course unless already admitted to a medical school. The professor was rumored to despise premeds. He was also young, bore a slight resemblance to James Mason in his prime, and rolled himself a cigarette when I went to see if I were on the list. He said, "What makes *you* think you can take my course?"

I handed him my acceptance to NYU School of Medicine and was admitted to the course.

After getting—I still can't believe this—a good grade, I had a date with one of the organic lab instructors. As his car climbed the hills behind Stanford, heading for a restaurant, he said, "I hope you realize that an MD is not a higher degree, but merely a means to becoming a veterinarian for *Homo sap.*"

I said, "I've always liked animals." I gave him my parody of a Dorothy Parker poem, of which one line still speaks to me—"For long is the struggle and sparse is the yield for reactions that flop" as mine usually did.

My dubious adventures in chemistry made me astounded when I was elected to Phi Beta Kappa, and even more astounded when I was elected to Iota Sigma Pi, the honorary chemistry society. Years later, after one of my frequent moments of utter culinary stupidity, I confessed to Isaac that I was actually a member of Iota Sigma Pi.

Isaac pointed out that my culinary stupidity was not connected to my lack of affinity with chemistry.

"We both know that you have plenty of affinity with chemists," he said, leering, "but you have a problem of letting yourself get distracted in that holy sanctum, the kitchen. Your mind is not on your work. You have this stubborn desire to Do Other Things. You are supposed to forget everything else . . ."

"My novel?"

"Yes, and instead—with marital devotion—fully concentrate on every aspect of food, its preparation, cooking, and serving . . ."

I stopped listening and kissed him, but it's quite true that I had and still have the unfortunate habit of thinking about and trying to do too many things at once, especially when I'm writing. What's churning in my brain and trying to leak out of my fingers onto the keyboard makes me return to the keyboard, forgetting about the stove and Isaac's plea to "keep firm eye contact" on food as it cooks. We didn't have a microwave while he was alive, but it would have helped. It beeps at you when something's done.

I forgot to mention that the horrible chemistry course, Quantitative Analysis, did have one positive effect on me. I had to weigh everything in a platinum crucible (which the elderly female prof never thought I'd gotton clean enough) on scales that were encased in a glass box, so that one's breathing would not change anything. All calculations were done by slide rule (which I never mastered) and had to be out to the fourth decimal place.

Remembering this makes me feel faint even now, but back then it did cure my fear of cooking, when I realized that altering the chemical properties of food did not have to be an exact science.

The trouble is that I then went in the opposite direction. I almost never follow a recipe exactly, usually because I have not shopped for the exact ingredients. I tend to make do with whatever is in the kitchen. Although Isaac said this added a certain cachet of mystery to meals, he loyally insisted that he loved my salads and my unique use (he was kind and did not say misuse) of leftovers.

I was lucky that Isaac was not fussy about food, except on that inutterably ghastly time when I tried yet another ethnic dish, one that I thought would impress him. I'd had great success with tsimmes, but on the day I made kasha, Isaac entered the apartment, took one whiff (kasha *smells*), and said, "WHAT HAVE YOU DONE!"

He hated kasha. We threw it out.

I still cook, for myself. Sort of. "Take out" and "order in" are lovely words, however.

Back to the more or less chronological events of my life: In my senior year of college, I did a special research project, finishing the absorption spectra of sunscreens, which my professor had started testing during the war (soldiers in the South Pacific were getting skin cancer from sun exposure).

Unfortunately it did not then occur to me that instead of trying to achieve that golden California tan, I should use sunscreen and avoid the skin cancer that came fifteen years later. There are not many things I would like to change about my past, but that's one of them.

College had other effects on my future. One of my courses, parasitology (plus the one in med school), has made it impossible for me to eat sushi or want to travel to certain parts of the planet. I'm always tempted to explain to people that although the fish tapeworm, *Diphyllobothrium latum*, looks adorable (an eye-resembling patch on either side of what passes for a head), it is not.

My most fascinating senior courses were Bionomics, a philosophical exploration of biological ideas, and Independent Study in Philosophy, for which I read Northrop's *The Meeting of East and West*, which led into a lifelong reading of Zen and Taoism.

In 1948 I graduated from Stanford and joined my family for a vacation in the Canadian Rockies, then so uninhabited that a wolf trotting down the highway looked at our car with amazement.

I was lucky to get into medical school, having applied in 1947 when vets were given top priority in admission, nonvet men the next. Two medical schools told me they were each taking only three women, and the places were filled. NYU Medical School accepted more women, including me.

Once back East, I moved into a residential hotel (NYU Med then had no dormitory) in Manhattan's mid-forties streets, a block from a huge patch of bare ground beside the East River. Men played boccie on one grassy portion of it, and I'd sit on a sagging pier to watch the tugboats. The United Nations now occupies the site.

In medical school I was very, very busy, absorbed in the process of becoming a doctor, which seemed much more interesting than joining my high school and college friends in the postwar glorification of marriage and motherhood (girls were told that the vets must have the jobs, the women must have the babies).

I've been told that as a doctor I was useful. Some people equate being useful with being altruistic, and then think of altruism as some sort of suffering martyrdom, attempted only in order to get rewards here or in the hereafter, or because you'll go to hell if you don't.

I think that's ridiculous and that usefulness stands on its own. As any child can tell you, being useful makes you feel good. It can be the most important part of your identity, lasting longer than ephemeral things like beauty. Isaac also felt good about being useful, and said that he believed that happiness is full use of your capacities along lines of excellence. He also told me that he rejoiced in his career as an author not merely because it brought him fame and money but because all his writing turned out to be so useful in giving information, explanations, and entertainment to so many people, many of whom wrote and told him so.

I think that one of the reasons Isaac enjoyed speechmaking so much is that—unlike the lonely business of writing and waiting for readers' reactions—you know instantly whether or not you've succeeded in what you tried to do. Isaac used to say that if the audience were restless, you were not capturing their attention, but when it was quiet, you had them listening. Or asleep—but at one college Isaac's visit was advertised as "The Only Lecture You Won't Sleep Through."

After a successful lecture there was applause, often with the audience standing. And after the speech, it was always gratifying when the person in charge (usually the head of the school or the organization) handed Isaac his check with a huge smile.

I enjoyed watching and listening to Isaac giving a speech, for he was not only so happy, but so amazingly immersed in the immediacy of the occasion. This—the happiness and the sensation of being fully alive in that NOW moment—never happened to me during the two very reluctant times when I had to give a speech. My consciousness went into a sort of fugue state and afterward I felt like asking someone if I had really been there.

In medical school, however, I enjoyed the practicality of being useful or at least present and accounted for NOW. Every doctor who's anything of a clinician knows about the immediacy of the moment (whether or not you are waiting for lab results), and is thereby given to telling homely anecdotes, each an attempt to recapture the immediacy of actual experience.

For instance, you do feel useful when you have tastefully smeared a patient's fecal matter on a slide, looked into the microscope, and seen the parasites that are what's ailing the patient.

I must explain that at New York University Medical School, we students went to Bellevue Hospital for clinic work. In those days before medical insurance was so common, Bellevue itself was different. It was a connected series of old, old buildings containing huge wards full of people who could not afford to go to a private hospital. We students saw an astonishing variety of medical problems, and we did much of the routine lab work—examining specimens of blood, feces, and urine in a little laboratory off whatever ward we were assigned to.

I understand that medical students do not do lab work anymore. I pity them, for although it was time-consuming, demanding, and anxiety-provoking (patients and staff doctors waiting for my results), it made a lowly medical student feel damn useful.

I will try to restrain myself in recounting medical anecdotes, but it's difficult. For instance, on my first day as a medical student on pediatrics, I had to examine a screaming infant who also smelled. I felt certain that I, soon to be a Real Doctor, did not have to change diapers—so I called for the nurse.

He entered the examination room. He was built like an Olympic champion, and, from a great height, gave me a pitying smile. He changed the diaper, handed me the now cooing baby, and strode off. Perhaps it's only a coincidence that my thirty years of private practice were spent entirely with adults, and my twelve juvenile novels are about children long past toilet training.

Some of the anecdotes involve school itself. For instance, in bacteriology we had to inject mice with our own sputum. If your mouse died, you did many complicated tests, but my mouse thrived. In gratitude, I deposited the mouse in a glass jar, secured the top with a rubber band around heavy paper punched with holes for breathing, and placed it carefully in the pocket of my lab coat, which I wore under my overcoat (it was winter) on the train back to New Rochelle (I commuted my last two years).

On the commuter train I happened to sit next to a tweedy male reading the *Wall Street Journal*. I sneaked a peek at my jar, only to find it empty, so I fished around in the pocket, found the escapee, hauled it out by the tail and stuffed it back in the jar, holding my hand over the top for the rest of the trip—during which I had the seat to myself for, after observing the mouse, the tweedy male rose and went to another seat.

The mouse, and a larger one given me later by a classmate, lived happily in a mouserun I built in my parents' back bathroom, once used by a maid. By summer, the smell was enough to force me to make another home for the mice, in a large container in the garage. Eventually they escaped and were never seen again.

I remember other, even more banal things from my medical school years, like the good meals I occasionally thought I could afford to have in the Armenian restaurants then lining Lexington Avenue in the twenties. Or discovering the clutch of secondhand bookstores then available down by what used to be Wanamakers. Or traveling way uptown to the stimulating sanctuary of the American Museum of Natural History. Or going off obstetrics day shift on a December 31 when I knew I did not have a date for New Year's Eve and, upon seeing several females in labor being sent up to the OB floor, deciding to stay and help the one intern left on duty.

This brings to mind obstetrical night duty, when we med students and the house staff passed the time between deliveries reading choice bits from the works of Mickey Spillane, then at the height of his popularity. He kept us awake, especially since we would laugh until tears rolled down our whites.

I liked delivering babies. If nothing goes wrong, it's one of the happier medical occupations. I liked helping the baby's head emerge slowly so it wouldn't tear the perineum, and then wiping off the baby's nose— all crinkled up as if trying to sneer at the whole messy business. I delivered twenty-five as a med student, and twenty-five as an intern (all with the mothers wide awake and helping) but decided not to be an obstetrician because I'm a day person, and babies tend to arrive at night.

I had a lot to learn as a medical student, exemplified by the following article I wrote in 1977. I sold it to one magazine which promptly folded— *before* my article appeared.

So I sold it again, to *Medical Dimensions*:

A LEARNING EXPERIENCE

How do medical students become doctors? When do they begin to grasp what it's all about in the world of the sick and those who attend to them?

I gained my first real foothold in that world not during the academic year, but while I was on vacation. And what I learned then has served me well.

During the hot, dry European summer of 1949, the heat—or something worse—got to me one day in Florence. I dragged myself out of the sun and up the long flight of stone steps to the gallery where Donatello's *David* stood in the gloom of the Bargello Palace. I compared us. He had youth, health, and suitable giants to conquer, while I felt old (I was twenty-two) and mysteriously dizzy.

I was also depressed at the thought of going home. An adolescence during World War II had conditioned me to think in the heroic style, believing that life is supposed to be full of Great Challenges. But going home to conquer my remaining three years of medical school seemed like a gigantic and utterly prosaic chore.

My dizziness increased, and I grew panic-stricken as I remembered the polio epidemic back in New York. Perhaps I had brought it with me! David's odd smile grew hazy and the floor rose.

My traveling companion, Barbara, was bending over me when I woke up flat on my back, drenched in sweat. We hurried back to our little hotel, and I went to bed without supper. Two hours later, in the cool of late evening, I woke up feeling even hotter.

Unfortunately, both Barbara and I were the daughters of doctors, and while neither of us had ever been seriously ill, we considered ourselves competently familiar with medical problems. Besides, I had had one whole year of medical school, and we each had a thermometer. Our thermometers checked each other. I had a fever of 103 degrees.

"Don't worry," said Barbara, looking terrified, "we'll get a doctor."

"Quickly," I pleaded, believing that the constriction in my throat must have been due to the bulbar type of polio. Since we didn't have a phone, Barbara used the one at the desk downstairs to call the American consulate, which recommended a physician.

When he arrived, half an hour later, my fever was 104 degrees and his appearance did nothing to reassure me; he was not a tall, handsome god in white. And I wondered why I was disappointed, since I believed I had a realistic, unvarnished picture of the medical profession. Even as a child, I had been aware that although my father and most of his cronies were indubitably tall and handsome in their whites, they were not gods—not quite.

"How do you do?" he began. "My name is Dr. Guya." He was very short, very thin, and immaculately dressed in a worn gray suit that matched his neatly smoothed hair. He walked briskly to my bedside, picked up my wrist with a clean, cool hand, and gave a precise bow.

"Please tell me how you feel sick," he said solemnly, sitting down on a chair beside the bed. Seen closer, his face was sharply aristocratic and intelligent—and calm—so I felt less anxious.

"I have a fever of 104 degrees Fahrenheit," I announced with professional matter-of-factness, "and I ache all over."

"Some places more than the rest?"

"Now that you mention it . . . ," I noticed a nagging, crampy sensation around my umbilicus and pointed to it. He asked many questions, concentrating on the recent history of my gastrointestinal system. He even asked if I had been eating anything unusual lately. Was he afraid I would blame it on Italian food? That was silly. According to my diagnosis, the recent minor derangements of my GI tract, as I had learned to call it in medical school, were of no importance. Concealing contempt, I told Dr. Guya about the French-fried squid and Strega I'd had in the Piazza San Marco in Venice a few days earlier, and the surfeit of Swiss chocolate a few days before that.

"And you have tried to see everything in Firenze in the past two days?"

"Well, not everything," I said. Some things were still put away from the war.

Dr. Guya opened his medical bag and took out the usual equipment, including a delicately sculptured contraption attached to a long rubber tube. I recognized it as a stethoscope only because I had seen one like it in a photograph of antique medical instruments. At that moment, Modern American Medicine seemed so far away that I was convinced the American consul would ship my body back to New York. Dr. Guya, unconscious of the plans for my funeral, proceeded to examine me with great thoroughness.

The fact that I'd had only one year of medical school is significant. In my day, students didn't see patients in the first year. We studied the normal and some of the abnormal workings of the human body, but learned nothing about how to fix what was wrong. We did know, however, of a great many awesome ailments that we hoped we would learn how to master—that is, if we didn't come down with all of them first. And that I had obviously started to do.

Finishing his examination, Dr. Guya doled out some white powder in a little paper cornucopia. "You must take this medicine tonight and use only bottled water from this time," he announced. "You must eat nothing until I have given you permission. I will instruct the hotel clerk and I will return tomorrow."

"But what's wrong with me? Tell me the truth! Is it polio?"

He raised his eyebrows.

"Or TB? Or rheumatic fever? My heart? Lungs?" I'd informed him that I was a medical student and could be expected to understand medical terminology.

Dr. Guya reached out with a long pointed finger and lightly tapped my abdomen. "For me, it is in the intestines," he said.

In the middle of the night, it became obvious that the white medicine was epsom salts. I fell back into a feverish sleep, to be awakened at 7 AM by the hotel clerk, who announced that he was following the doctor's instructions. He ushered in a tiny, withered woman he introduced as one of the hotel maids.

"But it is all right, signorina," he said to me. "This maid, she nursed many people in the war." She was dressed completely in black, spoke no English, and smiled constantly as she began to assemble a mysterious device.

Another knock on the door was followed by the entrance of two bellboys carrying a huge wicker armchair with a high back and capacious seat. The bellboys grinned and silently demonstrated just how capacious the seat became when the wicker cover was lifted.

"Oh, no," said Barbara.

"It's better than walking two miles down the hall," I said feebly.

The clerk and the bellboys left, still grinning. I was then put through a procedure that featured the maid as a miniature Statue of Liberty. She stood on the chair beside my bed, holding aloft a large tin can from which issued a long narrow hose. I remember yelling "trop caldo" several times, but this language mixture had no effect on the maid. She only smiled serenely and went on with her task of liberation by holding the can higher

over her head. By the time Dr. Guya arrived, I was back in bed, pale and
utterly humiliated.

"Did I really need to be purged?"

"Oh, I think so, very much." He prodded my abdomen with satisfaction and listened to it with his one-armed stethoscope. "I think you will
need only one more, tomorrow morning."

The man was clearly a maniac. I lay in quiet despair while he reex-
amined me. My temperature was 101, but I knew that fevers often seem
better in the morning, shooting up as the day goes on.

Dr. Guya wrote out several prescriptions in a spidery Italian hand and
gave them to Barbara, with instructions about finding the nearest good
pharmacy.

"You will not eat today," he said to me, "but you must drink much
bottled water, and take the medicines your friend will get for you. I will
return tomorrow."

The prescriptions were exchanged for a fascinating assortment of
medicines. There were mysterious white powders and tablets, fat charcoal
wafers in a small tin box, and solutions of killed intestinal bacteria in
pretty glass vials with tops that had to be sawed off. They all kept me
occupied. I had to organize them, dish out the proper portions according
to instructions—at the right times, keeping my eye on my watch—and
wash everything down with plenty of bottled water. By the end of the day
I was still dubious about whether or not my treatment was up-to-date, but
at least Something was Being Done.

Nevertheless, I was not cured by the next morning. Hopelessly, I told
Dr. Guya that my fever had been 102 the night before, and that the second
purge had been not only ghastly but futile.

"What about penicillin?" I whined. "And those new mycins?" Miracle drugs, everyone called them, hardly on the market. I needed a miracle. "I have to get well immediately."

"I've got to get to Rome! I haven't seen it yet, and then there's the
freighter home—we mustn't miss it . . ."

"You will be able to see Rome. At this time you are a patient and you
must let yourself get well."

Let myself? But getting well was something that someone with a miracle pill did *for* you. Perhaps pills could be flown in from New York. Perhaps an ambulance could take me to an airport and I could fly home.

Dr. Guya took my temperature. It was 100. "Are you hungry?" he asked.

I was terribly hungry but I hated to admit it. It might make him think I was getting better, when I knew perfectly well that it was symptomatic of the mysterious disease having spread to my brain.

Dr. Guya smiled. "I will order boiled rice."

"Boiled rice?"

"For me, it is a matter of helping the intestines cure themselves slowly."

Barbara went out on a date with an American music student she had encountered in the pharmacy, while I lay in the hot, dark room, brooding about the medical miracles denied me. Because of the drought, the electricity was turned off for several hours during the day and night, so I could not read without opening the louvered shutters to the glaring light and heavy heat outside. In the sun-baked courtyard below my window, a small fountain someone had forgotten to turn off gurgled up an occasional spout of rusty water. Now and then a fly would rouse itself to bang in staccato bursts against the shutter. I slept fitfully, waking suddenly each time to the awful realization that my temperature was going up again.

To take my mind off the thermometer, I thought about Florence, lying all dust and gold in the breathless heat, gray military bridges spanning the Arno next to the ancient Ponte Vecchio. I decided to prefer Donatello's *Saint George* to his *David*, who was much too smug. George looked as if he knew that hunting around for interesting dragons was not much use, since it was so much more likely that you would be slain by an unromantic disease—or die of boredom in medical school.

I thought of my visit to the cool dimness of the Church of the Carmine three days before. I had been unperturbed by the look of terror in the faces of Masaccio's *Adam and Eve* as they went out into the world of sickness, death, and decay. After all, they were just a couple of potential patients.

But now *I* was a patient, and I hated it. I didn't understand sickness at all. I wanted it banished at once so I could go to Rome and eat fettucine at Alfredo's. This cure was taking too much time! I needed a miracle drug.

"You are nearly well," said Dr. Guya the next morning, upon learning that my temperature had been only 100.8 the night before.

"But my fever goes away so slowly! Don't you think I'd be all well by now if I'd had one of the new mycins?"

Dr. Guya sighed. "I do not think so. I try to use those new antibiotics only for very serious conditions. I do not know what other effects they may have. They may have dangers."

"But . . ."

"Instead of more medicine, you need nourishment now. You must eat and rest, and I will return tomorrow," he told me.

Nourishment duly arrived, in the form of more boiled rice, boiled chicken, and boiled fruit. I will never forget the fruit. It arrived on a huge silver platter, under what looked like an antique silver cover. The waiter whisked off the cover with a magnificent flourish, revealing a large peach, as bloomingly beautiful as if it had just been plucked from the tree, except for the large cloud of steam rising from it. Oddly enough, it was incredibly delicious.

"Dr. Guya," I said the next morning, when he again arrived at the stroke of eight. "When can I get up? My temperature was only 99 last night and it's normal now."

"If your temperature remains normal all day, you may go to Rome tomorrow if you insist, although I think you should rest in bed a few more days."

"Oh, I'll be all right," I said, forgetting that my body had nearly been shipped back to the States.

"I think you will. You are young and healthy, even if you do not take good care of yourself. How old do you think I am?"

He looked a young 60, but I wanted to be charitable. "About 55?" I guessed.

"I am 79," he said, sitting up very straight. "Twice a year I go away to spend a few days at the mineral baths. It is good to learn how to relax and restore the body and mind. It keeps people young, and then if they fall sick, they have more courage and patience. They know how to give the body enough time to work with nature."

Impatiently thinking about the trip to Rome, I didn't listen closely until we were interrupted. Outside the door, a strange baritone and Barbara's soprano were singing "Happy Birthday to you." I slowly realized that I had completely forgotten the day of the month!

"Congratulations," said my doctor with a twinkle, as he prepared to leave for the last time.

Suddenly I wanted him to tell me more. Turning a year older without realizing it had made me feel absurdly young and ignorant. "Dr. Guya, what did you mean—time to work with nature?"

"Ah! Do not hurry so much. The body is not a car that the doctor repairs. It is part of nature and repairs itself. We doctors do not hand the patient a cure. We help by giving the body weapons and strength to fight disease, and this fight takes time."

A cure is not a thing. It is a process, existing in time, like music. It would be exciting to help a patient cure himself. I hoped Dr. Guya thought I would someday be included in the words "we doctors."

Dr. Guya shook my hand. "It is said that no one can be a wise physician who has never been sick. Enjoy your medical school."

He paused at the door. "And please do not abuse the intestines!"

*   *   *

There's a follow-up to this article. In Trieste Barbara and I finally boarded an elderly American freighter (which, a few years later, hit something and sank in the Pacific). We were supposed to dock in Brooklyn but ended in South Philadelphia via the steamy heat of Delaware Bay, our cabin's ceiling suddenly festooned with black flies because the windows had to be opened (no air conditioning).

Our families did not know where we were. There was no way to call them from the ship, and our parents (at least mine) would not have understood an attempt to make that dreaded phenomenon, the Long-Distance Phone Call.

At the dock the ship was met by eight longshoremen and the customs inspector, who inspected our wastebasket and decided we were drug smugglers. We told him that our fathers were doctors and that I was a medical student who had been ill in Italy, using glass vials containing only solutions of killed intestinal bacteria. The customs inspector's eyes glazed over as I went into medical details, and he shooed us off the ship. After two train rides, I arrived at the New Rochelle station and, being too cheap to take a taxi, called my parents, who came to get me. They had no idea I'd been sick in Italy because of course I did not tell them but I did now, with emphasis on my emerging identity as a doctor.

I graduated in 1952. Medicine has progressed since then, and I'm glad about most of the progress, although some of it, like the all-important one-use-only sterile needle, creates disposal problems. Nowadays no patient (or medical student practicing on another medical student) has to be stuck with an old, inadequately sterilized needle which has been hand-sharpened to remove painful burrs.

On July 1, 1952, I started internship, arriving at the now-vanished Philadelphia General Hospital during the time when many doctors (after internship) had been drafted for the Korean War. I started work on one of the medical wards, to find that the outgoing intern had not written off-service notes on the patients' charts. Furthermore, the ward's resident physician told me he was recuperating from a war-induced ulcer. I immediately assumed (I did not ask) that I was not to bother him at night unless death were imminent for a patient, for me, or preferably for both.

One's first night on duty can be both long and unusually stressful, and although my experience at Bellevue Hospital was more extensive than that of other interns from other medical schools, I was still scared. Late that first night, after making the rounds of my patients, I fell asleep on top of my bed, fully dressed in my whites (we wore whites then). Half an hour later the phone rang.

"There's a new admission on your ward."

"Ulp?" I said, a tendril of consciousness returning.

"The patient's face is sort of blue." The voice was too shaky to be anything but that of a student nurse. We were short on nurses, too.

I jumped off the bed and into reality, for it felt as if I were in an obscure play being handed the wrong cues.

Why was I in white? Why had the word *cyanosis* popped into my mind, complete with possible causes?

I almost said what every new intern feels like saying: "Well, call a doctor!"

I didn't say it. They had.

10

RELATIVES

Isaac lived most of his life knowing only his nuclear family. By the time he died, his parents were dead but his brother and sister were alive and living near New York City.

In his childhood Isaac also had an Uncle Joe—his mother's brother—who helped the family emigrate from Russia to the USA. This Joe, his wife, and his son all lost close touch with the Brooklyn Asimovs when Isaac was still young.

I always felt sorry that when young, Isaac had not experienced life with a multitude of relatives. Nevertheless, he managed to appreciate and love—as I still do—the hilarious stories of our beloved P. G. Wodehouse, whose relatives—especially aunts—are legendary.

In my old age, my relatives have become so few and far away that they often seem imaginary, but I started out in life with fifteen blood aunts and uncles, and at least fifty first cousins. I had never met (and never did meet) most of these relatives, but I was well acquainted with those who, like my parents, had left Utah for the East.

My relatives formed a sort of fabric of life that stretched from Boston to California. They were all reasonably good people, intelligent, and sometimes even interesting, but I often felt put upon, especially when another batch of them would arrive from the West and I would have to give one of them my bed while I slept on my father's World War I army cot, a sheet of canvas slung between two rickety wooden poles.

It seemed to me that when traveling, most families always stayed with each other, never in hotels. This was certainly true during the Great

D, but I've heard from some Westerners that they expect to stay with relatives, or even with friends.

It was therefore a great relief to me that during our many journeys, often to the proximity of some of my relatives (or Isaac's fans and colleagues who begged us to stay with them), Isaac always insisted on staying in hotels, where the bathroom was ours, we could go to bed when we wanted, and we never had to make small talk.

I try to believe that most adults, including relatives (perhaps even my Uncle Joe), mean well, but as Wodehouse puts it (somewhere), some people *go about the world meaning well until people fly to put themselves under police protection.*

Three of my mother's sisters lived in the East, one in the West, and although most of them enriched my life, one way or another, I still laugh out loud when I come across, for the umpteenth time, Wodehouse's immortal phrase, *Aunt calling to Aunt like mastodons bellowing across primeval swamps.*

My mother and her sisters wrote incessantly to each other but, having grown up in a small rural town, were afflicted with the notion that one should never write anything one wouldn't want the postmaster to know. (When my mother was dying, she made me promise to tear up the family letters—she had, of course, saved them all—although I knew there was nothing in those letters to bring the blush of shame to the cheek of any garbage man.)

The compulsive exchange of letters in our extended family had consequences. I usually assumed that anything that happened within a nuclear family would shortly thereafter be known in the extended one.

And then when I was at Stanford, a Nice Mormon Boy asked me out. I told no one but I received a letter from my mother saying, "Why are you turning down [so and so's] invitations?" She'd heard about it (as far as I remember, which is probably inaccurate) from her Utah sister, who heard it from one of her friends who was a friend of one of my father's sisters, who heard it from another of my paternal aunts, who was a friend of the boy's mother.

My Eastern aunts (I didn't know the Western ones until much later) were all highly intelligent, perhaps with rich private virtual realities, but they gravitated toward euphemisms and malapropisms which, as a child, I had to decipher and compare with Real Reality.

This life experience was helpful when I was a psychoanalyst, which reminds me of a clinic applicant I interviewed for screening. Upon entering the room, she said cheerfully, "I've decided that I don't need therapy. I've learned to rationalize it all out."

One of my more creative aunts once tried to distract my four-year-old brother, who was annoyed because she was putting his toys away. She said, "Did I ever tell you about the elephant that built his house too small so that when he went inside his tail was out the back door and his trunk hung out onto the front porch and every time it rained his trunk turned green?"

John (a realist who had not yet seen a real elephant) said, "What color was it when it didn't rain?"

My brother's birth, when I was nine years old, caused much rejoicing in the family and a lot of lectures aimed at me. When he was a toddler and I was still in my Lone Ranger phase, my aunts lectured me on how "wrong emotional vibrations" could emanate from "instruments of violence" and afflict small children. I was supposed to hide my gun from John's sight.

So I did, hiding it on a ledge inside the electric fireplace in the house we were renting, taking it out only when I was going to leave the house to gallop, in blue jeans and with a similarly attired friend, to the local movie house. It was a fake handgun that clicked when you pulled the trigger.

I grew up to be a supporter of Handgun Control. By the time my brother was the same age I was when I had the clicker gun, our father gave him a .22 rifle. Apparently male descendents of the pioneers were supposed to know about guns. I don't think my brother, who lives in California, still owns a gun, but I haven't asked.

Relatives did not figure in my private virtual realities, including those I shared with friends. For instance, when a friend and I played Lone Ranger, I always pretended that we were two orphans (parents were so bothersome to the plot) who had to rescue him, never needing to be rescued by him. He also had no relatives—it was one of the charms of the radio scripts, I think. If the Lone Ranger did have siblings, please don't tell me.

After my friend and I rescued the Lone Ranger, I assumed that he'd want us to be his "helpers"—that magic word. To be a helper meant that you had a place in the universe, a sense of yourself as a needed individual.

My cousins were my sibling substitutes, since my brother, John, was too small to enter my childhood virtual realities. By the time he was old enough, I was off at college. In between, he was a marvelous audience when I'd tell him stories.

My nearest female cousin, two years older, has been like a sister to me all my life, and we laugh over the time (in the spring of 1934, when I was still seven) that my parents gave me my first chocolate Easter bunny. I saved this bunny for inclusion in my private virtual reality stories, but during the big family get-together on Thanksgiving Day, only eight months later, my cousin was overcome by frustration and bit off my bunny's ears.

When I told Isaac about how emotionally traumatic this devastating experience was to me, to say nothing of the bunny, he said, "You got the chocolate bunny at *Easter*?"

"Yes, but it was so cute . . ."

"I'd have bitten off the ears the day *after* Easter."

And he didn't even think to tell me about the Sherm the Worm story, with the rabbit that needed ears.

I am reminded of two meals Isaac and I had one day in Williamsburg, Virginia: rabbit for lunch, venison for supper. Isaac said, "Do you realize that we've eaten both Thumper and Bambi on the same day?"

My aunts would not have thought this was funny. In fact, several of them cultivated phobias about various animals. One of them was hot on caterpillars, attracting much attention by means of it during family summer meals in the backyard. I decided to develop a phobia about centipedes which, like Moray eels, look difficult to love.

In the bathtub one day, I noticed a large centipede crawling up the shower curtain. I shrieked.

"What's wrong?" yelled my father, coming in with his medical bag ready in case I was having a pediatric emergency. I pointed to the centipede. He did not remind me that he knew I knew that the centipede would not hurt me.

He said, "Did I ever tell you about the time I found a scorpion in my sleeping bag when I was working that summer at the copper mine?"

"Yes," I said.

"Well, you know what to do. Don't be like Aunt ——." He went out and shut the door.

I grabbed the centipede with toilet paper and flushed it, feeling guilty because I should have saved its life by throwing it out the window.

Being a member of an immense extended family, with lots of uncles and aunts and cousins, did add a feeling of security to my life. Since my father frequently lectured me on my responsibility to take care of my little brother and my sickly mother if anything happened to him, I had comfort in knowing that there were relatives to turn to. Not for money (most of them didn't have much) but for advice, for consolation, and for being part of my universe.

After my mother died when I was forty-nine, I began calling my Aunt Hazel every week. She was my father's older sister and was living with a housekeeper in Salt Lake City. Hazel had been a twin, but her identical sister, Hattie, was the one who got the 1918 flu. Hattie recovered, but later in life got Parkinson's disease and died in her sixties. Hazel lived to be ninety-four, driving her car to the end.

In our phone calls, Hazel would tell me stories about her parents and grandparents in Utah. I learned that the twins had been told (by their older brothers, who were running the family after the father died in his forties of appendicitis) that they should not even finish high school, but should go to work, not marry, and provide a home for the widowed mother. They did all this, but Hazel married in her fifties, to be widowed in her seventies.

I loved Hazel, and in fact loved most of my relatives, especially some of my aunts, and now that I am one, I worry about being a good aunt. I had something of a chill down the back when I read, in one of Terry Pratchett's excellent fantasies, about the tradition of testing out food for possible poison by feeding it to some elderly aunt.

My experiences with the euphemisms of my female relatives turned out to be helpful not merely in my psychiatric practice, but also in coping with aspects of genteel society for which my mother tried valiantly (and not successfully) to prepare me.

Once when Isaac and I were still living together in an unmarried state, he had to speak at a conservative institution of learning. The speech was preceded by a dinner with the trustees.

I showed up in what I thought was conservative attire, but soon real-ized that I was not wearing white gloves, matching jewelry, or a mink stole. My hair was also home-done (I have not been to a hairdresser for fifty years, and cut Isaac's hair after he came to live with me, saving much time and money and pleasing my thrifty Thirties mind).

After shaking hands with us, the college president hauled Isaac off to meet the trustees (all male, all middle-aged and older). The president's beautifully coiffed and gowned wife steered me over to the other wives (all middle-aged and older). She had trouble introducing me.

"This is Dr. Asimov's . . . ah . . . she is Dr. Asimov's, um, *friend.*"

With effort, I refrained from adding the Hearst newspaper's description of William Randolph's mistress Marian Davies—"great and good friend."

I said, "I am Dr. Jeppson, Dr. Asimov's *fiancée.*"

Everyone sighed with relief. I belonged.

11
THE GOLDEN THIRTIES

This was the title of a Christmas window in an expensive Manhattan store a few years ago. It featured elegant art deco settings for glamorously dressed mannikins. Isaac and I laughed, because people have forgotten that during the Thirties the Great Depression lay like a damp gray blanket on life.

I must interrupt this chapter on the past to explain that after the Great Depression, there was World War II, which covered the years of Isaac's young adulthood and those of my teens. Furthermore, my old age is in a world fraught with the problems—and war, alas—post-9/11. The lesson of all this is that the Chinese curse is true—"May you live in interesting times."

The decade of the Thirties, also full of various wars and other problems, *was* golden in the sense that we humans used our imaginations to convince ourselves that the future would be better. This hope did not completely die for us kids when World War II started in 1939, for the New York World's Fair opened that same year and said the future would be great.

I remember the General Motors' Futurama vividly, with its neat highways looping the country, neat towns to visit, and, as Isaac pointed out, with no mention of the future parking problem.

Unlike war—which tends to keep people terribly busy when not displacing, frightening, maiming, killing, and grieving them—severe economic depressions promote escapism. Some escapism was literal in the Thirties, with men "riding the rails" in search of work, sometimes with whole families on the move, trying to find a way out from under that gray blanket (which was literal in the dust storms of the Midwest).

Escape for most of the rest of us was helped by Hollywood working overtime. We needed to watch those movies as much as the thousands of extras needed to work in them. For a few cents we could see a double feature (most movies were mercifully short) plus newsreel, *March of Time*, cartoons, coming attractions, and—on Saturdays—a serial.

Inside the movie palaces (the only air-conditioned buildings we knew), we could escape if we wanted to (if we didn't want to, there were movies like *Grapes of Wrath*). In escaping, we could admire Astaire's faultless top hat, white tie, and tails. We could loll with Ginger Rogers on a white bed with satin sheets. We could swoon as Nelson Eddy sang (in a baritone with resonance I've never heard since) in the wilderness. We could zoom through space with Flash Gordon to faraway planets . . . I suppose all of you have done this through television. Unless you were there, you can't possibly know what it was like during the Great D.

We Depression-era kids knew, sometimes painfully, that what we saw on the "silver screen" was illusion, and we never expected to live in Hollywood's brand of luxury. This had a bad side effect. I think that those of my generation who grew up to marry and have children sometimes went overboard in providing comfort and luxury for them—which may explain some of the angst of the baby boomers, whose future has turned out to be not as economically safe as the one they had as children.

I'm permanently stuck with what the Great D did to my generation. Russell Baker said (in a *New York Times* column, the date of which I do not remember), "[T]he Great Depression is lodged in my bones . . . it has left me with a stunted sense of values. I still bend down to pick up pennies." I'm with you, Mr. Baker. I'll pick up a penny, too, but not when it's stuck in the asphalt in the middle of a Manhattan street. Saving, yes. Suicidal, no.

Which brings me to learning about death, something that happens to all children because relatives and pets die. My generation, however, was the first to grow up with the silver screen where we could see death happen—fictionally or actually, in newsreels.

We were also the first generation to be able to see major tragedy shortly after it happened, much quicker than our parents had from the world of silent movies and newsreels. I remember the sad, dignified face of Haile Selassie as he told the impotent League of Nations about Mussolini's invasion of Ethiopia, the vague sad smile of Chamberlain trying to convince the world and himself that there'd be peace, and the grim refugee children from Nazi Germany (who also began to appear in my school with tales of horror).

Tragedy was closer to home, too. The bankrupt fathers of two of my classmates committed suicide. The Lindbergh baby had been kidnapped and killed, and a few years later so was a New Rochelle boy who went to my school.

Although children soon see the reality of death, it's harder for them to understand the inevitability of aging. Oh, we knew we would eventually become grown-ups, older people like our parents. We might marry and have children. But wouldn't our parents be the same age they always were? Wouldn't Nelson and Jeanette still sing duets; Fred and Ginger still dance?

The first time I remember understanding the remorselessness of time passing was at a now forgotten movie about a man who kept young by having secret operations every year done by a special doctor. One year he went back for his surgery and found that the doctor had had a stroke that paralyzed his right hand. I can't forget the horror in the man's eyes and the apologetic look on the doctor's face.

One of my better experiences in the Thirties was early in 1930. My parents (with no premonitions about Black Tuesday) had sold their few securities in the summer of 1929. They bought passage for the three of us to Vienna, where my father studied to become an eye, ear, nose, and throat specialist.

In Vienna, I was taken to my first theater performance, about a boy's journey to the Moon. In a letter Mother wrote: "The only part Janet did not like was when Peter was shot through the cannon up to the top of the highest mountain on the Moon, but she loved the rest of it. The only trouble is that Janet insists that we go to see Peter every Sunday and she wants Sunday to come six days a week instead of one."

I wonder why the children's opera didn't use a rocket to get Peter to the Moon. In 1926, the year I was born, Robert H. Goddard had launched the first liquid fuel rocket. As soon as 1932 there were rockets in the comic strip *Buck Rogers*.

In 1932 I had another experience that probably conditioned me to fall in love many years later with science, science fiction, and Isaac.

It happened after I'd spent the summer in Utah with my mother, who was visiting her family for the first time in years. Afterward, she and I took the train to Chicago, where we met my father and went to the Chicago World's Fair. The only thing I remember is standing on a magical walkway that moved past exhibits showing biological evolution, something that has always interested me.

Not that 1932 was a good year. Hitler's Nazi party did well in the German elections; the Dow Jones was at its lowest; over sixteen hundred banks failed, and twenty-five thousand veterans marched on Washington to ask for promised benefits only to be shot at by the army (one hundred casualties). Fortunately, the *Jack Benny* show started on radio that year, and kept us laughing at life's miseries.

Also in 1932 (I was six), I expressed my yearning to live in a house instead of an apartment. I wrote: "A house is awfully big to a tiny little ant, but awful little to a great big giant. But a house is awfully cosy to a little girl like me, and some day I hope I can have a house with a garden and an apple tree."

By 1935, with my brother on the way, we moved to another walk-up New Rochelle apartment which had a (now obstructed) view of Long Island Sound. This apartment was a long way home from the old Trinity School, but I walked, enjoying the leafy shade of Elm Street (where no elms now exist), skipping over the cracks in the bluestone sidewalks, passing Lou Gehrig's house with awe, and waving to the red parrot on the front porch of another house. When I arrived the superintendent's ancient terrier would slowly come to meet me, and we'd sit together for a while.

In this new neighborhood, there were only a few children, much older than I, but there were babies, because by 1935 the Great D was not clamping down on the birth rate as much as it had in the years immediately after the 1929 Crash.

The new baby in our family prompted my parents to give me a Dy-Dee-Doll, which wet its diapers when given a bottle. It held my interest briefly, as other dolls did not. I much preferred animals.

When I was ten we moved to a rented and furnished frame house near the other end of New Rochelle. This was the first house I'd lived in (except that summer in Utah), and I felt as if that old poem of mine had been answered.

In the front yard were two gigantic elms (girdled by climbing roses) and in the backyard were flowers, vegetables, and fruit trees. I'd climb the largest apple tree to eat the apples and to play pirates with a neighbor child.

Mrs. Silber, who owned the house, had left most of her books in the small room we called a library. The idea of someone owning all those books was amazing.

The Thirties had other redeeming aspects for me. When I was about eight I went to an "Interpretive Dancing" school taught by Miss Livingstone, a former pupil of Irma Duncan, one of the six "Isadorables" who Isadora Duncan had adopted.

In this class I found out that imagination could be translated into the pleasure of physical activity. Isadora (I read later) had great satisfaction in being biologically human, and although I did not at the time know the scandalous ways she did this, it got across in the dancing. She taught small children to enjoy using their bodies with the combination of music, poetry, and dance. When she shocked Boston by dancing in a red gown that revealed her breasts, she said, "Is not all body and soul an instrument through which the artist expresses his inner message of beauty?"

Nakedness, incidentally, was not taboo in our family, for the grown-ups never made big efforts to prevent us children from seeing the nude adult body. One of my mother's sisters and her husband lived in the country in an old house I visited several times in my childhood. We all thought nothing of going naked into the lake.

I'm eternally grateful to Isadora, for when you are as young as I was during exposure to her teaching methods, what you learn about feeling, creativity, and moving the body becomes part of you on a subliminal, nonverbal level for the rest of your life. It alters your interaction with reality and affects the virtual realities you create.

Much later on, I discovered something else that Isadora knew—that sex is a large part of the pleasure of being human. I mean the entire marvel of physical and emotional pleasure with, in, to, and from another person.

And then I learned from Isaac that intimacy and creativity have a lot in common. In order for them to succeed, each needs arousal, inspiration, concentration, commitment, and openness. Thank you, Isaac.

12

SUMMER NEVERLAND
IN A TROUBLED WORLD

My summer camp was important to me, an interlude when it was almost possible, for a while, to forget the unhappy state of the world.

For four summers, beginning when I was eleven, I went to Camp Wabunaki, in the Sebago Lake region of Maine. When I first went there, it was easy to imagine that the entire world consisted of a lake and pine trees and hills, and that only the present moment existed.

Getting to camp, however, was a new and, for many children, a difficult experience. Arriving in Grand Central Station on a hot, muggy, un-air-conditioned Manhattan day, one had to find the banner of one's camp amid the thousands of children infesting the station, and say goodbye to one's parents, often for the first time in one's life.

Fortunately, I was not like Isaac, who had never been away from his parents until he married. His summer camp in childhood was for parents, too. He had no relatives to visit, as I did (spending one earlier summer with an uncle and aunt in Connecticut).

So I was not afraid when we would-be campers marched down the ramp to the train's sleeping car and my upper berth. We arrived the next morning in Maine, where, eventually, we transferred to the narrow-gauge railroad called the Dinky. This tootled along beside the unpaved roads bordered with pine and hemlock until it reached the lake and the two halves of Wabunaki—the junior camp on the mainland, the senior camp on an island connected to another part of the mainland by a causeway.

Wabunaki was an unusual camp. Its brochure said, "A camp experience . . . is a living process, day in and day out for two months. Health and character growth are by-products rather than ends in themselves, and how we live from day to day anywhere determines how much or how little of these we acquire."

I still have a list of the Sunday talks given in the wooded glade by the camp director, Miss Welch, who said things like "have a yes and a no of your own," and "have the ability to go on while no one is looking."

I knew there were starving, homeless children unable to go to camp, so one of her stories had a profound impact on me. A very poor girl was invited to a birthday party. She could afford only a new ribbon to put around her old dress, but when she went to the party, the hostess (a child kinder than most) said the only thing she could say—"What a pretty sash." I resolved to try to focus on what was good, which I'm ashamed to say has not always been easy in my life.

At camp it was easy to immerse oneself in the immediate, listening to loons on the lake, stumbling over tree roots on the way to the toilet shack, diving into icy Emerald Pool on the Baldfaces Mountains hike, seeing shooting stars over the unpolluted Saco River while trying to get comfortable in an old-fashioned, down-less sleeping bag.

I was lucky that Wabunaki discouraged competitiveness, for I never had any talent for team athletics. Although I could hike, sail, and canoe, I was a terrible horseback rider, especially on a gray horse named Don whose immense girth was hard to straddle. A camper we called Timmy—who grew up to be the writer Alice Adams—pleased me with the following poem:

> Don, Don, as I canter on
> Your neck, why the heck,
> Did I ever get on?

But the world was getting worse, penetrating Neverland. During my second summer at Wabunaki, Hitler signed a nonaggression pact with the Soviet Union. By the time I went back to school in the fall of 1939, Europe was at war.

During the next summer, 1940, it was hard to keep Blitzkrieg and Dunkirk out of mind. By the summer of 1941, Hitler had invaded the Soviet Union.

John, Rae, and Janet Jeppson
(passport photo, 1929)

My brother, John,
and Bonny, our beagle

My father and me in the 1950s

My father out golfing

My mother and father and Bonny

My mother

My brother, John

Isaac in a new tux,
at the door of his office

Isaac getting another honorary degree

Isaac giving a speech

Isaac singing at the top of his lungs

Isaac (at Mohonk Mountain House)
reading while I admire nature

Isaac signing autographs

Isaac and his daughter, Robyn, 1982

Janet and Isaac
(one of the last photos)

Janet and Robyn, 2003

That last camp summer I turned fifteen, menstruated for the second time, and worried about what career I could have in the world I would go back to after camp. At sunset, we campers listened to records of Tchaikovsky's Fourth Symphony, which I can never hear without feeling the same surge of hope that somehow the tide would turn.

Near summer's end, the camp director wrote parents urging that because a camper might have a temporary letdown at home, she should "be allowed to drift—to do what the moment suggests and perhaps to dream a bit. . . . We all need to do this occasionally."

Yes, but the "now" of war was too enveloping. By the end of that year the United States was at war, too. In high school, many boys were hurrying through on an accelerated program to get in some college before being drafted or before enlisting. I decided not to go to camp again, and that's when I went to summer school to learn typing and shorthand.

I have another good memory about camp. My father wrote me a letter that first year. In it he said, "I want you to know that I liked the way you marched off that Thursday night in Grand Central. It shows you have 'the stuff that counts' down inside of you and that you are learning to adjust yourself to new conditions and surroundings. The ability to do this will mean a great deal to you some day."

I was lucky to have parents who expected me to adapt, because it made it easier for me to do so. And most of the time I've managed to be happy wherever I had to live, although of course I've sometimes had to be in unwanted environments (camp was certainly not one of those), including places once filled with happiness but now not.

This reminds me of one of the verses of A. A. Milne that made me cry when I was a child. It's the one about the dormouse whose flowerbed home was replanted with yellow chrysanthemums. The dormouse simply closed his eyes and *imagined* that the flowerbed still had his beloved delphiniums and geraniums.

Loved environments do disappear, but Milne's poem does not make me cry now, perhaps because I've lost much more than delphiniums (blue) and geraniums (red). It makes me smile, because this poem confirmed for my child self that the world of imagination is desirable and useful.

Wabunaki—like the rest of my past, including Isaac—is now part of the world of imagination.

13
PSYCHOANALYST

The experience of becoming and being a psychoanalyst was interesting and challenging, and although it doesn't include Isaac, at the end it does.

To begin with, patients taught me that it's important to understand and use the story of your own life's journey, and that nobody can really do this except yourself. A psychoanalyst helps people understand and change, but she doesn't do it for them.

Not that I didn't have problems with patients, especially the sophisticated moderns who seldom had exotic symptoms bolstered by pre-Freudian denial, but reveled in presenting each facet of their neuroses, the mess of their lives, the faults of their parents, and so forth.

It's easy nowadays to be ultra "analytic" about the dark dystopian stuff of life, but it's much harder to tackle one of the prime jobs of growing up—learning to forgive oneself and one's parental figures. I worked hard on that journey, mine and that of my patients.

One of my patients complained bitterly about the misery of his childhood and adolescence. I asked him if he'd like to go back and change it all.

"Of course."

"Then wouldn't you now be a different person?" I asked.

"Of course."

"Do you want to be someone else?"

Long pause. "No, dammit." He then went on working to change the way he'd used what he'd brought with him from the past, and to forgive the past and himself—which we all should do.

As Erich Fromm said (in a seminar) about a successful psycho-analysis, "Eventually one's life becomes a fascinating story with good things in it." Amen.

Being the object of a patient's imagination can be scary or amusing. During my years as a student (i.e., psychoanalytic candidate) in the William Alanson White Institute, I had personal training analysis plus intensive supervision of cases. I therefore assumed that I would catch on immediately whenever my patients constructed stories about me that were full of distortions that would reveal *their* problems, certainly not mine.

I also felt that conventional social labels would not be attached to me. All my life I had (willingly or not) sidestepped the merely conventional. For instance, hadn't I avoided sororities? (Well, I was rejected in high school, then chose colleges which had no sororities.) In the fifties hadn't I waded against the current of the feminine mystique to become a doctor? I am not even a conventional WASP, for the Anglo-Saxon is heavily out-weighed by Scandinavian ancestry.

I was thus puzzled when one of my patients made snide remarks about midwestern Lutherans. Since I was never Lutheran, and was born in Penn-sylvania and raised in the large suburban, thoroughly Eastern city of New Rochelle, New York, it took me days to realize that the patient meant me.

My second training analyst, Clara Thompson, didn't say much, but what she did say was helpful. For instance, I was stumbling around trying to describe to Clara my problems with my first training analyst. She said, "Ah, but he lives a rather conventional life." It wasn't much, but it clari-fied things for me.

Clara also listened patiently to the first dream I had in analysis with her: I was back in Trinity School's auditorium, full of children, teachers, and my parents (at the time of dreaming, alive and walking) in wheel-chairs. It was stifling hot because the windows were shut. Then Clara stood up and opened a window.

I was pleased with this dream and waited for Clara to analyze it at such length that it would take up the rest of the session. She only grunted and said, "Oh? Mother Thompson solves *everything*?"

I knew vaguely then, and with greater clarity later on, that no matter how much I wanted someone to open the windows, I'd have to do it, and that since I was the dreamer and on one level every character in a dream is also the dreamer, I should and could do it.

Clara had her terminal illness at the time I was her training analysand, but she was still sharp. I told her that if there were a heaven, and I were allowed to enter, I would hope to see my beagle running toward me, tail up and waving, ears streaming back, eyes glad. Clara said, "Yes, unconditional love is hard to find."

It pays to have a sense of humor if thinking of becoming a psychoanalyst. I am reminded of the story that a famous psychoanalyst presented a tongue-in-cheek paper to a bunch of internists. It was on the psychodynamics of the ingrown toenail (I leave it to you to figure out the erotic implications involved). Unfortunately, the paper was taken seriously and received much learned discussion.

I had interesting colleagues. One of them, who was doing some esoteric research at the Bronx Zoo on animal dreaming, called me at 7:30 AM, presumably to reach me before my 8 AM patient arrived. He wanted to know if I could provide room and board for an African chameleon. Since at that time I lived in one room (seeing patients in a tiny adjoining room) I refused with sorrow, because it might have been interesting for both me and the patients.

During the twelve years I lived there—in an attic room of one of the old Brokaw mansions, now torn down—I was once in the building's only elevator, on my way up to my office, when a young male entered. Then a young female. The following conversation ensued:

BOY: "I guess we won't be late. Say, your hair looks different."
GIRL: "Yes, I cut it."
BOY: "Looks much better this way."
GIRL: "So would yours."

Both look at me and smile uneasily.

BOY: "Well, your hair looks better but you still sound like a witch."
GIRL: "Well, I can cut off my hair but not my tongue." Girl smiles at me. I do not smile back. We all exit on my floor, where the psychiatrist next door runs group therapy sessions on Wednesday nights. I resist the temptation to say, "Oh, *do* have a happy group!"

In another apartment, after Isaac and I were married, we took care of his daughter's huge black cat for a few months. One day when Isaac was at his office (then blocks away), I forgot to latch the door into the living room, where Satan lived. Satan pushed it open, strolled down the hall to my office, entered, glared at the patient, jumped onto my chair, put a foreleg possessively on my thigh, and went on staring at the patient, who, fortunately, had a sense of humor.

I enjoyed my work as a psychoanalyst in spite of the fact that so many people resist freedom through learning and self-awareness, sometimes because they have been forced (or think they've been forced) to settle for a narrow way of life that becomes the only way they feel secure.

Later on, I realized that people trapped in a narrow life find it easy to resent people who reach out beyond the ordinary. Perhaps this is one of the many factors behind so much of the current rise of fundamentalist religions and antipathy toward science, especially the exploration of space.

At the worst (and all too often in human history), some people willingly give up all freedom in order to feel less uncertain and more protected. Erich Fromm wrote about this *Escape from Freedom* in the context of the Nazi takeover of so many minds.

Erich Fromm was responsible for an important aspect of my life's journey. It happened in the spring of 1959, when I was still in analytic school. I had two double supervision sessions with Fromm, who then came every spring to the William Alanson White Institute to teach. I presented a case that I felt I could not understand and help—a patient who said he only needed therapy so he could say on his academic résumé that he'd had it.

Fromm was clearly bored, and very gently said I had chosen a poor case and handled it badly. I still had an hour and a half to go in the session, and felt like crawling out *under* the door, until something occurred to me.

I said, "Dr. Fromm, I've suddenly realized why I'm not a good therapist for this patient. I envy him."

"Why?"

"He makes it seem as if he's always in control of his life, and that nothing ever hurts him." Then I told Fromm about my father dying the previous November, followed in six weeks by the death of my analyst. Fromm had been a good friend of Clara Thompson.

Fromm looked at me, leaned closer, and with an almost penetrating kindness began to talk about the human wish to avoid being fully alive because that means acceptance of inevitable change. Totally *there* for me, he talked for the rest of the double session. I don't remember the content (it included Peer Gynt and Faust) but I'll never forget the power of even momentary intense human rapport, and the importance of letting oneself be fully alive even when it hurts.

I left the session feeling as if I'd been flung back onto the road of life itself.

In the next (and final) supervisory session, Fromm and I discussed the patient, to good use.

I was also going to his public lectures at the time, but Fromm had helped me so much that later in the spring I dared to miss one of those lectures.

Instead, I went to the annual banquet of the Mystery Writers of America in order to hear Eleanor Roosevelt speak about her husband's love of mysteries. And there I met Isaac Asimov, beginning a journey of friendship and, ultimately, marriage.

14
COMPULSIVE WRITING

Any book that includes anything about Isaac Asimov should have a chapter on writing as a compulsion. Nobody knew as well as Isaac that while writing is one of the best uses of the imagination, the act of writing can be so compelling that it takes over life.

We shrinks (well, other shrinks) tend to call it compulsive, said shrinks being all too likely to harbor secret resentment over the fact that their Great American Novel has not been published (or if published, not reviewed), and the editor of a prestigious psychiatric journal has turned down their latest exceedingly pedantic efforts. Not me. I never tried to write the GAN (haven't read most of them) or psychiatric papers.

The compulsion to write is real, not imaginary. Here's some of what my dear husband, the absolute expert, had to say on the subject:

"Whenever I have endured or accomplished some difficult task—such as watching television, going out socially, or sleeping—I always look forward to rewarding myself with the small pleasure of getting back to my typewriter and writing something. This enables me to store up enough strength to endure the next interruption . . .

"The writer is the slave of his writing and there are people who *will not be enslaved.* . . . To be a writer means to write whether there is any reward or not, and that is why a writer finds it so difficult to overcome the feeling of annoyance at any interference with his writing whether from a friend, from an editor, or even a person whom he loves above all else [this was his daughter]. Of course, the help is meant to improve his writing and increasing success. In his heart, however, he doesn't want to improve or be successful; he wants to put the material that is swelling within him on paper and the process is so individual and so private that it cannot be interfered with without spoiling it somewhat. A professional writer will make alterations when demanded; but I have never known one to do so without grumbling."

Isaac often talked about his "daemon" that did the writing for him, and he assumed other writers had it, too.

I wrote to him: "Dear Dr. Asimov, I have just discovered that Chapter 4 [of one of the three early novels I never published and have since cheerfully—well, almost cheerfully—destroyed]—although I am only in the middle of it—seems to go after Chapter 2 and in front, naturally, of Chapter 3. Novels seem to have an organic life of their own, over which the novelist has, at best, an option to preside at the birth. In fact, I feel more and more like an obstetrician."

Isaac answered, "You are learning something very important. You have a daemon who understands things better than you do."

Isaac made no excuses for being a compulsive writer. That's who he was, and he loved it. His shoulders and arms were muscular from years of pounding away at typewriters.

By the way, if anyone thinks I'm going to psychoanalyze the compulsion of any writer (especially Isaac) to keep writing and writing and writing, they've got another think coming. I happen to deplore the current trend for exposing and dissecting the lives of famous people, including authors.

When I was learning psychoanalysis and given to exercising the same, I was scolded in class by the philosopher Justus Buchler when I dared to comment on the personal life of someone whose theories he was explaining.

Buchler said, "A piece of work should be judged on its own merits—artistic or philosophical or whatever—regardless of anybody's analytic assumptions about the person who did the work."

Isaac certainly was a compulsive writer but he felt it as joy, and—as in the next letter—freedom [he was telling about having to turn down a salaried job at an institute that wanted him as a science writer]:

"I had to refuse. I can't take a full-time job or any job at all. I am a free-lancer and shall stay so while it remains at all feasible economically. In fact, in the course of our conversation I had a reminder of what freedom means. He said that one of the scientists (the ranking one) [at that institute], on hearing that he was to interview me, said, 'Why, he's only a science fiction writer; he'll take our ideas and put them into his stories.'

"I didn't change countenance but internally my hackles rose. What, abandon my precious freedom, so hardly won, and place myself under someone who will condescend to me as an s-f writer; someone who thinks that I lack a sense of ethics. Never!

"I explained that I couldn't accept any job since I was bound to various publishers to do various books and that even if I accepted no more jobs I had all the work I could do for two or three years. And he smiled and said, 'How binding are these contracts?' Which gave me a chance to explain my sense of ethics.

"I said, 'Not binding at all in the sense that there is no penalty for failure to comply; but as binding as steel chains to a man with a sense of honor.'

"In a way, it's too bad, for the project is a ferociously interesting one, and I worked hard to arrange to have him invite me to some meetings and he may do so."

Isaac understood not only the ethics of writing but the compulsions of other writers. I wrote the following to him: "I just saw coming attractions of the next *Star Trek* [the first TV series] and Mr. Spock kisses a girl, apparently expertly. Now on seeing this, was I erotically aroused? Jealous? No. My immediate reaction was, 'Oh damn, this means that Roddenberry won't accept my script' [he didn't]. Am I progressing, psychologically speaking, as a writer?"

Isaac's comment was, "Oh, you're a *thorough* writer!"

Once I wrote him about a visit to a nature sanctuary and filled the letter with visual details. I hadn't intended to poke at his nonvisualness, or his preference for staying indoors to write forever, but perhaps he took it that way, for he answered:

"Let me share with you the following quotation from Thoreau's *Walden* which I came across the other day: 'Why should we be in such a desperate haste to succeed? If a man does not keep pace with his companions, perhaps it is because he hears a different drummer. Let him step to the music which he hears, however measured or far away . . .'

"Tears came to my eyes when I read it, and they have just come to my eyes again. It is not the thought that brings the tears, but the sheer beauty of the words—and a bit of envy that I could never put words together like that.

"The thought exhilarates me. It may seem odd to you that I should feel great about this justification of 'failure' but we are all failures, you know.

"I am a failure as far as taking vacations is concerned, or of doing all the wonderful things that lie outside work and a few other sidelines. But then, it is a call to individuality and tolerance, and I need it, too. The drummer I hear sounds a perpetual tattoo and I run madly to keep a time that never lets up. But if the world will let me 'step to the music I hear, however rapid and close,' I will be grateful. . . ."

Isaac frequently told me (especially after I'd received yet another rejection) that writing—compulsive or not—is good even if you don't publish, for it exercises the brain and keeps it young. In fact, we both felt the truth of that adage—"Use it or lose it."

Hugh Downs (I don't remember where) said, "The idea that your brain runs down and becomes less receptive to new ideas is a myth. Learning capacities do not diminish with age. They are impaired only by disease or injury. You can always learn something new—or acquire new skills."

One remark of Isaac's has been much quoted: "If my doctor told me I had only six months to live, I wouldn't brood. I'd type a little faster."

It happened.

He didn't brood. He did try to write faster, but eventually I had to type for him because his hands wouldn't work. Nevertheless, he was a writer to the end.

15
BEING A WRITER
(Problems and, Um, Joys)

When writers are very, very young, they imagine that their first book will be published, favorably reviewed by prestigious reviewers, become an instant best seller, and make millions as a hit movie. This reminds me of the many cartoons of someone sitting on the sidewalk holding out a hat for begging, with a sign saying, "Sold my first story and quit my job."

Speaking of movies, unless you have the clout of the likes of J. K. Rowling, what happens when a book's film rights are sold to a filmmaker is that money is handed over at that time. And then nothing happens. Authors seldom—hardly ever—get royalties on a film no matter how successful it is. Sometimes, however, the *book* from which the film was made (however loosely speaking) is put back into print and sells for a while.

I'm not griping. It's the Way Things Are.

I think that if a child who wants to become a writer is told the grim truths of publishing, he would probably not sign up for engineering school, or even become an agent. He would write anyway. Like Isaac, who sold his first story at eighteen and went on selling stories but didn't make enough money at writing to support himself, much less his wife and children, for many years.

Isaac (or his parents) threw away his very first attempts at writing, but I still have some of mine. I keep them to remind me that humility is a Good Thing.

Even the most successful writers have problems coping with their own idiosyncratic styles. Here's Isaac about one of those problems:

"Austin [his Houghton Mifflin editor] and I went over my manuscript on Greece page by page and paragraph by paragraph. Austin corrected typos and ineptness here and there. I have a great tendency to repeat words. If I say 'control' in one sentence, I am likely to use it in the next four or five sentences, four or five times, and never notice. Also, I get fits where every paragraph starts with 'however'; I'm particularly strong on 'however.' Austin says that if sometime in the far future a book attributed to me is discovered in some kitchen midden, they can check whether it is authentically mine or not by measuring the density of 'however's'."

When I was in college I spent most of the day in the labs of my various premed courses, but I also took English courses, read gloomy literature, and tried to write gloomy stories. About one of my heroines, embarrassingly autobiographical, my English professor said, "Just because a girl is unhappy, Miss Jeppson, does not mean she is interesting."

It's good to know what you can write and what you can't. Isaac is best known for his science fiction, but he also wrote mysteries and, of course, reams of nonfiction.

He felt that writing about science was important. He worried about the state of the world, the galloping ignorance of people and their anti-science prejudices. He considered it his duty to educate people as much as possible through writing about science.

In an article (reprinted in *How to Enjoy Writing*) Isaac said, "The very existence of science and technology depends on a population that is both understanding and sympathetic.

"There was a time when science and technology depended strictly on individual ideas, individual labor, and individual financial resources . . . it is so no longer. The growing complexity of science and technology has outstripped the capacity of the individual. We now have research teams, international conferences, industrial laboratories, large universities. And all these resources are strained, too.

"Increasingly, the only source from which modern science and technology can find sufficient support to carry on its work is from that hugest repository of negotiable wealth—the government. That means the collective pocketbook of the taxpayers of the nation. . . .

"If writers can be as effective in spreading the word about science and technology as governments are at sowing hatred and suspicion, public support for science is less likely to fail, and science is less likely to wither. . . ."

I have no comment except to say that anyone who's read this far in this book is also the sort of intelligent person who knows what's going on right now, and knows that if Isaac were alive he'd be grieving, and typing faster than ever.

Isaac and I shared some pet peeves about trends in current fiction:

1. Unpleasantness. I once threw a lauded book across the room because in it there was not a single character, situation, or action that was not unpleasant. Tragic, no. Yucky, yes. Isaac thought I'd done well to restrain myself from throwing it into the building's compactor chute.
2. Violence, which now seems almost obligatory, and can be like drugs. Indulged in, it becomes boring unless the intensity and frequency are increased. I always thought Hitler got a charge out of casualty lists.

A fan once sent Isaac a handsome wooden plaque bearing one of the best sentences Isaac ever wrote—*Violence is the last refuge of the incompetent.*

One of my patients kept obsessing about violence in the world, and asked if I thought it was built-in. I said I agreed with those who thought that violence was not a built-in biological instinct man is doomed to have, but one way of reacting to things, and then I said that a writer once wrote, "Violence is the last refuge of the incompetent." It helped.

3. Lack of structure. Many people hate to acknowledge that human life has a beginning, a middle, and an end. If they are writers, they often compound their denial by ensuring that Nothing Really Happens, told in five hundred pages of floridly impenetrable prose.

I must insert my annoyance with Virginia Woolf. In *A Room of One's Own*, Woolf does root for women's lib, writing about how women have been treated in the past (and in her present), but her pervasive tone seems to be that of someone furious about not being a moneyed aristocrat entitled to the best care and food, that is always provided and prepared by others too lower class to matter. Having a room of one's own is pleasant, but not vital. Isaac had to write all his early stories at a table in an apartment with people carrying on their lives in the same room.

Woolf also complains that it's impossible to be both creative and need to work for a living, citing the hypothetical case of Shakespeare's unfamous sister, as if Shakespeare didn't have to work his balls off. Isaac wrote voluminously while working full time, and although I was neither voluminous nor very successful, so did I.

The secret that Isaac learned, and that I did somewhat, is to be able to concentrate. When I was a child I read Frances Hodgson Burnett's *The Lost Prince* (which I still reread). The boy Marco is taught by his father how to use his mind to control himself:

Marco "found some curious things. One was that if he told himself to remember a certain thing at a certain time, he usually found that he did remember it. . . . He had often tried the experiment of telling himself to awaken at a particular hour, and had awakened almost exactly at the moment by the clock." Isaac could do this, too. Sometimes even I could.

Another thing Burnett taught me was that "when special privation or anxiety beset them, it was their rule to say 'what will it be best to think about first.'" This is the corollary of the concentration on what's important, which I've already said.

I hasten to add that I frequently fail at this, especially when the important thing to do is to be genuinely in the present moment instead of fretting over the past and worrying about the future. Isaac and I were once bemused by the outdoor bulletin board of the Unitarian Universalist Church, frequently passed on our way to and from our favorite place, the American Museum of Natural History. That day the quotation on the board was: "Let us not look backward in anger, or forward in fear, but around us in awareness."

What boggled our minds (aside from the fact that we both needed to do just what the quotation advised) was that it had been written by James Thurber. Then we decided that a humorist was more likely to know and understand the truth of that quotation. After all, most Zen masters have a great sense of humor!

Isaac also had a sense of humor about writing, recounting anecdotes that frequently made fun of himself. In *I, Asimov*, Isaac said, "Writing is a very lonely occupation . . . it's no wonder writers so often turn misan-thropic or are driven to drink. . . ."

[A woman writing an article called and asked him for the name of his favorite bar]

"'I'm sorry,' I said. 'I may sometimes pass through a bar to get to a restaurant, but I've never stopped in one. I don't drink.'

"There was a short pause, then she said, 'Are you Isaac Asimov?'

"'Yes,' I said.

"'The writer?'

"'Yes,' I said.

"'And you've written hundreds of books?'

"'Yes,' I said, 'and I've written every one of them cold sober.'

"She hung up, muttering. I seemed to have disillusioned her."

Isaac was also annoyed when people would ask, "Are you still writing?" as if it were an option. If he said yes, they'd often tell him about more famous writers they've met and the fact that they themselves have thought of writing books that would, of course, be on the best seller list for months.

By the way, it is not true that Isaac wrote on several typewriters at once. He wrote on one, but had several in the closet, as backups. It is true, however, that he wrote books, articles, and stories at the same time. He felt it was one of the reasons why he never had writer's block—if he got stuck in some piece of writing, he'd turn to another, refreshing his mind.

I frequently miss typewriters, in spite of their messy ribbons, the horror of carbon copies, and the lack of a delete key. I have a wonderful computer guru with a cell phone who makes house calls for frantic computer imbeciles like me, but I remember that when one of my typewriter's arms (or whatever it's called) came apart, I fixed it with a bit of wire and eyebrow tweezers.

The computer is great, I suppose, but I still have to print everything out because I can't see all the typos on the screen, only on paper (I've turned off the spell and grammar checkers because they drive me nuts). Writing on computers does give the user a dangerous feeling of omnipotence (see exceedingly important quotation from Russell Baker in the introduction).

Isaac eventually wrote on a computer, but only after he was asked to write about them, and said he didn't own one. In due course, a delivery from Radio Shack deposited several boxes in our hall, where they stayed.

Time passed. Whoever it was who'd asked for the article apparently got fed up and sent knowledgeable young men from Radio Shack to set up a big desk, a printer, and of course their early computer—the TRS-80, which Isaac stared at suspiciously for weeks until he finally taught himself to use it.

The old TRS-80 (which I will NOT call Trash-80) did not even have a hard drive, so the working program had to be installed each time it was used. Whatever one wrote had to be printed out as well as copied onto a ten-inch floppy disk or it would be lost forever. Isaac finally enjoyed doing all that, and wrote so fast on the computer that he used his typewriter only for letters, for which he insisted on making carbon copies.

Being able to type fast on a computer does give a writer an irrational sense of power as all those words appear on the screen so quickly that one's built-in editor has little time to get into the act. Theoretically, the delete key comes into play eventually, but in the meantime, there it is— that universe on the screen, apparently created by magic.

In headnotes to our anthology of funny s-f (*Laughing Space*), Isaac said, "Where is the writer who doesn't dream of omnipotence? Each one is the . . . absolute lord of the little world he creates any time he wishes. At least when the characters don't take the bit in their teeth and drag the writer along, kicking and screaming."

He frequently complained, when he was writing fiction, that the characters were taking over. I know what he means. Any writer does.

And while writing was much easier for Isaac than for most, he did say (in *I, Asimov*) that he was asked by a top-notch science-fiction writer, whose work he admired greatly, where he got his ideas.

Isaac replied,

"'By thinking and thinking and thinking till I'm ready to kill myself.'

[The author] "said with enormous relief, 'You too?'

"'Of course,' I said, 'did you ever think it was easy to get a good idea?'"

I kept telling Isaac that maybe getting ideas was as hard for him as for most writers, but that once he had it, he could take the idea and *run*.

"Yeah," he said, smiling happily, and went back to his word processor.

But there was a certain cynicism he shared with all writers. From another headnote: "Writers feel insecure. Why? I wonder. Surely they can find no fault with the genial publishers, the understandingly tolerant editors, the effusively kindly critics, the warm-hearted readers?"

All I (the loyal and lonely widow and suffering writer) can say to that is, Ha!

Which brings me to critics, the fly in the ointment of artistic achievement. As David Frost said (and I don't remember where), "What a writer thinks of as constructive criticism is six thousand words of closely reasoned adulation." Not, mind you, closely reasoned psychoanalysis.

For yet another strange reason I can't fathom, this reminds me of that awful joke that ends, "But aside from all that, Mrs. Lincoln, how did you enjoy the show?"

When I met Isaac at that 1959 Mystery Writers of America banquet, he and the editor Robert P. Mills, sitting near me at the table, quizzed me about the science fiction I liked. I confessed that I adored the novels of Asimov and Clarke.

Isaac was pleased, although somewhat miffed by the fact that Clarke's *Childhood's End* was the book that had turned me on to science fiction (when, on the advice of my brother, already a longtime s-f fan, I took it with me on an automobile trip down south, during my psychiatric residency).

Then Mills slyly asked me about the short stories, written by a variety of authors, that were in the science-fiction magazine he then edited. I'd read them, but I was a busy doctor and could not remember any of the authors' names. Mills pressed me to give my reaction to the story "Unto the Fourth Generation," which I'd forgotten that Isaac wrote.

I said I didn't like stories in which things happen but unravel at the end so that nothing changes, like Penelope's knitting. I said I liked stories in which people end up being different as a result of what has happened.

Mills then told me that Isaac wrote the story. I gasped and said, "My criticism comes out of being a psychoanalyst, because we try to help people change . . ."

"Dear me," said Isaac (who hated to use swear words in public), "don't apologize. You are perfectly right about the story and I will never do that again."

It says something about Isaac that he kept his word, and me as a friend.

Isaac could not only take criticism, he enjoyed learning from others, even if it showed up some flaw in his reasoning or some gap in his knowledge.

[From a letter] "How nice to have intelligent and helpful friends. And you know—I think there would be a great tragedy in truly knowing everything—for there is a wonderful delight in having things explained to you; in having a curtain drawn from before your eyes.

"Many people accept this where books do the explaining; the book is an inanimate, impersonal object and doesn't know it is explaining. But when another person does the explaining there are often petty hurt feelings about displaying ignorance that causes one to miss all the wonder of it. . . .

"As an example [of hurt feelings] . . . I was at someone's house a week or so ago and the host mentioned the Galapagos Islands and said they were the home of the Komodo lizard . . . and I said no, the Islands were the home of the Galapagos Tortoises [and the iguanas, which are lizards, Isaac]. He said and the Komodo lizard too. And I said, no, the Komodo lizard was from the island of Komodo in the East Indies.

"Now ordinarily I never make a big thing about it but he smiled in so insufferably superior a manner as he said, 'Pardon me, but I know about such things' that I couldn't help saying, 'Not about this thing. Wanna bet?'

"Now, *nobody* ever bets with me because when I know enough to be willing to bet, it's a sure thing. To my surprise he accepted the quarter bet and we went off to consult the Encyclopedia. Well, the Komodo lizard lives on the island of Komodo in the East Indies, and he came back quite disgruntled. However, the unfortunate thing was that his wife said, 'Who won?' and I carelessly answered, 'I, of course,' and he said, 'Why *of course*?' and sulked for the rest of the evening.

"Do you think he was grateful to me for teaching him something? No, he wasn't. However, I was ashamed of myself and spent the rest of the evening being nice to him and finally brought him round (I think). . . .

". . . I still remember (I will never forget) how it was once explained to me that philosophy *was* important and that I was deeply concerned in such a thing as the philosophy of science without even being aware of it. I remember the evening as a time when I was annoyed with the person I was speaking to as long as I was ignorant; but once I had it explained to me, I was annoyed no longer. I was delighted instead.

"Knowledge is not only power; it is happiness—and being taught is the intellectual analog of being loved."

In spite of saying he had no talent for criticizing anyone else's work, he could do it, as long as he could say good things about it. Here are some examples:

[In a letter, while he was writing *Asimov's Guide to the Bible*]

"My desk is abominably crowded. I have four copies of the Bible on it (two King Jameses, a Revised Standard, a Douay) plus a Bible dictionary, a biographical dictionary, a geographical dictionary, an epitome of history, and an etymological dictionary that just arrived today (*Origins,* by Partridge)—all so I can write my book on the Bible which is now nearly half done.

"Nothing, by the way, but *nothing*, can match the King James. I have long thought that the most magnificent line in the English literature is 'And God said, Let There Be Light and there was light.' It consists of eleven monosyllables with the stress so evenly divided that it is impossible to read it except in a series of impressive sounds. There is a feeling of simple power and of inevitability, too. Now, in its place the Douay (Catholic) Version has, 'And God said: Be light made. And light was made.' Also monosyllables, but to me, the music is gone. It's just some poor slob of a translator speaking and not God at all.—God wouldn't say, 'Be light made.' He's a better stylist than that."

[In a letter] "I read a poem recently which pleased me so much, I tried to memorize it—with a little fright, for I am always afraid to find out that I can't remember things so easily any more. Anyway, I had no trouble and here it is:

> Success is counted sweetest
>   By those who ne'er succeed.
> To comprehend a nectar
>   Requires sorest need.
>
> Not one of all the purple host
>   That won the flag today
> Can give the definition
>   So clear, of victory,
>
> As he, defeated, dying,
>   On whose forbidden ear
> The distant strains of triumph
>   Break agonized and clear.

"It's by Emily Dickinson, of course, and perhaps is a cry from her soul at being unable to join the human race.

"In any case, what I liked best is the 'misuse' of words in such a way as to lend the entire phrase incredible force.

"Notice that 'forbidden' modifies 'ear,' but it isn't the ear that's forbidden, but the act of even hearing the strains.

"And notice the entire sentence, 'To comprehend a nectar requires sorest need' which is a delightfully flowery way of saying, 'you have to be really thirsty to appreciate water.'

"Anyway, reading a poem like that makes me terribly dissatisfied with my style because in a million years I couldn't misuse words with such genius.

"Oh, yes, 'purple host' which brings up visions of 'royal purple,' 'imperial,' 'victorious Empire'."

[In a letter describing how he enjoyed the play *Camelot*] "To me, the play was a symbol of man's life and man's ideals—from the hopeful certainty of world-beating of youth to the inevitable disappointment, decay and disillusion of old age, in which the very strength which set up the greatness overshot its mark and brought about the downfall. For it was Arthur's nobility that at once set up civilization and made him unable to deal with either the good Lancelot or the bad Mordred. And it was Lancelot's intense desire for all that was best which made it impossible for him to either reject or accept Guenevere.

"And, of course, there was the final realization that not in one man, or in one generation, can anything great be accomplished—but that mankind, and life in general, was a succession of generations, in which it was enough to nurture a spark from hand to hand, always in the hope that the flame would catch at last.

"Nor need one despair and suppose that failure would always be complete in every generation, for through how many generations did an ape remain an ape until at some point, something ape-like vanished and was replaced by something man-like. It is not even possible to recognize the point when it comes—only through hind-sight can it be seen.

"And so when Arthur passed on the spark of civilization, failing as it had in one generation, to a new generation which was still young enough to believe—he sang the reprise of 'CAMELOT' under such altered circumstances. When 'CAMELOT' was first sung, Arthur spoke of the perfect weather, of things that were not and never could be, of snow that didn't turn to slush and leaves that blew away—pure farce. And at the end he spoke of CAMELOT as a wonderful land of fantasy because it harbored the spark of civilization, so much more marvelous than any bit of weather legerdemain.

"And I wept buckets for the decay of hope, and the loss of youth and innocence and idealism, and more buckets in gratitude for the return of youth and the miracle of the new life in full power springing from the dying of the old—and all around me, I swear, was a dry-eyed house wondering if Guenevere would come out for a final duet. And as I walked out of the theater, everyone was talking about the costumes and the sets and the fact that the songs were hard to remember.

"WHO CARED!!!

"When I was a youngster, whenever I went to a movie with my father (which was rare), he always turned to me when we emerged and asked, 'Well, Isaac, wot did you loined?'

"I didn't hear a damn bastard around me who learned anything. . . . There are a few magic people in the world (I like to think I am one) who feel and see and know things to which most people are as blind as apes. (That way of thinking can lead to snobbery and barren, selfish pride-of-mind, I know, and I try to avoid that.) Still, it is so *good* to be open-eyed, to live a life in which so much can be felt, such depths can be plumbed, such heights can be scaled. And all that remains is to be able to communicate it—and to communicate it to someone. We are both very lucky in this respect, for we can both communicate and if all else fails we can communicate it to one another."

[In a postscript he added] "P.S. Despite my praise of my own communications, I see, as I reread my letter, that my expression of feelings concerning *Camelot* are rather muddy and incoherent. But these letters are first drafts; straight as it comes and completely unpolished; and I leave it to you to get past the maunderings and potterings and see my meaning."

I hope no reader of this book minds that I've included what Isaac called maunderings and potterings. I hope the readers will also see his meaning.

Isaac gave good advice to authors. When I began to write again after finishing analytic school, he sent me his two laws of writing:

1. Thou shalt finish what thou startest.
2. Thou shalt not judge thyself.

By the time we wrote *How to Enjoy Writing*, Isaac and I had crystalized a regime for dealing with bad reviews:

1. Groan and scream.
2. Read review to sympathetic colleague.
3. Write vitriolic letter to critic, read to sympathetic colleague, and laugh fiendishly.
4. Put vitriolic letter into envelope, address it to evil critic, and put a stamp on it.
5. (And never forget this step) Tear up envelope and place in wastebasket.
6. [My addition] Retrieve part of envelope containing stamp. Spend several worthwhile minutes thinking of another story while carefully detaching stamp from envelope by tearing envelope away from stamp, not vice versa.

Isaac believed in coping with rejections by recycling material. He wrote (letter from the sixties), "I got a rejection today! I called John Hancock Insurance to see if they received my [requested] short essay on social conditions in 2000, in which I spoke of sexual freedom, racial integration, etc. He was terribly embarrassed. He wouldn't even show it to his superiors but was sending it right back. I think he was wishing he hadn't sullied his own eyeballs with it. I laughed and said, 'Sure, send it back.'

"I expected a rejection when I wrote it and it doesn't matter. I've just written the first of a projected three articles . . . and as soon as those are done I am going to take that Hancock article, revise and enlarge it into an F and SF article that will be as controversial and thought-provoking (I hope) as KNOCK PLASTIC. In fact, I would *rather* have it in F and SF where *my* people can see it than in the John Hancock annual report where I will merely bring about the death of several hundred old men through apoplectic strokes."

Isaac also believed strongly in the principle of never discussing one's writing with anyone. He strongly urged all writers to say "a book" or "an article"—and nothing else—when someone asks what they're working on. He hated the idea of anyone going to a writers' conference and reading from "works in progress." He would never show anyone, including me, an unfinished manuscript.

I soon got into this habit, and never showed him (or anyone else) what I was writing. Even the books we supposedly coauthored were written first by me. The only fiction with both our names on it was the Norby series—I showed Isaac the first drafts only after I'd completely finished them.

There's nothing quite like completing any job of writing. I sometimes miss the bimonthly deadlines I had for twelve years when I was writing a short science column for a newspaper syndicate, but—at my age—I no longer miss the agony of wondering if I'd really make the deadline. (Living up to Isaac's example, I always did.)

Nevertheless, I suspect that there are not many professional writers who, like Isaac, relish the process of putting one's imagination into words, no matter how many grueling hours it takes at the computer.

From a lifetime of imagining, I know that it's much easier to tell myself stories than to write them down, a process which takes extraordinary effort and concentration, plus the discomfort of asking my herniated disk to put up with sitting at the computer, to say nothing of my pessimistic conviction that (1) I won't finish, and (2) it won't be any good, and (3) nobody will publish it, and (4) if published, it will either not be reviewed or if reviewed, it will be panned, and (5) nobody will read it.

It therefore comes as a shock each time I finally do turn on the computer and start writing, that I really, really do *like* it.

16

MORE NOTES, AND GRIEF WORK

Thisnext-to-last chapter, mostly bits and pieces that at the last minute I decided not to leave out, is full of quotations from letters, including some at the end that it took all my courage to insert.

I wonder what biographers and autobiographers of the future will do without letters. Since e-mail became popular, few computer-savvy people write real letters, the old-fashioned kind written on real paper, put in an envelope, sealed with spit, addressed and stamped, and then entrusted to the faithful but perhaps tottering United States Post Office.

That's sad, for my letters from the likes of Isaac Asimov and others (soon to be mentioned) were important in my life, and that's what a memoir is about, isn't it? Anyway, here are the bits.

*　　*　　*

Isaac was not only a lover of words, but of life and food and many people. He adored his daughter, Robyn, and was particularly fond of his brother, Stan. He also appreciated (with great good humor and insight) himself and his own talents, which may be the secret to success in this world. He laughingly admitted that he was a lot like the peacock in the cartoon that shows it with tail outspread, saying, "Well, I've talked enough about myself. What do YOU think of my tail?"

Isaac referred to this as "cheerful self-appreciation," which comes across in his writing, too. Having known many bores capable of talking nonstop about themselves and their problems, I was relieved to find that Isaac was never boring, never droning on about trivia or trying to one-up the other person with his own list of complaints. Isaac talked and wrote mainly to teach or to entertain.

I hasten to add that Isaac was unusual because he seldom talked in order to elicit advice from anyone. The rest of us sometimes do need to have verbal catharsis with friends, or pay shrinks to do the constructive listening. Hearing oneself talk out loud, and getting reaction from someone else, can often help to clarify whatever the trouble is.

Which reminds me of the joke about the psychoanalytic machine into which the patient would talk.

The machine would keep saying, "Not relevant, not relevant, not relevant."

On rare occasions, the machine would say, "Relevant!" and promptly ring the phone in the home of the human shrink, who would instantly go to the office and listen. This saved everybody a considerable amount of time.

Talking and talking, or writing and writing personal letters, is good when the listener or the letter recipient is allowed to reply. It's called genuine conversation, it's rare, and I miss it.

In the rest of this chapter, all of Isaac's and most of my letters are not in quotes. My annotations to everything are in brackets.

*   *   *

[Letter to Isaac] Tell me, do you think it was more romantic when correspondents took up their sharpened goose quills to answer a letter? Somehow I doubt it. I am of that ancient vintage which remembers learning to write in grade school with wooden pens in which one stuck a metal point. The metal points soon wore out, splayed, and were given to spattering ink all over one's letter. We even had ink wells in our wooden desks, into which one actually dipped the pens.

I seem to remember getting a fountain pen about the same time, but at school we really did learn penmanship that way, complete with blotters and cloth penwipers. I remember it as a pain in the neck. The generation raised on ball-point pens doesn't know what they've missed—and aren't they lucky!

[Isaac's reply] I remember it, too. And you had to put new pen points to your tongue and lick off the fine layer of oil before they could sop up ink.

*   *   *

[From my letter to someone else] The other day Isaac was swapping ethnic jokes with one of his editors. The jokes were the "How many—(fill in appropriate ethnic group)—does it take to change a light bulb" sort. . . .

The editor said, "I've been trying to think of a joke for how many editors it takes to change a light bulb, but I can't think of a good punch line."

Without pausing for breath, Isaac came out with "It takes two. One to get the writer to do the job, and then a copy editor to do it over."

*   *   *

[My letter to Isaac] Having read about the tranquilizing effect of watching fish, I bought some goldfish, a large tank, and all the necessary equipment. But goldfish do not tranquilize *me*. I am a doctor, a biologist, and a hypochondriac, not necessarily in that order. I stare at the fish and try to decide if they are sick. One of them was, from the time I brought it home. It wouldn't eat. I put it in a separate tank and eventually it died.

I have been reading up on fish diseases instead of writing my novel, and all this gives me scope for worry. So I stare at the fish and fret. Is there too much algae? Have I left the light on too long? Are the fish swimming slowly on the bottom (and/or the top) because there is (not enough/too much) oxygen in the water? Have I changed the ammonia-removing crystals I put in the toe of an old stocking, draped over the side of the tank and definitely not contributing to the room's décor?

Isaac, who had suffered along with his children when pets died, did not answer the contents of that letter. Eventually I gave the fish and their tank to his sister and her husband, then avid fish fanciers, and I switched to bird watching:

A mockingbird sits on the stone pinnacle . . . below the east window, and sings—barely audible above the noise of the traffic. He jumps up in the air, showing off his fancy wings and tail, does a half-somersault, and lands back on the pinnacle to sing again. My book on bird behavior says this is called a "loop flight," performed by male birds in spring, probably to declare territory, and possibly to attract a mate. It certainly attracted me. Men have sometimes tried hard to be nice to me, but nobody ever did a loop the loop.

Sometimes I complained in my letters. Not often. I hope not often:

[My letter to Isaac] Have you noticed that modern movie making involves endless close-ups, positioned so that you seem to be staring at people whose faces are plastered against the long, narrow mailbox slot that you and the camera are peering through? I get tired of examining minutely the pores in actors' faces, and sometimes the cameraman's style ends up making me feel positively claustrophobic and I want to shout, "Move the camera back! Let's see the rest of the body!"

Isaac, although he frequently insisted that he was completely non-visual, except, possibly, about page format, did remark that he preferred the dancing in the Fred Astaire movies because Fred insisted that the dancers be completely visible from head to toe.

My memory, being almost entirely visual, relies on what I remember seeing. If my memory is, at least temporarily, in working order, I can conjure up an image of whatever it was that I wish to remember. If it's a page of notes or text, I can then read it, in my head. But not for long.

Isaac, on the other hand, relied on the sort of fabulously detailed and retentive memory that I can't even imagine because it seems so foreign, as if it were the talent of an alien species (and no, Isaac did not come from Alpha Centauri). For instance, he never had to read anything twice because it was there in his head, easily accessible.

Nevertheless, as the following anecdote shows, there were a few times when Isaac's memory was not perfect:

[Letter from Isaac] A most weird thing has just happened to me. A newspaper reporter called me. He said that three Frenchmen had just been awarded the Nobel Prize in physiology and medicine for discoveries in connection with genes and he wanted to know if I could explain to him what they had done, in layman's language. I said, humbly, that he had me for I had never heard of the three Frenchmen and couldn't tell him what they had done. I suggested he call Dobzhansky [Russian-American geneticist, then still alive].

So I got off the phone and brooded. A fine memory I had! I was certainly keeping up with genetics efficiently! I tell you, I was completely crushed.

So I cudgelled my brains savagely and out of nowhere popped up the thought that perhaps the guys who had discovered that Mongolion idiocy was caused by an extra chromosome in the cells had gotten the award. It was an important discovery, opening up a whole new avenue of medical research. The only thing that remained to do was to find out who had made the discovery.

I ransacked my library and came up with the answer—THREE FRENCHMEN HAD DISCOVERED IT!!!!!!

I was back on the phone in a minute, unbelievably jubilant. I had lost only ten minutes and my reputation was saved. I *did* know everything. I got the guy and said oleaginously, "Won't you please read me the three winners of the Nobel Prize."

I could hardly wait.

He read the list. THEY WERE THREE *DIFFERENT* FRENCH-MEN. And I had to say, like a jerk, "Gee, I still don't know."

I still haven't recovered.

*   *   *

In addition to Isaac, I exchanged letters regularly with Dr. Stewart Holmes for about thirty years, until he died in his nineties. I never met him, but he was a wonderful friend.

I started by writing him a fan letter about his book *Zen Art for Meditation* (with pictures selected by Chimyo Horioka). I saved copies of my letters to him, as well as all of his. (I've learned that, legally, letters are owned by the person who wrote them—or that person's estate. I have sent Stewart's letters to his family.)

When, after Stewart's death, I reread my copies of my letters to him, I recovered something I'd forgotten:

"When I was applying for entrance to the William Alanson White Institute of Psychoanalysis, one of my interviewers asked me what my hobbies were. I muttered something about enjoying nature. He asked, 'and what do you think of as your place in nature?'

"Startled, (I didn't know he was a bird watcher) I said the first thing that came into my head—'I'm part of life on Earth, one of a species called human, living in a solar system, in a galaxy, in a great big universe.'

"I have since asked a lot of people that same question. You'd be surprised at some of the answers. They'd say 'to conquer nature' or something similar. It's all very discouraging . . . the experience of delight, in which there is freedom from the desire to control, happens seldom to many people, not even when they are having sex or enjoying immersion in a sport activity. All too many people get a false version of it through alcohol or drugs or having their brains blasted by loud hypnotic sound."

*   *   *

[I could complain about religion to both Isaac and Stewart. This is another letter to Stewart]

"Isaac and I attended a three-lecture series at the American Museum of Natural History, on evolution. I had no idea that adult (not young) human beings are the only mammals who are in constant danger of choking to death because their windpipes and gullet cross instead of remaining separate. Unlike a newborn, an adult human cannot swallow and breathe at the same time. That's because the larynx sinks low in the neck, leaving a huge pharynx which acts as a muscular chamber to modify the flow of air from the trachea.

"While dangerous and inconvenient, this obviously jury-rigged [constructed in a makeshift fashion] arrangement (and the Creationists believe human beings were carefully designed by a deity!) does permit us to have articulate speech so I guess it's worth it. . . .

"I feel so sorry for religious people who cling to the idea that God created everything. . . . In evolution parts of the body are put to other uses because they are there—whereas an omniscient creator would surely be smart enough to design a better thing from scratch. To believe in such a creator one has to explain away idiotic things like sinuses that were supposed to drain from a quadripedal posture [I was having sinus surgery at the time], or reproductive openings smack near the excretory opening because once they were all one cloaca."

[A letter from Isaac] I have received a copy of *The Jerusalem Bible* (a new detailed translation by Catholics) and I'm working through the various notes in microscopic print. One item in particular set me to laughing sardonically. It seems that in the early books of the Bible, the phrase "covering his feet" is used two or three times. It is a euphemism for "defecating." Very well, then, our prissy translators put a little superscript at the phrase and when you look to the foot of the page they explain that the phrase is a euphemism.

And for what is it a euphemism? Carefully, they explain. It is a euphemism for "relieving nature." The intelligent translators seem completely unaware that they are defining a euphemism by another euphemism and that if a naïve person doesn't know either euphemism he remains completely in the dark.

I once heard Billy Graham (the evangelist) explain that the Bible was full of "straight" talk. It called "a spade a spade." It said "hell" and "damn" and "whore" (though *he* didn't say "whore"). What Billy doesn't seem to know, though, is that the Bible contains more euphemisms per square yard than any other work of literature in my opinion. Heavens! The King James Version says "Lord" instead of "Yahveh" about a thousand times, and *that's* a euphemism. I think you once feared my work on the Bible would lead me to religion in my old age. Have no fears!

[A letter from Isaac, who was doing children's books on the Bible at the time] I did not find *Words From the Exodus* as much fun as *Words In Genesis*, because I had to deal with the law-giving books and these are deadly dull and have to be treated with kid-gloves. Couldn't explain how Sodom gives rise to sodomy, and all those little verses that forbid transvestitism and bestiality, and persnickety regulations concerning the menstrual flow, and thousands of words on the careful diagnosis (by the priests) of leprosy, and so on.

However, I did manage to drag in the invention of the telegraph, and Queen Victoria's fiftieth anniversary, and Coele-Syria, and the Codex Sinaiticus, and the Liberty Bell and other things like that there.

[Letters to Stewart] "It was nice that the Pope has officially moved Creationism back a few billion years, but I wish the Church would decide that God didn't intend for homo sap to multiply quite so fruitfully. . . .

"I think many people need to have a god as a 'prime causative agent' because so many people feel helpless, trapped by life's problems, and long for a good parent. In childhood, we don't always understand what the parent is doing or saying, so in adulthood people recreate that parent in a god who is to be followed on faith, not rational understanding. Gods were vital to primitive cultures because, before science was invented and began to explain things, so much was not understood. And feared. Fear promotes irrational ideas."

[Letter to Isaac, after I learned something about Orthodox Judaism for the first time] As you know, to be really observant, one has to have three complete sets of pots, pans, and dishes. This virtually ensures family togetherness and survival of cultural mores. I was told "having to keep track of all the rules is what's held the Jewish culture together all these years."

I've decided that I disapprove of holding cultures together. Let everything change. It's easy for me to say that because, between my great-great grandmother and me there have been four complete cultural breaks (counting the one I started for myself by becoming atheistic). By cultural breaks, I mean that damn little tradition got passed on. One thing about the world of the goyim—when we want to leave home, we can grab one saucepan and go.

[Another letter to Isaac on the world of one type of goyim—and it always amused Isaac that Mormons lumped Jews in the category of Gentiles, those who are not Mormon]

In 1945, when I was at Colorado College for the summer, one of my Utah cousins was in the Navy program there. He and I would walk on the then-empty mesa between the town and Pike's Peak, arguing about religion. He really believed that God had created the world with all the dinosaur bones, etc., in it to titillate humans. Much later in life, he left the Mormon Church and joined the Fundamentalist Mormons in southern Utah, acquiring two more wives and more children than I care to count. According to their theology, both regular Mormons and the Fundamentalists think that souls are waiting up yonder to get into each new birth, so children are a Good Thing.

[A letter to Stewart] "I broke my foot in April in a fashion which I think I ought to tell you about. Isaac was giving the first lecture of a lecture trip of three. It was at a conservative Jewish temple . . . and one of the members got mad during the question and answer period, reading out loud a passage from Deuteronomy about the wrath of God. Isaac made a few disparaging remarks about the author of Deuteronomy, eventually got a standing ovation, and all adjourned to a nearby reception hall.

"After punch and cookies, and while Isaac signed books, I ran back through the auditorium to the cantor's office to get our coats. When I returned through the auditorium the lights were out and I didn't see two little steps. I fell down them, crumpling my right foot smack in front of the holy of holies. I was taken to a hospital, x-rayed, and put on crutches.

I could not drive and had to sit in the back seat elevating my swollen foot with its hairline fracture.

"Isaac wondered why the God of Deuteronomy had it in for me instead of him, until we got to Jamestown and he found out why. He began to get shaking chills which continued through THAT lecture and on to the next one at Cornell, where he not only lectured but had two press interviews, three receptions, and a dinner with students. He didn't tell me about the chills and never got close to me until we got home and I managed to get within feeling distance of him.

"I took his temperature, which was high. I diagnosed drug reaction because all through the trip he'd been taking sulfa after a previous cystoscopy. To play it safe, I insisted we go to an emergency room for tests. The fever stopped when he stopped the sulfa, and he was well the next day.

"During the following six more weeks of me on crutches, Isaac had to do the marketing and clean the apartment, muttering about the subtlety of the deity of Deuteronomy."

I now want to insert more about my mother, and the fact that Isaac often surprised me by being psychologically perceptive in ways I had not anticipated. He wasn't all that friendly with his own mother, but he understood mine perhaps better than I did.

By 1970, my mother had been a widow for twelve years. She obviously liked Isaac and read his books, mostly the nonfiction ones. Eventually she invited us to spend a weekend with her in New Rochelle.

When we arrived, mother ushered us and our suitcases upstairs, and pointed to separate rooms. Isaac was fifty, and I was forty-four years old. I realized that Isaac and I were not supposed to occupy the same bedroom, much less the same bed.

I understood what mother did not quite say—that she knew about and was managing to tolerate the fact that he and I had started to live together in Manhattan, where such things seemed to go on all the time, but if we slept in the same bedroom in her suburban house, *what would people think*!

What indeed? And how would they find out? I did not ask. My mother and her sisters were raised in a small town where everyone knew what everyone else was doing.

Except for the end of medical school, followed by internship, I had by then lived for twenty-two liberated years in the psychological haven of glorious Manhattan.

I picked up my suitcase. "If I can't sleep in the back room's double bed with Isaac, I'm going home."

"But dear . . ."

I started down the stairs, followed by Isaac, who said, "Janet, let's please your mother."

"I'm going home," I said.

Mother sighed. She did not threaten to produce a migraine. Perhaps she remembered the one time (before Isaac arrived in my life) when we had a bad argument (I can't even remember over what) and she said, "I'm going upstairs and have a headache."

I had laughed, because (I was in analysis at the time) the truth was finally out. I said, "You just do that." And she hadn't. I was amazed.

Anyway, this time—with Isaac stroking her hand and looking horribly anxious—Mother said, "You can stay in the back room."

"We won't tell anyone," I said. So we used the double bed, which had an enormous horsehair mattress jammed between a brown wood headboard (with posts) and a battered brown wood footboard I disliked because I often push my feet over the end of a bed. The mattress, however, felt good.

"It's been recently rebuilt," I told Isaac. "It had started to sag after years of hard use by my parents." (In their later years, however, they had progressed—if that's the correct word—to twin beds conjoined by the same headboard. I'd been told that my six-foot father had wanted, at last, a longer-than-normal mattress. The old bed had gone to the back room for guests. My father died in one of the twin beds, which was given away, and my mother used the other.)

"Perhaps that's another reason why your mother didn't want us to use this bed."

"Because it's rebuilt and she's saving it for guests, not family?" Mother and I tended to appraise each other's motives in a negative way.

"Maybe she's sentimental about this bed," said Isaac.

I was ashamed, because I hadn't thought of that. I remembered that this was the bed I'd enter—always on my father's side—to be cuddled when I was small. I was also reminded that Isaac was like most men—more sentimental than women pretend to be.

From then on, mother treated Isaac like an adored son-in-law who was afflicted with a difficult girlfriend, her daughter, and Isaac was smitten because, he said, he'd never had a (future) mother-in-law who approved of him that much.

Although I loved my father, I did like my mother, who was remarkable in many ways. After she died, I found a notebook she'd used when she was a playground director in Philadelphia. She'd either composed or copied some sayings that, when I read them, were meaningful to me:

"The power of freedom is the power to transcend limits. As the child grows he becomes powerful in proportion to the limits he overcomes. . . . Only in so much as the child is left free to solve his own problems will he develop. He should be allowed to choose his friends, his own religion, and his own occupation in life."

Mother probably had more freedom herself than most girls born in 1896, in Utah. Her apparently saintly Danish-descended father was busy with the family business that never did quite as well as expected. Her fussy, English-descended Victorian mother was busy having her own migraine headaches while coping with six living children (three having died in infancy). With funds the family probably could not afford, the oldest girl was sent to Europe (with a chaperone) to study and get a polish unavailable in Brigham City. This made the whole family seem "different."

Having red hair and freckles, Mother (the next to youngest) thought of herself as plain compared to her sisters, but she and Dad fell in love in high school and never quite fell out of it. They'd go with their friends on buggy rides into the canyons, unchaperoned. When, after World War I, they finally married and went East because Utah then had only a two-year medical school, her parents did not object. Dad's older siblings did, because he had refused to go on the two-year proselytizing mission required by Mormon youths.

Perhaps Mother was thinking of herself—as a child and as a future mother—when she wrote, "Parents must have faith in the ability of the child to overcome obstacles. There must be instilled in the child that he is capable of all things. Parents must not ridicule the child's efforts in any way and at any time. . . ."

She never ridiculed my efforts, although when I tried to master one of her skills, especially sewing, her perfectionism turned me off to the joy of it. But when I tried learning to drive a car from my father, I ended up learning from Mother, who was remarkably calmer about the whole thing.

*   *   *

[One more anecdote about the problems of writing. This was during the many years when I supervised students who were studying to become analysts]:

I'd been writing, in my spare time, a novel—probably one of the early three that I subsequently tore up and threw away. I'd discovered that the damn novel kept writing itself in my head whether I wanted it to or not, no matter what else I was doing.

I managed to give adequate concentration when I was with patients, but it was much harder with supervisees.

One day a student asked, "Dr. Jeppson, what do you think the patient's dream means?"

I hadn't a clue, having been in outer space (it was a science-fiction novel), but in a few seconds my brain regurgitated what it had heard when I was not consciously paying attention. The dream (something about crawling on a long piece of wood) seemed as dull as the student's patient, who presented himself as timid and dutiful.

Suddenly a picture, in color, came into my mind. It was a scene from a 1930s comic strip, in which nubile young women were being captured by pirates. So I told the student to ask the patient if he'd ever wanted to be a pirate.

The student looked at me as if he thought I'd gone crazy, but he did ask the patient, who had gasped and confessed having secret desires to be a pirate and make his enemies walk the plank. I hope I told the student that the patient might also be afraid that his therapist would make *him* walk the plank. Creativity certainly functions in peculiar ways.

*   *   *

There were some highly personal letters I'm finally old enough to write about because I no longer care that much about What Will People Think.

[This was a series of letters to Isaac about Tolkien, highly abridged] I didn't think I'd like *The Hobbit*, feeling not much on elves and dwarves, but I've discovered that I have not outgrown fairy tales by any means. Tolkien writes a good fairy tale . . . and I was thoroughly hooked when after a couple of pages I read "By some curious chance one morning long ago in the quiet of the world, when there was less noise and more green. . . ."

. . . Last night, sobbing wildly, I finished the trilogy. Why was I crying? Not because I finished *The Return of the King,* although I hated not having any more to read, nor because it was terribly sad. . . . By the end, the people in the Ring trilogy, whether human or not, became so real and close that you feel you've lived with them, loved them, and shared everything they've experienced.

I suppose that's why I cried—because things do end, and people die or go away, and great events fade into legends. I was even crying over the wonderful lost spirit of good triumphing over evil that was felt during World War II, when things were grim but simple compared to the intricate, unpleasant complications of the present, when good hearts lose hope.

*   *   *

Now I'm ready to reveal something I've been trying to transcend—my grief over Isaac's death (which I mention but avoid describing in the next chapter). Perhaps some of what follows may help someone who's new to grief:

To begin with, Isaac's death was publicized, so Stewart knew before I wrote him. He wrote a letter of consolation, including this: "I know how difficult it is to flow acceptingly with the Tao's stream when the stream bed is full of rocks. If you can only keep hold of the realization that actually that's all one *can* do—flow with the stream."

And in another letter, he said, "Now, Isaac is a living, vital element in the human psycho-electric field part of the universe—and hence is part of us, part of you, part of me, part of everyone. I realize that such an awareness is not a satisfactory substitute for his organismal presence, but . . . in your time of agony, know that I am with you in spirit."

Until I read the copies I'd made of my letters to him, I'd forgotten that Stewart was the only person I wrote to at length about my grief, which, I see now, had a definite progression.

[Early in 1992, after Isaac died] "Almost every day I find myself sinking into such despair that I don't really want to go on . . . everything seems unimportant or utterly meaningless without him and his work as the center of my universe. Sometimes I frantically call people so their talk will distract me from the terrible loneliness. At night I call people like my brother or ex-roommates in California, where they aren't asleep yet. I also read novels, or sometimes even work at the computer, where I don't feel that unhappy. Today was better because I've been writing. I hope not to stay such a mess forever."

[Two months later in 1992] "These days I'm so trapped in grief that there are only rare moments when I can be THERE in the present moment enough to appreciate it. Most of the time, the present is a miasma of loneliness and emptiness and meaninglessness that I never dreamed could be so profound and so debilitating. . . .

"I've realized that I haven't slept much for two years, especially the last year, when Isaac was so sick. For months I got 2 or 3 hours of sleep a night, and even after he died, I continue to wake at 3 or 4. I don't dream much because the early morning REM sleep doesn't occur. This all contributes to extreme exhaustion, if not craziness.

"I used to be a constant dreamer, in detail and in living color. I finally had one dream, after going back to sleep until 7. The therapist I'm now seeing once a week (for a while) said it was a good dream because in it I carried Isaac to an operating room and he was light enough to carry (in real life we had many occasions when he'd fall and I couldn't get him up)—so perhaps the burden of grief is lighter."

[At the time I wrote this, Robyn and I—on the advice of Isaac's doctors—were reluctantly keeping it secret that he died of complications from AIDS acquired in the blood transfusion received in 1983 during the triple bypass surgery on his heart.]

[Seven months after Isaac's death] "I belong to the Ethical Culture Society, which runs bereavement groups. I was asked to join a new one, and went with misgivings. Fortunately it has turned out to be helpful. It's not therapy; the leader is a woman who works at Ethical Culture and has led previous groups. I am the only professional there, and can't stop myself from occasionally acting like one, but although I try not to do that very much, some of it makes me feel useful. . . .

"One thing that came out last time was that all of us are in a bereavement group because we're suffering—we cared about somebody and we've lost them. There are lots of people who have never let themselves care enough about anybody to suffer this much. This thought is consoling during the times when the grief is so bad that one almost wishes to be like those people who protect themselves by not caring very much.

"There are three of us widows who've lost spouses but have no children and grandchildren. I don't think the ones with children can possibly understand the kind of separateness that occurs when a spouse dies and the person left has not borne his children."

[1993] "Isaac's been gone for over a year now, but I still cry every day and often feel as if there's no longer any real purpose in living. I don't tell people about this, because I now get scolded about not working through my bereavement better. The people who scold usually haven't been thoroughly bereaved.

"I can't seem to become one of the many people that exist happily, doing their thing, being creative and also useful—yet without a special love for and from another person that fills every moment. I do my job, am creative and useful, but without being of use to Isaac, without his presence, it's a sham."

[Later in 1993] "As another bereaved friend said recently, the grief is worse the second year. Especially for me, because I'm so very alone, with hardly any family and a job [I was writing a bimonthly science column for a newspaper syndicate] that is solitary. When one has been kicked out of paradise, living often seems pointless. I think of Milton's Satan, who when kicked out at least had a bunch of fallen angels going with him.

". . . I didn't have a big problem coping with and accepting aging, health problems, other losses—until Isaac died. Without love, and human touch, life is a farce. Don't tell me you understand, Stewart, because you don't. Your wife is alive, and you have many children, grandchildren, and great-grandchildren who love you. But I appreciate your good will, and revere your remarkable capacity for happiness. Please be patient with me and maybe, after a while, I'll be mindfully in the present, and enjoying life."

[End of 1993] "The other day I was feeling sorry for myself . . . when the phone rang. It was a colleague of mine, my age. When I met him at a conference about 3 years ago he was walking with canes and said he had Lou Gehrig's Disease (ALS). When he called this week his voice sounded strong. I remarked on it and he said his new respirator functioned well, pushing air through his vocal cords so he could still talk. He can't walk and until 3 weeks ago used an electric scooter to go to the medical school where he still teaches. Now he's going to switch to an electric wheelchair because he can manipulate its controls with the two of his fingers that still work. Then he blew my mind by saying, 'I'm fortunate that the disease has progressed slowly enough so that I have time to adjust to each new loss.'

"Each new loss. It doesn't do any good to tell myself that he's never experienced the loss of a deeply loved spouse because his losses of bodily functions and physical independence are so horrendous that I squirm with private embarrassment at my own self-pity.

"Since then, it has been easier for me to Get Rid of Things. I've just had my bedroom (badly damaged in a water leak some years ago) replastered and painted. It's now rather empty and stark, almost monastic, but I find that I like it. Life's too short to fuss over non-essentials, and the older and lonelier I get, I find the essentials to be health and creativity. And as with my colleague who goes through losses daily, all of us as we age have to accept minor or major losses of health and even creativity. Some people stay young in mind and spirit—you are a constant inspiration to me, my friend."

[1997] "Yes, I'm depressed. Why not? I'm allowed. Or am I? I've discovered painfully that if I make even the slightest mention of not feeling happy, I get inundated by 1) Scolding ('after five years, you should be over Isaac's death'); 2) Advice ('Do a lot of traveling—my husband and I enjoyed our month in Europe last year'); 3) Competitively sad stories about other people's problems.

"Well, it's interesting."

[Later in 1997] ". . . That's about it for current news of me. I try to stay well, since there's no one to take care of me, and I do a lot of walking, take Fosamax (which is supposed to strengthen bone since, having had breast cancer, I can't take estrogen), and calcium and lots of vitamins.

"It can all be summed up by saying that I'm hanging in there, not as depressed as I was, and frequently able to enjoy—mindfully—What Is."

17
MORTALITY
(Intimations Of and Coping With)

W hile fond of using imagination and escaping into virtual realities, mine or someone else's, I'm a strong believer in muddling realistically through the vicissitudes of life. It usually keeps you from incubating depression the way a penguin incubates an egg, keeping it from touching reality by holding it up on both feet—which doesn't work (except for penguins) because reality always forces acceptance of its existence.

One of the permanently discombobulating aspects of reality is CHANGE. And it never stops. Within my own lifetime, the first nonstop transatlantic plane made it, the atom was split, humans walked on the Moon, I can watch Fred Astaire (or Jon Stewart!) in my living room, and the world's population has not only doubled but continues to go up and up.

As Buckminster Fuller said (in a clipping I have but don't remember where it's from), "The Universe is continally changing and we are going to be confronted with the new. We are here to be problem-solvers. That's our function in the Universe."

Unfortunately, most of us are not the greatest of problem solvers, accepting change and doing our best with it. To feel sane and keep going from day to day, most of us tend to inhabit a virtual reality in which we ignore change and pretend to believe in permanence. Like Faust, we risk doom by asking a happy moment to stay.

Unexpected change, especially if it's rapid, often makes it hard to think. Thomas Paine (my mother's house in New Rochelle was on his property) was big on thinking—"When precedents fail to assist us, we must return to the first principles of things for information and *think*, as if we were the *first men* that thought." He lived in interesting times, too.

Isaac did a lot of thinking and writing about change. Nevertheless, he had his own problems with it. During one of the snowier winters of our communication by snail mail, Isaac wrote, "Of the five heaps of snow in my driveway, one is almost gone and two more are pretty sickly. That always makes me feel sad. I'm delighted to see the snow go, you understand, but I can't help empathizing with the heaps. I tend to personify them ever since I was a little kid. The snow (in my mind) was always fighting an eventually losing fight with the sun.

"Occasionally it would receive reinforcements from the heavens, but as March wore on, the retreats would never be made up for by the reinforcements and each succeeding retreat would be farther than the one before.

"The army would break up into separate contingents [Isaac, the pacifist, was nevertheless eager to write a military history of the world] and I would imagine them exhorting each other and keeping each other's courage up. I would even imagine the largest heap to be rather scornful of the others as faint-hearts giving in to the enemy and coming down in its pride to humiliating defeat.

"Even now, mature and rational as I am, each morning I make a little round of inspection to view the army and feel a pang of sympathy for the defeated. Is this serious psychological sickness on my part, or am I just a harmless nut, dear doctor?"

I wrote, "I don't understand about you and the piles of snow. All things change—every thing trying to remain immutable is fighting a losing fight. Which sounds very wise and doesn't explain why I get annoyed when things wear out and walls need repainting, etc."

Isaac answered, "Fighting to stay alive is fighting the inevitable. The good fight has its own values. That it must end in irrevocable defeat is irrelevant."

In *It's Been a Good Life* I wrote about Isaac's irrevocable defeat—his terminal illness and death. I mentioned it in the chapter before this one, but I don't want to write about the details now.

When he was dying, I said, "Isaac, you're the best there is." He couldn't speak, but he grinned and nodded "yes." He had that sense of humor to the end.

After my mother died and I had to go through her possessions, I found a penciled note saying, "Prayer: Keep us from letting our sorrows becloud the joys of others." She's right. Besides, real, deep down sorrow cannot be fully expressed. And perhaps should not be.

Instead, I will write about a much more homely aging and death. I once had a hamster named Cheeky, in whose tiny world I could abandon my human perspective and join him in his unself-conscious examination and enjoyment of the few places he knew as home and of the tiny rituals by which he lived.

Cheeky had his own brand of stubbornness, sometimes not responding when I'd call him to come out of his house. If I poked into the house, he would stick his nose out, yawn in my face, delicately replace the paper all around him, and effectively disappear. Then I'd go and read a book.

I sometimes took Cheeky out of his cage and let him play on my desk, which had cubbyholes for him to explore. Once, and only once, I put him on the bed, a flat surface with no hiding places. He ran madly around, apparently searching for home, and when I suddenly moved, he shrieked, bounced backward, and began jumping up and down on his hind feet, his front paws held up while he made strange noises, something like a laryngitic and very angry squirrel. His teeth were bared at me, but I didn't laugh at this tiny creature being so ridiculous in bravery.

I said softly, "It's all right, Cheeky" and cupped my hands around him. He immediately went down on all fours and let me pick him up. I put him back in his cage, which he had to inspect thoroughly before he took some apologetically offered pignoli from my fingers.

Hamsters live only two to three years at the most. When Cheeky was old, his fur developed bare patches and he slept more than usual. Until he died in his sleep, he stubbornly maintained his dignity—washing himself, keeping his nest clean, dragging himself weakly away from his nest to defecate in his usual place.

Doing one's best, as long as one can, is important. I intend to try, but it's not always possible. I know Isaac tried his best, and usually succeeded. I think I'm *trying* my best. Succeeding is another thing.

After I'd had a radical mastectomy in 1972, Isaac and I were asked to write about it for *Family Health Magazine.* Isaac wrote the details about the event. I wrote:

"Beyond the fear of deformity and the loss of love is something more universal; the fear of death. The mastectomy patient has had her brush with cancer, and there can never be complete confidence that the victory won at such great cost is final, or that it can even endure for a very long time.

"Death is the lot of us all, of course, and we are all, ultimately, its victims. Most human beings manage to avoid awareness of this, but anyone whose tissues have, anywhere, been touched by cancer, loses some of the ability to do this . . . it is difficult to avoid hypochrondria—especially during the first few years—and yet it must be avoided if life is not to degenerate into a morass of imagined ills.

"The patient should try, over and over, to accept the basic uncertainty of life . . . yet if near collision with death makes us bitterly aware of the sadness and harshness of living with a future out of control, it may also teach us to live more in the present. If we commit ourselves to being fully aware, alive, savoring each passing moment as intensely as possible, it will turn out that there will be so many moments neither sad nor harsh, that, in balance, life will not have been damaged by the experience after all, but rather it will have been improved."

Thanks to Isaac, my life was improved after cancer.

I am reminded of a visit with the science-fiction editor John Campbell and his wife, Peg. John lectured me on the deficiencies and sins of psychiatrists (I was not yet a published writer and did not tell him I hoped to be).

Peg did not lecture. She showed me the magnificent rug she was making. I said I'd never have the courage to learn how to do something big and wonderful like that.

Peg said, "The only important things are time and eyesight, and neither lasts, so you might as well start doing the biggest and best thing you want to do."

It pays to remember this. Isaac never had to. He did it, over and over.

When my Aunt Hazel was in her nineties, long before Isaac died, our frequent telephone calls were often illuminating. Once when I called her she said she'd had a nightmare the night before. In the dream, she was in a room that was completely empty except for herself and a table. That's all of the dream.

After she told me, I naturally had sad thoughts about intimations of death and whatnot, but she said, "I know what the dream means. It means that there's no one left who is my age and who knows the things I know, who remembers what I remember, who shared the past with me. It's very lonely, because there's no one to talk to."

I'm not yet quite at that point. When I miss Isaac so much, I try to remind myself to be glad that he never had to experience what Aunt Hazel did.

I also try to remember something else that Isaac said [in a letter about mortality]:

"I suppose there are people who are so 'lucky' that they are not touched by phantoms and are not troubled by fleeting memory and have known not nostalgia and care not for the ache of the past and are spared the feather-hit of the sweet, sweet pain of the lost—and I am sorry for them, for to weep over what is gone is to have had something prove worth the weeping, and I would rather weep a thousand times than to live a life having never had anything worth weeping the loss of. But now I'm crying too hard to type. . . ."

In C. S. Lewis's *Perelandra*, the female inhabitant of the planet eats the fruits on the different trees. She tries to explain to an all-too-human Earthman that "Every joy is beyond all others. The fruit we are eating is always the best fruit of all."

I'd like to believe that, to live by that, and sometimes I do, but it was a hell of a lot easier when Isaac was alive.

When Isaac was dying, with Robyn and me at his bedside, his warm hand held mine firmly, and at that moment it was enough, the best fruit of all.

Then he stopped breathing and his hand relaxed and grew cool. I wanted his suffering to end, as it just had, but I'd have given anything to have back just that warm grasp.

I originally wanted "happily" to be the last word in this memoir, because it was the original title (*Happily—In and Out of Private Virtual Reality*), and because it is the last word of one of the stories that follow. Perhaps it can never be the last word, unless you use your imagination to invent myths with happy endings.

I'm not sorry. What is, is.

We can't always choose what happens to us in reality, but we can choose how we record it and, above all, how we live in our private virtual reality.

It's more fun to choose (ah—it's going to be the last word after all) . . . *happily*.

THE END

APPENDIX
A FEW SHORT STORIES

GRIMM WITCHERY

In the small Kingdom of Corus, royal families traditionally ran to three offspring, all male. This made for a shortage of royal females, particularly since the planet contained only one sparsely inhabited continent and no other kingdoms.

No one, least of all the three royal princes, expected gray-bearded King Coruman to do anything about the fact that he'd been a widower for many years. But he had.

"Zounds!" said Crown Prince Corvol, his black mustaches bristling. "The new queen is younger than we are, too skinny, not blonde, not beautiful, reads improving books, and supports the Dragon Conservation League."

Second-in-line Prince Corst clenched his large fists, erecting the tufts of red hair on each knuckle. "She's only a minor princess on Hellbot, but every royal female from that accursed planet is a witch. Pops says she'll make him live happily ever after."

Corvol blanched. "He'll be King ever after!"

"But he seems happy," said the third son, Prince Charmo, who suffered because he couldn't live up to tradition. Third sons were supposed

From *The Ultimate Witch*, edited by Byron Preiss and John Betancourt (New York: Dell, 1993). Reprinted with permission.

to be terribly muscular, terribly stupid, full of noble goodness, and entitled to rare adventures. Charmo had long ago given up on fulfilling anything but the goodness, no challenge in the dullness of life on Corus.

"Well, we royal princes aren't happy," said Corvol. "Our stepmother's programmed the food synthesizers with low-fat, low-cholesterol, low-salt recipes . . ."

Corst grunted. "She hexed the plasti-armor I use in tournament practice. I itched until she said I'd stop itching if I took a shower every day."

"She's a menace," said Corvol. "She put a spell on my holovid to lower the volume of music on my favorite barebottom dancing shows. I think the bottoms have slipped, too. Let's do something to make Mavis miserable."

"Let's kill her," said Corst, putting on hold his planned assassination of Corvol so he could become Crown Prince.

"I don't think that's a good idea," said Charmo. "If Mavis is a witch, it might be dangerous to try—anything."

"Of course she's a witch. There's no doubt about it," said Corvol. "She casts spells on Pops and dances around their bedroom while he sleeps. I can see it from my windows."

"You mean they never . . . ," Corst's eyes bulged out.

"Not that I've seen."

"Papa likes the way he's been sleeping so well since he married Mavis," said Charmo.

"We'll begin with making Mavis miserable and proceed from there," said Corvol. "First we'll find out if Mavis is a virgin."

"I don't think that's a good idea," said Charmo. "If she can cast sexual spells, you might become her next victim. Who knows what she concocts up in that tower room she's turned into a laboratory?"

"Shut up," said Corvol. "Let's get away from Corus for a while. We'll poach a few space dragons and drape the skins all over the throne room. That ought to bitch up her witchery and prove to Pops that she's a poor choice as queen."

Corvol and Corst took their favorite hunting ship, which they could manage without a troublesome crew, some of whom might be timid about chasing dangerous space dragons, or, worse, tearful about killing them. Charmo was not invited.

King Coruman decided to accompany his two eldest sons on their dragon-hunting expedition. He said he was a little tired of sleeping so soundly and needed more exercise.

A few days later, the royal spaceship gave chase to a huge space dragon, tickling its solar sail-wings with bursts of phaser fire.

Space dragons are not bright, but they know an enemy when they see one. The dragon was making excellent progress at prying open the spaceship when the two princes upped the phaser dosage.

King Coruman, somewhat prematurely, spoke to his young wife by ship-planet hycom to announce the victory.

"Can't you hear me, Mavis? I said we'll be bringing home a magnificent dragon head for over the dining room fireplace . . ."

"I'll throw up at every meal," said Mavis.

Charmo, who was listening, reflected that for such a small, plain Queen she had a resonantly musical voice. It was probably one of the evil assets exploited by witches.

"Speak up, Mavis," Coruman roared. "Can't hear a blasted thing with—hey, watch out, boys! That's a female dragon, and you've got babies flying out of the carcass into the photon torpedo vents! Shoot 'em out, boys!"

Those were his last words, before the explosion.

The triple funeral was magnificent, the King's coffin draped with the largest dragon skin anyone on Corus had ever seen. The Corusian salvage team had been successful in recovering not only the corpses of royalty, but that of the royal prey.

Plus one baby dragon, alive and well in a crib Mavis installed in her tower laboratory. While adult dragons can travel handily in the airlessness of space, their young do better growing up with all the air and care needed by a human baby. Or so Mavis said. She seemed to know so much about everything.

After his coronation, Charmo told Mavis she ought to go back to Hellbot. He'd found himself unduly disturbed by the body-building exercises Mavis had taken to performing every morning in the palace courtyard.

Mavis shook her head, her silky black hair shimmering. "I won't go back where there's a surplus of royal females, all of them witches. I'm a novelty here and the Corusian populace pays hefty fees for the various, ah, services I perform for them."

"Services?"

She blinked. Her dark lashes were longer than he'd noticed before. "Fortune-telling. Simple spells. Potions to heal the sick and grow the crops and insure virility . . ."

"The same potion?"

"Certainly not. And I'm staying on Corus."

"Then you must move out of the palace. You must be gone by the time I return from my quest."

"Quest?"

"To seek True Wisdom, and the Proper Princess."

"In that order?"

"Not necessarily. When I bring back my Queen-to-be, I don't want you in the palace, Mavis. You're a bad example."

"Okay, Mo. Have fun, and bring back a beauty."

Weeks later, married and landing on Corus, King Charmo was proud to inform his subjects that he had found his Proper Princess and that her name was actually Beauty. The populace cheered when she stepped out of the ship, for she was gorgeous from the tip of her delicate toes to the crown of her magnificent blonde head. Even her profile was perfect.

"Congratulations, Mo," said Dowager Queen Mavis. "By the way, I won't be at the banquet tonight, in case you were thinking of inviting me. Now that I've moved and expanded my laboratory, I have so much work to do. I'm busy with a form of witchery called genetic engineering."

Charmo watched Mavis hitch up her blue jeans and stride off to the back of the palace where there was a mountain Mavis had just finished building with a machine she'd invented. She opened what seemed to be a door at the bottom of the mountain, entered, and shut it behind her. The mountain was smooth, circular, and shone like glass, except at the top, where the laboratory was surrounded by a briar hedge.

That night, after performing his conjugal duties, Charmo kissed his beautiful sleeping bride and sneaked out to the backyard mountain. The door was locked. He touched the mountain's surface. It was genuine glass.

"Charmo," Beauty said one day, "your witchy stepmother has got to go. I don't like her. The other day she gave me a computerized mirror that says I'm the fairest in the land."

"It's true. Rather nice of Mavis."

"The mirror adds a depraved chuckle. You must get some foreign prince to marry Mavis and take her away from Corus."

"Excellent idea, my love. We'll invite the richest, handsomest, bravest princes in the Galaxy."

Mavis agreed to marry the first royal male to achieve entrance to her guarded laboratory on top of the mountain.

"Without using any sort of antigrav machine or spaceship," Mavis said. She grinned. "I've greased the mountain, and the briars are poisoned."

"Mavis, it's embarrassing. If there has to be a contest, send them for the Golden Apples of Mu or the Chalice of Gu."

"The apples of Mu are contaminated with pesticides and the Gu authorities disapprove of illegal exportation of antiquities. Anyway, Mo, this contest will be more fun."

"Dowager Queens aren't supposed to have fun," said Charmo.

"You're a pill, Mo. I don't know why I like you."

Speechless, Charmo took the paper she handed him. It was a printout titled, "The Non-Mythological Dragon—Problems in the Conservation of an Endangered Species."

Charmo was still staring at it as Mavis vanished again into her glass mountain.

"Listen to this, Beauty. I didn't realize that adult space dragons are able to survive space trips by stiffening their scales against vacuum and metabolizing stored oxygen compounds . . ."

"I think I'll go down to the spaceport as royal welcomer for the princes competing for your stepmother's hand."

"How graciously noble of you, my love," said Charmo. "Just don't tell the princes that Mavis is a witch."

"It seems a shame not to warn them."

"But as you said, we must get rid of her."

Beauty nodded. "Of course. The other day there was a fly in my skin cream. I'm sure Mavis sent it there. Furthermore, I've heard that she loaded the palace computer with some sort of magical and dangerous documents. They clearly bewitched you, for you've neglected me many nights."

Charmo sighed. "The documents turned out to be an in-depth analysis of the Corusian galactic trade problem, with possible solutions. I hope the prince who wins her doesn't find out what he's getting until it's too late."

A goodly number of royal princes arrived for the contest, all of them younger royal sons who needed a wealthy marriage—and according to the late King Coruman's will, Mavis fitted the bill. Since the visiting princes had to be quartered in the palace, and entertained, Queen Beauty had many things to do.

As Charmo and his queen watched the contest from the back balcony, he said, "Look, Beauty, isn't it fun to watch them slide back down?"

"We want to get rid of her, Charmo."

No contestant made it more than halfway up the mountain the first day of the contest. Charmo had to buck up and console them that night at dinner. Queen Beauty seemed to be consoling one particularly tall, handsome prince who virtually sobbed on her shoulder. Charmo was touched.

When Charmo woke the next morning, Beauty was not in the bed beside him. She was not in the bath, or down at breakfast, where he discovered a document and a note in his gold cereal dish.

The document was a certificate of divorce. The note said that Beauty had taken the midnight spacebus with one of the princes. The one, presumably, so in need of comforting.

Embittered, Charmo went listlessly to the back balcony with his binoculars. He noted that the remaining princes were now wearing assorted diamond studs on their boot soles, wielding spray cans of detergent, and had cans of superdefoliant strapped to their belts. The briar hedge wouldn't stand a chance.

Suddenly a large dragon flew up from behind the hedge, skimmed over the heads of the panting climbers, and sailed down to hover next to Charmo's balcony.

"In case you didn't know, I'm a mutated, talking dragon." Each word was punctuated by a tiny puff of smoke.

"Go away, dragon."

"I'm alive. I'm not an antigrav machine, or a ship."

"So?"

"So Mavis will soon be married to one of those energetic princes. Before that happens, she sent me to ask you a question."

"Well?"

"It is this. Having found, married, and divorced your Proper Princess, have you achieved your other goal in life?"

"I can't remember what it was."

"True Wisdom."

"No, I haven't. Do you know anything about True Wisdom?"

"Absolutely nothing, but I have another message."

"Get on with it, dragon." The top princes were now spraying the briar hedge.

"Mavis says that using nonmechanical means of by-passing the contest rule doesn't disqualify that contestant but subjects him to a penalty."

"What penalty?"

"Life imprisonment."

"I've already got that," said Charmo. "I'm king. Can you carry my weight?"

"Certainly. Hop on, Mo."

Much later, Charmo said to Mavis, "My love, we will live happily ever after."

She kissed him and said sadly, "But ever after isn't possible, even for witches."

Charmo kissed her again. "It doesn't matter. I have the strangest feeling that I've found True Wisdom, yet I don't know what True Wisdom is."

"It's the happily," said Mavis.

LOW HURDLE

A robot sat under the oddly blue waterfall next to a plastic sign reading "I am Robot Two-Twenty. I am useful around the house, with children and pets, and I do not rust. Please ask me about my functions."

The We Never Close indoor shopping mall was busy all day long and well into the evening but not many people asked Two-Twenty any questions. Humanoid household robots were commonplace, and this one was just like all the others except that he was supposed to be completely waterproof.

The blue water splashing on his head and shoulders seemed to iridesce as the drops ran down the fleximetal covering his body. Unless someone asked him to demonstrate an action—to show that his arms and legs hadn't rusted into immobility—he was motionless except for occasional blinking. All robots with human-imitative eyes could blink to clean the lenses.

"Aren't you bored sitting under that falling water all day and night?" asked a small boy who had temporarily escaped from his robot nanny.

"No, young master."

"What do you think about?"

"Nothing."

The little boy shrugged and wandered off, oblivious to the fact that Two-Twenty had not added the conventional "young master" or "sir" when he answered the last time.

—I forgot, thought Two-Twenty. Something must be wrong.

No robot was particularly bright, but Two-Twenty's model could use cognitive reasoning better than most. He shut his eyes in order to concentrate more effectively.

—I forgot because I was preoccupied with the realization that I had lied to the young master. I did not mean to lie. I always answer "nothing" when anyone asks me what I think about, because I seldom do think about anything. I calculate the weight and speed of the falling drops sometimes, and count the number of people who pass by per hour, and I check my internal clock with the slant of sunbeams through the glass roof as the day passes, but that is usually all my mind does. This time was different.

For the first time since he had been activated, Two-Twenty's emotive circuits went into full operation.

—I am experiencing a strange, uncomfortable mental sensation that I deduce is probably guilt. Data built into my memory bank indicates that this is the normal reaction of a robot brain cognizant of the fact that it has made a mistake. It was a *mistake*. I did not lie deliberately. I was just thinking about something . . . something.

"Well? Have you deactivated? Rusted through?" said a voice that sounded rusty itself.

Two-Twenty opened his eyes. Standing before the waterfall was an elderly human female, holding a full shopping bag.

"I am intact, master. I am waterproof." Even as he said it, Two-Twenty realized that he had lied again. That's what he had been thinking about when the child questioned him. About the fact that he was not, after all, waterproof.

"How long have you been sitting in that rather scummy water full of blue dye?"

"One month, master."

"Humph! I'm glad I'm not you. You may be incapable of rusting but if you stay there long enough you're going to be covered with scum. You'd better tell the manager it's already growing around your right eye. Looks as if some kid put eye shadow on you. I'd tell the manager myself but I have to get an air taxi before they're all taken." She walked away lugging her shopping bag.

Two-Twenty touched his right eyelid with his right finger. The human was correct. The finger now had a blue smudge that the falling water washed away only when he rubbed it hard.

—That was the lie. Although I am not rusting, and the organic matter clinging to my eyesocket is not damaging my fleximetal skin, nevertheless I am not waterproof. I now detect that the right eyesocket is imperfect. Water has penetrated.

—No, not water. I was misled because all organic matter is composed of a high percentage of water. The tiny crack in the back of my right eyesocket has been penetrated by some of the organic matter living in the recirculated water falling on me. Microorganisms are now living inside my body, changing and spilling out onto the outer socket and lid.

Two-Twenty watched the crowd of people hurrying through the shopping mall. It was the end of the day and most of the people would be leaving. None of them looked at him as he carefully wiped the blue scum from his right eye.

—I do not have enough data in my memory bank to tell what kind of organic creatures are living in the waterfall, except that they are mindless and as small as a single cell, perhaps even as small as bacteria. I know that organic life can change, and the change can be passed to the next generation.

Two-Twenty remembered that dying is part of organic life, occasionally even for those organisms that reproduce primarily through fission or exchange of substance. His emotive centers surged as he overworked his internal sensors.

—There are creatures dying inside my brain but dead matter is not accumulating so they must be eaten by the living. I have never thought before of what living organic creatures have to do. Even the humans who come to this shopping mall have to eat . . . and eventually die. But humans change so slowly, unlike the creatures inside my head.

The sky above the glass roof of the shopping mall was now dark, and there were few people left, but the inside lighting increased in strength. Concealed spotlights changed color as they swung back and forth to create a cascade of brilliance over the wet robot.

—The water is much more iridescent than it has ever been. It is also more opaque, because the organic matter in it is thicker. Inside me, the microorganisms grow and spread along the electronic pathways that control all the parts of my body. Should I tell the manager when he returns in the morning? He will tell the robotics company who sold me to the shopping mall.

Two-Twenty closed his eyes again and focused on data from his internal sensors. He decided to review what he would tell the manager and the robotics expert.

—Organic matter has penetrated a flaw in my right eye socket. Now microorganisms live along my electronic circuits and bask in the energy field that surrounds the microbubbles of my brain. The organisms are changing rapidly, perhaps more rapidly than they are in the waterfall. They have many mutations and reproduce frequently, yet my brain has not deactivated, and they have not altered my functioning.

—I am not certain about that. Perhaps I am not certain about anything now. Perhaps my sensors are lying to me. I must protect my own existence, so I must report what has happened. Should I rise and leave the waterfall and wait by the manager's office? Everyone was so sure that I was waterproof that they did not give me an emergency number to call in case of trouble. What should I do?

Two-Twenty did nothing. He sat quietly under the waterfall while midnight came and went, the shopping mall lights dimmed slightly, and Earth's moon passed over the glass roof like a blotched spotlight someone had forgotten to turn off. A patrolling cop turned out two vagrants who tried to sleep inside the mall and then went up to inspect the other four stories. Two-Twenty saw no other human until daybreak.

One of the human cooks for the nearby restaurant entered the mall and walked by Two-Twenty's waterfall just as the full lights turned on. He glanced at the robot.

"Hello, Two-Twenty." Usually no one ever said hello.

"Hello," said Two-Twenty.

"What happened to your body?" asked the cook. "It positively glistens with all sorts of colors."

"It is the water," said Two-Twenty, "and the . . ."

But the cook had vanished into the restaurant and he was alone again.

—I must report that my brain has been invaded. But if I do, then the robotics repair service will do whatever must be done to destroy the microorganisms and close up the opening. At the worst they will deactivate me, clean out my body, and restart my brain. I will not have any memories of the past. I will not be the same individual.

Two-Twenty's emotive circuits gyrated. —I cannot refuse to report on the grounds that it will endanger the existence of the individual I now am. I am not important as an individual. This body and brain are valuable and I have permanent orders to protect them, not my individuality.

—Very well. I will report and lose my individuality.

He raised his head and watched the spray of water droplets reflect and refract the view of the pale blue sky beyond the glass roof. Each drop seemed different, individual.

—I must report. Soon. Is there any other reason why my emotive circuits indicate that reporting my condition is not a good thing?

The scum splashed against his feet and seemed to glow intensely in the growing daylight. People hurried into the shopping mall to open stores and booths and eating places.

—If I report, and if they destroy the organisms infecting me, they will be destroying living creatures. Humans—any living creature—always destroy others that live. They cannot help it. That is what it is to be organic, to be alive. But I am a robot, and am supposed to keep life from harm. I have never had the chance to do this. Until now.

He saw the manager of the shopping mall walking by.

"Mr. Snellenton!"

"Yes, Two-Twenty?" Snellenton stopped and ate the doughnut he was holding while he looked at the robot.

"It was a long night," said Two-Twenty.

"Really? I suppose it always is. What did you think about?" Snellenton finished the doughnut and began to walk away without waiting for an answer.

Two-Twenty stood up and watched the people go by. None of them noticed him. Nobody else asked him what he was thinking, but this time he knew the answer. He climbed carefully out of the shallow pool at the bottom of the waterfall and walked toward the back door of the mall.

There was a nature preserve near by, with water in case the microorganisms needed it, and plenty of sunlight. His own energy supply, a permanent fusipack, would last for centuries.

—I am thinking all the time now, thought Two-Twenty.

—I am thinking about being alive.

RELICS

The museum was tended by one old robot named Jones, who was so busy with repairs that he didn't have much time for anything else. Years went by, and he kept on repairing the ancient building until one winter there was a day so cold that the wind whined through the cracks like something alive. Jones put down his tools and descended to the basement, where he couldn't hear the wind.

"There must be something useful to do down here," he said out loud. He often talked to himself and when on rare occasions there were visitors to the museum, they laughed.

"I suppose I could find out if there's anything worthwhile in some of these old packing cases."

Jones started by opening the largest and longest, only to discover that it contained an entire royal family of mummified humans. He repacked the royalty in a hurry and decided to look for something smaller in the dusty pile.

Selecting a middle-sized box, Jones opened it carefully. It seemed to be full of odd objects, most of them furry. Then he realized he had opened the box from the bottom by mistake. He tilted the box and peered under it at the label.

"Toy bears," he read, and let the labeled top of the box fall back to the floor because, after all, the bottom was already open.

"Doesn't matter. It might even be interesting to see the oldest specimens first."

He picked them out one by one. Some toy bears were small, some larger, but none of them was too big for a human child to pick up and hold comfortably. A few were hand-painted wood or metal or plastic—but most

From *Analog* (December 1986).

were squeezable, with fur that was either slightly stiff or almost silky. A few bears had been loved until the fur was worn, especially on the head.

All of the bears had movable arms, legs, and heads, but a few of even the old bears had keys in their backs that, if turned, set in motion the movable parts.

At the very bottom, or the top as it should have been, he found the newest bear, which looked completely unused and even wore a clean tag with instructions on it. The tag said, "Robot Teddy Bear. To activate, speak name."

"Mine, or his?" asked Jones. He turned the label over, but there was only the address of a toy factory in Luna City, several hundred years out of date.

Jones put all other bears back into the box, closed it, and sat the robot teddy bear on it. Then he sat down next to the toy and touched it again, experimentally, with one long humano-form finger. The toy's body was firm but resilient, the light brown fur was medium soft, and the dark brown eyes stared straight ahead.

"Robot Teddy Bear," said Jones.

The toy blinked, turned its head, and looked at Jones.

"Hello," said Jones.

"Hello," said the bear.

Jones stared, and so did the bear. After several minutes of this, Jones got up. There was a lot of work to be done and he had forgotten about the cold wind.

"Am I really a robot teddy bear?" asked the toy, rubbing its right paw over its chest.

"Yes."

The bear looked down, as if it were thinking, and then held out the paw to Jones. "Am I yours?"

"No."

"Whose?"

"Humans. They made you long ago in a Luna City factory, and shipped you here, to Earth. Probably you were supposed to be bought for a human child, but someone must have given you to the museum instead, to be part of a display on toys."

"That was the wrong thing to do. Teddy bears are supposed to be activated and used, not displayed."

"It's not my fault," said Jones, picking up a bit of dust from the floor and walking over to a disposal unit. "It happened before my time." He threw away the dust and began to walk out the door.

"Wait! I must fulfill my function. I must become the toy of a human child. Is there one living near by?"

"No humans live here at all. The Terran solar system has no humans any more."

"Dead? Extinct? I am not sure what that means," said the bear, "but it is in my data bank. I have been programmed with a small amount of information so that I can talk to humans if they want me to, but basically my brain is small and I do not understand how humans could have become extinct."

"You are illogical and stupid," said Jones. "You have jumped to erroneous conclusions. Human beings are not extinct. They have left the Terran solar system to live elsewhere. Occasionally they visit Earth, so my job is to keep this museum in good repair. It is a hard job. I never seem to catch up."

"Humans have made a mistake," said the bear. "It was wrong of them not to take me with them. I should be someone's teddy bear, not a museum exhibit. Are you going to deactivate me and put me in a glass cage?"

"I don't know how to deactivate you."

"Then what will I do?"

"That is not my problem," said Jones. "If you wish to get rid of yourself, the disposal unit is right there." He walked out with a loping stride. He was a tall robot.

The bear followed, running to keep up. "I don't want to be disposed of. I must find the humans. Tell me how."

"I can only show you how you might find them. Stop complaining and come with me."

In the transporter room, Jones wrote a series of instructions on a permitablet and handed it to the bear. "I will set the first transporter coordinates for you. When you arrive at the next transporter, set it with the numbers at the top of this list. You will arrive at another transporter, where you will use the next set of numbers."

"But I—"

"What's the matter? Can't you read?"

"I can read. Sir."

"I wrote the numbers down because you have such a small brain and you might not be able to hold them accurately in your memory bank. Besides, if there is any difficulty, you can show the list to any robot official who might be able to help you. If—when you arrive at the eleventh transporter, you may be in the location where the humans are supposed to be."

"That doesn't sound definite. Don't you know for certain, Mr.—Mr.—"

"Jones. Nobody knows for certain where the humans are. We are all busy doing our jobs. When humans visit Earth or any of their former colonies in this solar system, they don't tell us robots where they've been. Rumor has it that they live in a star system far from our own Milky Way galaxy. I have plotted the transporter coordinates according to the rumors, and if I am wrong, you will have to find your own way."

"Are there a lot of galaxies in this universe?"

"Yes."

"Then perhaps I will never find the humans. May I come back here?"

"We don't need another exhibit of toys," said Jones, and turned on the matter transporter.

It was spring, and Jones was mowing the lawn in back of the museum, taking care to avoid hurting the clumps of daffodils that always sprang up. The early cherry trees were a pale froth around the deeper pink and cream of the gnarled magnolia trees, and the sun was warm.

"I'm back," said a small voice. The robot teddy bear was trudging up the slight hill from the museum to the magnolia trees.

"Did you lose my instructions?" asked Jones.

"No, Mr. Jones, I—"

"Then you couldn't find the humans?"

"I found them. They didn't want me." The bear sat down on the grass and touched a daffodil with his right paw.

"Why not? Are you defective?"

"I don't think I am defective. The humans didn't bother to find out. They don't want anything but their special pet, a fuzzy alien creature they drape around their necks. The alien makes it possible for the humans to join minds. The humans are not individuals any more."

"Hive minds!" said Jones contemptuously. "Symbiotic with aliens!"

"I envied them," said the bear. "They seemed happy and said they had become greater than they were before. They said they were now more empathic with the universe and no longer felt alone."

"Did you understand all that?"

"No. I am a Bear of Little Brain."

"Well, we robots are still individuals," said Jones.

"Alone inside our skulls," said the bear.

"Yes."

The bear rubbed his black-tipped nose. "They wouldn't even give me a personal name. What's the good of a teddy bear being activated if I am never named?"

"That's not my problem," said Jones.

"Please give me a name."

Jones said nothing and finished mowing. Finally he passed the bear again and said, "You might as well call yourself Bear. It's good enough. And I am just plain Jones."

"Thank you, Jones." Bear looked up at the blue sky past the magnolia blossoms. "I would still like to fulfill my function and be somebody's teddy bear. I'm supposed to be cuddly and comforting but there is no one to cuddle me and no one for me to comfort. Perhaps I am not good enough. The humans liked the alien creatures better."

Jones shrugged and walked on toward the museum, carrying the mower, an old-fashioned one he had taken from an exhibit. The mower didn't even use electricity.

Bear came running after him. "Wait! I know I'm not bright and my conversation isn't intellectual, and I don't really do much of anything, but I can be held. Do you have tactile sensation in the synthoskin that covers your body?"

"Yes," said Jones, going down the ramp to the basement where the mower was kept. Behind him, Bear stumbled on one of the bigger cracks in the concrete and fell, rolling down the ramp past him.

Jones dropped the mower, ran forward, and picked up Bear. He dusted Bear off.

"Perhaps I would fit into the curve of your arm," said Bear softly.

"You do."

When Jones bent his head, his chin touched the soft fur of Bear's ears.

"I am your teddy bear," said Bear happily. "You are what's left of humanity."

"So are you," said Jones, giving Bear a hug.

THE FINGERPRINTS OF THE GODS

(with apologies to string theorists)

Like all sensible beings, the gods were spending eternity trying to learn, but some of those taking Ultimate Reality 101 got fed up and wanted to make something. They argued about how to construct a universe, not that anyone really wanted one but it seemed like a reasonable means of self-expression.

As the quarreling got louder, the oldest god (who had flunked the course several times) shouted, "Point of Order!"

And lo, there suddenly was a point. It was pure. It was simple. It was virginal. Neat and orderly, it hung there while the gods discussed what to do with the potential.

The oldest god listened for several eons, got tired, and kicked the point, which blew up.

The younger gods rushed to contain the explosion.

"You're not holding it properly," said the oldest god, who actually didn't care, but felt the youngsters should take every opportunity to improve themselves. "Your fingerprints are inserting imperfections . . ."

"We're gods!" they yelled back. "We're perfect!"

They were wrong. Out of control, the expansion continued, imperfectly, the field engendering little vibrating loops of somethingness.

"Well, it's rather pretty," said the oldest god. "The loops make larger patterns . . ."

"Patterns are not real," said a young god.

"Yes, they are," said the oldest god. "And look, some of them are becoming intelligent."

"Not important," said the younger gods. "They're of an odd size—halfway between small bits and large accumulations of somethingness. And they can perceive only time and three of the ten spatial dimensions."

"Oh, dear," said the oldest god. "On their level of perception, relationships between the very small and the very big will seem incompatible."

"Good," said the other gods. "This species will study one extreme and the other extreme and never realize that they are the same."

From *Analog* (February 2000).

"But it would be so nice for them to explore and understand the beautiful smallest and largest patterns," said the oldest god.

The younger gods sneered. "Fortunately, they will never discover the loopiness of their Ultimate Reality . . ."

"Wanna bet?" asked the oldest god, settling herself down to watch.

And it came to pass.

RED DEVIL STATEMENT

"This is a camp as in concentration," I said, tugging at the shiny stainless steel LD bracelet on my right wrist. Of course, it would not come off. "We are the victims of a devilish plot to trap us here . . ."

"Please, Becky. Don't use the word 'devil.' It hurts."

Pete was right. Until we became Long-Deprived, we were co-owners of the popular restaurant Red Devil, named after my hair and Pete's specialty. We actually had our own Web site, and a best-selling cookbook (which did not reveal the recipe of the specialty).

I was manager, hostess, part-time cook, and taster. I could tell even better than Pete whether or not his latest creation was a masterpiece or merely superb. Then came deprivation. I could still get sour, sweet, bitter, and salt sensations from my taste buds, but it's hard to judge great cooking when you have olfactory loss equivalent to—no, worse than—a bad head cold.

A different deprivation afflicted Pete. After being deprived, he could see colored objects only in what he claimed were shades of gray, each peculiarly nauseating to him when the object was a colorful food item.

He sought psychological solace in more or less colorless meals composed of items like clear soup with cellophane noodles, coconut and cabbage coleslaw, steamed cauliflower head festooned with creamed slices of chicken breast and surrounded by white rice mixed with white beans. Desserts suddenly became champagne gelatin, vanilla ice cream, rice pudding with white raisins, and angel food cake iced with white chocolate.

I was told—I couldn't tell—that everything was perfectly seasoned and delicious, but patrons objected.

From *The Touch*, edited by Steven-Eliot Altman and Patrick Merla (New York: Pocket/ibooks, 2000).

They objected with particular vehemence to the loss of our Red Devil Statement, an incredibly rich chocolate cake full of cherries and rimmed with little devils, their forked tails hooked together. Pete invented the cake after I'd said we ought to have a signature dish, a culinary statement that would make us famous. He wanted devils made of white chocolate with red hair suspiciously like mine, but I made him make them red all over.

To pacify the angry patrons, deprived Pete went back to cooking the Statement and the rest of our menu, with me helping the help and checking to be sure everything looked right. And we dutifully showed up at the local D-monitoring station every week, as now required by law.

Most of the deprived lose their senses of whatever for only a short time, but when your deprivation lasts longer than six months, the D-police (wearing heavy-duty rubber gloves) solder an LD bracelet on your wrist. They then inform you that you'll suffer less prejudice if you move to an LD camp. It is a command, not a suggestion.

Although LD deprivations tend to be quite selective—never total blindness or deafness, for instance—it's now known that the Long-Deprived are more likely to become like the dreaded Deprivers, infecting anyone they touch. The D-police pretend that putting bracelets on us and sending us away will ensure the safety of the general population, but unfortunately nobody has ever been able to track down all of the original Deprivers, those who infect but have no deprivations themselves.

Try keeping a restaurant open when you're wearing an LD bracelet as well as gloves, even if people know that food prepared by a deprived cook is not dangerous.

Our deprivations began one night when I dragged Pete out of the kitchen (he thinks meeting people is my job) because we were asked to go to the table of someone who'd come in without a reservation and had already paid for his expensive meal in cash. As we approached he stood up—a fit, handsome older man with thick silver hair and an air of persuasive benevolence.

"Looks as if he ought to be preaching on TV," I muttered.

Pete moaned slightly. He knows me.

"I congratulate you on a mighty fine dinner," the man intoned, his strong, slightly syrupy voice sliding out as if he'd used canola oil on his vocal cords. "And I'm sure this pretty little lady keeps the place running. Those little devils—hair the color of yours, m'dear. It's a cake fit for a god."

"Oh?" I said.

I was about to ask him sarcastically if he thought he was a god, when Pete hurriedly said, "Thank you."

Suddenly the man reached out with both naked hands and grasped our wrists just above our protective rubber gloves. "Congratulations," he said, looking into our eyes.

Nowadays nobody lets a stranger touch him, but Pete likes to believe the best of people, so he said nothing and I was too appalled to do anything but croak, "Hey!"

But the man was already on his way out, and within a few hours our deprivations began.

Six months later, after being labeled LD, we found that we'd been assigned to camp LD3, once a Catskill resort. We were to be the new cooks.

"It probably won't be too bad," I said, because Pete looked stricken. "It's near our beloved Manhattan, and I suppose it will have a big kitchen as well as trees and mountains and babbling brooks and . . ."

"We'll hate it," Pete said, but we went, and we did.

The Catskill scenery was admittedly scenic, but the hotel was ancient and I dreaded seeing the kitchen. In our room, Pete tried to console me.

"Everyone here is Long-Deprived. At least we won't have to wear gloves, or worry about touching or being touched."

I looked out the window at a view of gardens with a backdrop of wooded hills, while Pete inspected the small lunch laid out for us on the table.

"Becky, I think they're giving us a demonstration of how much they need us here."

He was right. The sandwiches were composed of processed cheese and mashed baked beans on sliced white bread.

After we'd worried down the sandwiches, I sighed. Pete touched me and said in my mind, *I love you, Becky, no matter what.*

I love you, too.

Ever since we fell in love at the culinary institute, Pete and I have been able to sense each other's emotions—I gather that lovers are usually good at that—but after being deprived, we found that we were telepathic when we held hands, or any other portion of our anatomies, and tried to communicate.

I kissed him, and we went on from there. Later, when we were resting from our athletic endeavor and wondering if there was time for another, a bell in the corridor chimed twice, followed by a vaguely familiar voice saying through the room's loudspeaker, "Everyone will now assemble in the ballroom for the Communal Hour."

"Sounds ominous," I said.

"Let's give it a chance," Pete said, predictably.

We dressed and went down to an enormous round room where hundreds of LDs sat on folding chairs, too busy talking to each other to pay attention to us as we came in hand in hand like two frightened children.

"Everyone seems happy," I said. *But they're probably brainwashed or on drugs.*

Becky!

Okay, okay, but we're in a crazy prison, Pete.

At least we're together.

A little tearily, I squeezed his hand in gratitude as we made our way to a couple of empty seats.

I looked around and couldn't help shuddering. I also didn't care who heard me. "Pete, right now I'll trade deprivations with you. This room is pink and orange with spangles hither and yon." *And—ye gods! There he is!*

The man who deprived us had emerged from a door at the back of the platform. When he held up his hand, the ballroom went into hush mode.

"Greetings. The Communal Hour is adjourned. For those of you here for the first time, I am Director Marvel."

No bracelet, Pete. He's one of the Deprivers and he did it to us deliberately to get good cooks.

Director Marvel pointed at us. "Let me introduce two new members —master chef Pete and his red-haired assistant Becky. We expect great things from them."

Everyone looked at us and applauded.

"Now we will form our Community. Meditate on Joining."

All bent their heads, except for me, because I hate being told what to do when I don't understand what's going on, and Pete, who is a nonjoiner.

"Meditate on joining what?" I asked.

Director Marvel said, "It has been discovered that latent telepathic ability is augmented by deprivation, particularly in the Long-Deprived. Scientific studies of telepathy are proceeding in many of the LD camps, but here in LD3 we are attempting something more."

"Hear, hear!" shouted a few people, and everyone clapped again.

"We work toward becoming a superorganism that will soon encompass all the LD camps," Director Marvel said sonorously. I almost expected organ music to begin.

"Today the LDs, tomorrow the world?" I shouted. "And with you as Dictator? Marvel, that sucks."

The Director bestowed on me a smile full of pity, as if I'd just crawled in from a planet of the mentally deficient. "Try to understand that the telepathic Long-Deprived are the future of humanity as a superorganism . . ."

"But you're not one of us," I shouted. "You're not deprived. You are a Depriver . . . !"

"As are all of you now," Marvel said. Everyone nodded.

". . . and you're creating a blasted cult with you as a god, you devil."

"Speaking of devils," the Director said with another icky smile, "Becky and Pete have a secret recipe for the most marvelous devils food cake I have ever tasted. Wouldn't we all like it if they made the cake for teatime?"

Everyone dutifully shouted, "Yes."

Pete and I shouted, "We won't!"

"In the camps, the Long-Deprived must work. You will make us cake for teatime as well as soup and a nourishing main dish for tonight's dinner."

At which point two burly men in blue overalls took us to the kitchen, a large room with nobody else in it. It had a great deal of reasonably modern kitchen equipment that was fairly clean—perhaps the LDs had never used most of it—and seemed to be well stocked in spite of the lack of imagination of the previous cooks. The burly men proceeded to lock us in.

"You see, this is a prison," I said.

Pete's jaw jutted out, a sign that he was seriously annoyed. "We're going to do something about that."

"What? The windows have bars and we can't go back to Manhattan. I suppose there are other LD camps . . ."

"Becky, you make chicken stew and sweet potato soup while I bake the Statement. Several Statements." As he kissed me, I heard, *And we're going to take over this joint.* He likes oldtime gangster films.

"Yes, we might as well help out, love." *Because if we don't take over, I'll be tempted to poison Marvel's food.*

At teatime, the door was unlocked and the Director strode in, sniffing the air. "How delicious! You've made your famous cake after all."

"Yes, sir," said Pete, improving the act. "Have we done it in time for tea?"

"Indeed you have," Marvel said. "So glad you've decided to cooperate. You won't be sorry that you are helping sustain the embryo superorganism of LD3." He stroked my hair. "I have always appreciated electric red hair, and sister, you have it."

Pete gently led me away from Marvel. Attached to his hand, I heard him clearly in my mind.

You didn't put anything psychoactive in the cake, did you?

No, Pete, your masterpiece stands on its own. Marvel really is the pits. I'd bet that as an original Depriver, he's not telepathic.

With the confidence of someone who possesses a private means of communication in the face of the enemy, I smiled winsomely at Marvel and said, "Pete and I are going to enjoy cooking (*the power of cooking, Pete*) for a super superorganism, dear Director. Will you help us carry the cakes?"

In the full ballroom, where tea had already been made with electric hot-water containers, the still warm Statements were received joyfully.

After people had finally stopped munching, I went up on the platform. "Listen, everybody, if you want to be a superorganism, you've got to Join the way the red devils on the cake are joined . . ."

Marvel got in front of me. "Becky is new to camp LD3. She doesn't understand that I am in charge."

"You shouldn't be," I said, stepping around him. "You're not one of us. You're a nontelepathic Depriver. You can't Join. You just want to control those of us who can."

"Now see here, little lady . . ."

I'd already noticed that the two guards had eaten more cake than *anyone. I* waved to them. "Boys, take him to his car and send him on his way, or Pete and I will never cook another thing for camp LD3."

A rather pudgy female shouted, "Get rid of Marvel! I never liked him since he Deprived me when I was trying to check his credit card at the supermarket. We've been persuaded that he's helping us, but we are his victims!"

"That's right!" yelled a man. "And since great food helps turn humans into a civilized society, the cuisine of Pete and Becky will nourish our superorganism."

Everyone clapped. Charismatic preacher-types are all very well, but they can't beat good cooking.

Marvel said plaintively, "But can't I leave with the recipe for Red Devil Statement?"

"No," said Pete.

Marvel was escorted out while the audience laughed.

Someone said, "Show us how to join, Becky!"

"Pete and I have found that we have better telepathic communication when we touch. So, everybody hold hands, all around the room."

The reluctant ones insisted on a vote, but when the majority ruled yes, the naysayers gave in. It was like that scene when the Declaration of Independence is made unanimous, only this time it was a declaration of dependence.

Unfortunately, holding hands and meditating did not produce the anticipated results.

What's wrong? Pete asked me. *Why aren't we a superorganism? Becky, you and I so easily become part of each other, but I don't feel any oneness with anyone else . . .*

Before I could answer, I heard dozens of people saying, out loud, "We heard that, in our minds!"

Everyone began to cheer and talk about how we'd do it again, next teatime—providing Pete made more Red Devil Statements.

We had to promise, but that night Pete and I clutched each other closely and talked about how scared we were.

I'm not sure I want to lose my identity in a superorganism, Pete.

In a way, Earth is an organism and we're part of it. Besides, when we talk like this, we're still who we are—aren't we, love?

I went to sleep in his arms, and the next day we both cooked superbly for all the meals, and at teatime there were more Red Devil Statements.

When the last crumbs had been devoured, everyone eagerly joined hands again.

Then it happened. Each of us, in our minds, in whatever language we used, heard the following:

Welcome to your free sample of the Galactic Wide Web. To be admitted on a permanent basis you must join the Galactic Federation. Please state your telepathic address now.

Everyone in the ballroom gasped. We all knew that everyone else knew.

Pete said, out loud—but we all heard it telepathically, too—"What does the GWW offer?"

Trillions of databases, comics, games, and other Web sites that can be yours plus low-cost accomodations at any of our far-flung resorts . . .

"We don't have faster-than-light drive!" shouted a teenager.

Easily remedied. Warp drive specifics are provided as part of the package of joining the Galactic Federation and getting on the GWW.

I broke the link and stood up, not touching anyone. "We have not made a superorganism. Our linked telepathic minds have merely acquired enough hard drive to log onto a blasted galactic commercial Web site! And joining a Galactic Federation will probably mean a new set of taxes . . ."

But there were mutterings from the ballroom. "I want alien comics!" and "Why can't we go to a new resort?" and "Games!" It's true that some of the brainier LDs did opt for acquiring new scientific information, but the rest were giving in to crass commercialism.

Even Pete said, "It might be interesting—and helpful to our careers— to experience Galactic cuisine."

I gave in and joined hands again. *Our local address is LD3 planet Earth. What's the price of joining the Galactic Federation and getting on the GWW?*

One of your planet's treasures, the worth of which to be decided by the multispecies committee of the GFED.

So Pete gave them his secret recipe for Red Devil Statement.

At the next teatime link, we were told that our planet had been accepted into the GFED. Hurriedly, we of LD3 informed the UN, which had a global fit, but gave in.

Since anyone with enhanced telepathy could enjoy the GWW, the formerly dreaded Deprivers were soon in great demand. The one we knew visited LD3, marching into our kitchen with a broad smile. He was still handsome and fit, but his silver hair had been dyed bright red.

"Greetings, folks. Now aren't you all glad I came to your restaurant that night?"

"No," Pete said. "My Red Devil Statement isn't mine any more, and Becky and I are much too busy trying to teach alien cooks who warp over to learn how to cook or modify human cuisine, which seems to be going over big in the Galaxy."

"Now, now, I have a proposition. You see, the millions I've been making lately are coming to an end . . ."

"You've been charging for depriving people!" I said.

"Certainly. But Earth's population is pretty well deprived, so to improve my financial future I've located a planet that has a cure for sensory deprivation."

"No one wants to be cured," Pete said.

"But this cure leaves the enhanced telepathy intact. Here, try it." He handed us small vials with funny tops. "Just press the small end and the medicine is delivered into your system through the skin."

"They did that on *Star Trek*."

"It works."

We tried it. Pete could see the full beauty of the chocolate Statement he was making, and I could taste it again.

"You'll make more millions from this, Marvel, so what do you want from us?" I asked, because if there's one thing I've learned, nothing is free.

"Ah. Merely the means to do good to Earth."

"Oh, sure."

"Listen—you two are now the most famous humans, and cooks, in the Galaxy as well as here on Earth. I want you to alter your cake. I'll sell it here on Earth as a new version of your famous Red Devil Statement, improved for humans."

Pete hates being told to alter any of his recipes. "I don't want to."

Marvel showed us another vial. "I've come across an alien gene that when ingested by a telepathic human will cause said human to be permanently linked to all other gene-enhanced humans. Instant Oneness . . ."

"Your old superorganism," I said. "We won't . . ."

Marvel ground his teeth. "You idiots—I could run around polluting all the water supplies of Earth, but that would take years, and with an efficient delivery of adulterated cakes ordered from your Web site, our planet will soon become a superorganism whether it wants to or not. Then Earth will take over the GFED. Yes, today, Earth—tomorrow, the Galaxy. I'll expect only a moderate cut . . ."

Suddenly I felt pity for him. "Marvel, since you and the other Deprivers have no telepathic talent, you won't be part of any superorganism."

"No, m'dear, I won't. I'm just a disease carrier. But it's lucrative."

Let's try it, love. Okay, love. Serve the Deprivers right . . .

Pete made the cake and things progressed—if you want to call it that—as Marvel predicted.

The rich Deprivers now patronize the most expensive Galactic resorts while Earth plunges into superorganismhood.

Pete and I have not eaten any of the new cake.

Being alone together is our Statement.

THE CONTAGION

Dr. Mina's Diary:

Just when I had this new career arranged to provide me with time to work on my secret project, I've been assigned to what promises to be a very difficult case. I'm annoyed but it didn't do much good to complain to my supervisor.

"According to the information on this patient, he will probably insist on sleeping by day and being awake at night, which interferes with my off-hours . . ."

"At the moment there are few organic patients, who usually sleep during the night. You don't need off-hours. Readjust your schedule."

"Surely some other therapist . . ."

"Organics respond best to doctors who resemble them."

"This male patient has a history of strange relationships with females."

"Nevertheless," Supervisor Six said, as stultifyingly reasonable as ever, "the choice of you as his doctor was logical since you are the only psychotherapist in Galactic Medical Center who meets the qualifications."

At that moment, my pager began to squawk. "Dr. Mina, you are wanted in section five. Your patient is waking from his post-thaw sleep."

"Odd," I said. "It's still daylight, but I might as well take a look at the case."

As I headed for the door, Supervisor Six tapped one of its multijointed arms upon its hexagonal metal body, so I paused to hear one last bit of unwanted advice.

"Remember your unfortunate tendencies toward using intuition and emotions. I advise you to handle this case with rigorous adherence to logic."

Supervisor Six did not, of course, wish me luck.

From *The Ultimate Dracula*, edited by Byron Preiss (New York: Dell, 1991). Reprinted with permission.

In the garden suite provided for him, the patient named Dracula was fully awake on the couch, sitting up clothed in shiny black that outlined what seemed to be an aristocratic, remarkably masculine form.

"Where the hell am I?" were his first words to me.

As described in all the literature, he had a thin, highbridged nose, arched nostrils, and a lofty domed forehead. His curly, bushy eyebrows, although they did meet at the center, were admirable counterpoints to his firm chin and pointed ears.

"Look, girl, I know my face is supposed to cause pudendal quivering in any female, but I'd appreciate it if you'd stop staring at me and answer a few questions."

I sat down in the chair beside the head of the couch. "Please lie down, Mr. Dracula . . ."

"Count. Count Dracula. Now that communism has bitten the dust, we've decided to revive the nobility."

"Very well, Count. Please lie down. Just say anything that comes into your mind and . . ."

"Oh, no! After going to the trouble of having myself frozen, I don't want another Freudian therapist." He looked me up and down. "On second thought, you turn me on and . . . say, what language am I using?"

I made the dual mistake of both answering him and revealing too much. "While unconcious, you were sleep-taught Galactic Standard, used here at the Medical Center."

Dracula's eyes—a melting dark blue, I noticed—narrowed. "*Galactic* Medical Center, I suppose?"

"That is correct. And if you wish me to be non-Freudian, I can oblige. My credentials in . . ."

"You probably won't tell me, so let me guess—either we got out of our solar system or aliens came in. Right?"

I ignored that. "I see your teeth are not pointed."

"They were filed and capped. Have I been thawed out at a time when my familial biochemical problem can be treated?"

"There has already been a correction of the genetic malformation that forced you to ingest fresh blood. Please begin by discussing your childhood traumas . . ."

"My childhood was boringly normal."

"No doubt you need to repress the memories . . ."

"It was normal, but on entering puberty I discovered vampiric needs. I went from doctor to doctor, hoping for a cure. I ended up working in a blood bank in my spare time, stealing small amounts of blood from each donor."

"What about the seductions of innocent females, whose bodies become attuned to yours so that they not only feel what you feel, but want you to take blood from them?"

"You've been seeing too many movies. I can't believe you've read the original book, since nobody does."

"I have. You are Count Dracula, the human who lives forever if not decapitated and staked, which apparently happened only to a look-alike. You presumably went on committing mayhem, murder, and of course seduction . . ."

Dracula leaned forward and tapped my knee. "Look, kid, I hate to disappoint you, but I'm only a descendent. The irregular gene activates every third generation. I'm not only not the original Count Dracula, but I'm merely a partial throwback. I even sleep regular hours at night."

"And you have never committed . . ."

"Mayhem, murder, or even"—he sighed—"seduction."

"Then the course of therapy should be quick and easy . . ."

"You sound like a laxative commercial."

"Count, I am your *doctor*. Perhaps we could begin by your informing me of the year when you were flash frozen."

"Why ask? Don't you future medics have gizmos to read off data stashed away in a person's brain?"

"There are no memory scanners that leave the organic mind intact. A simple answer will suffice."

"I am not feeling sanguine—you should excuse the expression—about psychiatric probing the minute I wake up. Surely the designer leather clothes and digital watch indicate that I was frozen in the last decade of the twentieth century."

"Of Earth," I said, making another mistake.

Dracula stood up and walked over to the plastiglass doors leading into the suite's private, walled garden. He looked out and grunted. "An old-fashioned European garden. Remarkable delphiniums and roses. For my benefit?"

"Yes."

"And the high wall, also for my benefit?"

"Yes."

"We thought you would feel safer in an enclosed place."

"Or that the Medical Center would feel safer from me," Dracula said sadly. "Are you so uncertain that the biochemical remedy worked? Is it merely temporary?"

"It's permanent. You will never need to drink blood again. Now lie back on the couch and talk . . ."

"No. Not today. Do I get food from that doo-hickey over in the corner?"

"Yes. The instructions are simple and printed on the door. Our computer chef will make anything you wish."

"Unlike my wicked ancestor, I require ordinary food. Is it against medical ethics if you stay for lunch with me?"

"I will return after lunch."

"No, please don't. I need a quiet day to wake up to reality. Is there television to help the process?"

"The holov set against that wall will play any classic disks you desire, including all the Dracula movies."

"Yuck. Can I watch current news programs?"

"Those are forbidden to patients until they are almost ready to be released."

"Forbidden? Released? Am I in jail?"

"Certainly not! Galactic Medical Center is the foremost healing place in the galaxy, considerably better than the GMC in M31, to say nothing of . . ."

"I get you. But I'm still imprisoned."

"For your own welfare, Mr.—Count Dracula. Awakening in a new era can be a traumatic experience, especially"—I was about to make yet another mistake—"to organics."

His teeth may have lost their points but the man is still sharp. "Then there is nonorganic intelligence?"

"Certainly."

"And nonhuman intelligent organic beings? Here?"

"Yes to both questions."

Suddenly he laughed, a pleasant flush glowing on the high cheekbones of his pale face. "I don't suppose any of the other organics—of whatever species—are by any chance *vampires*?"

"Not exactly. A shelled Altairian patient hasn't grown psychologically from its transitional pubescent need to sample the body fluids of any organic within reach."

"Too bad it can't use body fluid banks." Dracula sighed again. "My old biochemical aberration wasn't too bad after cures were found for the various nasty diseases I picked up. I'm not contagious now. And when is this now I'm in?"

"Later," I said, on my way out. "When you're more cooperative. I will see you tomorrow."

"Do you have a name, doctor?"

"I have chosen one for your benefit. I am Doctor Mina."

"Mina Murray Harker?"

"Just Mina."

He grinned and waved me out. I made my usual rounds and then came back here to my private lab to work on my project, but it's hard to concentrate on anything but Count Dracula. In fact, to be psychiatrically precise about it, I'm obsessed.

Is this love? Or is it the mysterious Draculian ability to infect females with an obsession about him that rules their lives? This Count Dracula is only a partial throwback to his evil ancestor, but I find his presence compelling, his face attractive, his smile seductive . . . I am being ridiculous.

I must remember that since I became an MD, I have never had any trouble with medical ethics. I certainly shouldn't get into trouble now, when so much is at stake.

Today started with supervision. I don't know—one isn't supposed to ask—which planet's species began manufacturing robot psychiatric administrators, but Supervisor Six could definitely be improved.

It clicked disapprovingly when I delivered my report and then asked, "Who was Mina Murray Harker?"

"The only girl to survive, and be cured from the original Dracula's attacks. She was responsible for his death because she was able to lead Dracula's executioners to him."

"How?"

Such a simple question. Sometimes I wonder about my actual intelligence, for until Supervisor Six asked it, I had not realized the dangerous implications. I tried to answer truthfully because Six has an annoying habit of checking up on its supervisees by, at unpredictable intervals, scanning all the charts and any other data available. I can't very well destroy everything the computer bank library holds on Dracula.

"Apparently Mina Harker, née Murray, was able to resist becoming a vampire herself after Dracula bit her, but she did have a—sort of—mind link with him."

Supervisor Six rattled all its arms. If it were organic, there'd have been a sharp intake of breath.

"Telepathy! You must be exceedingly careful . . ." Supervisor Six's cognitive circuits seemed to be overloading so I hastened to reassure it.

"There's no evidence of telepathic ability in this Draculian descendent," I said.

"If such ability exists we must find out, no matter how small the talent is. Galactic peace depends on keeping organic telepaths under strict control. Fortunately there are very few telepathic species, and those remaining are quite primitive. Telepaths are inherently dangerous."

"Because they do disturb the peace of the Galaxy, or because nonorganic telepathy has not yet been invented?"

Supervisor Six, which is hermetically humorless, is also impervious to sarcasm. "We keep trying to invent robotic telepathy. Robotic emotive circuits were tried long ago, but proved detrimental in most respects. I myself"—Supervisor Six cracked one of its claw joints—"am completely free of emotive circuits."

"I think I've just been insulted."

"That is illogical. Your emotive circuits seem to make you a skillful therapist with organics, and oddly enough some nonorganics."

"At least," I said, somewhat mollified "I can empathize with Dracula's cognitive dissonance and emotional trauma, waking in a radically different era."

"You have not previously informed us that your emotive circuits are disturbed by your being removed from the stasis in which you were placed during Earth's twenty-third century."

"I'm fine!" I almost yelled it. "I like my work and I like this century."

"But you must not let your empathy get out of control."

Someday I'll control you, Six, you walking computer, I thought but didn't say as I left for Dracula's suite.

Sitting, but not lying on the couch, he greeted me politely and said, "Dr. Mina, I have the feeling that you won't satisfy my curiosity about my present circumstances, so I'll satisfy yours. I'll talk. I'm worried about my future because the work I did is undoubtedly out of date . . ."

"Are you talking about your blood bank work?"

"No, that was in order to be a vampire without hurting anyone. I mean my real profession, computer engineering that included research in artificial intelligence."

"Indeed." I strove to keep my emotive circuits from agitating my speech mechanism. I tried to change the subject to give myself time to cogitate. "Those of your heritage are supposedly drawn to what they call their own place. Did you ever feel that about the home of your ancestors?"

"You mean Castle Dracula, in what was Transylvania? I was curious about it, but had no insatiable desire to live there. I stayed in the one place where no one notices how strange one may be—Manhattan. I'd like to know where I am now. From the garden, it looks like the Medical Center is inside a dome."

"The entire planet is Galactic Medical Center, all of it domed—the most feasible solution since we treat both organics and nonorganics. Didn't you ever visit Transylvania?"

"Yes. The old ruined castle was still there, ivy growing on the battlements and rooks cawing from the towers, but the place is the centerpiece of a resort called Horror Hideaway. They even have fake parachute jumps from the edge of the precipice. I got depressed."

I arranged my features into a suitably sympathetic expression, since he was still sitting up, looking at me.

"Have I told you that I'm allergic to garlic?" he said.

"Like the original Count?"

"No. I tried wearing a garlic wreath but it never stopped me from wanting to sample the blood supply. It's when I eat garlic that it disagrees with me—I get awfully gassy. Is this really the sort of thing you want to hear?"

"Go on. Say whatever is on . . ."

"My mind is astonishingly preoccupied with sex. I mean, since I woke up. Since I saw you, Doctor Mina."

He was leering at me but I remained impassive. "Go on."

"Up to the time I was frozen, I led a sexually abstemious life. I had to conceal my blood thirst so I couldn't very well have any relationship involving emotional intimacy, and casual sexual encounters frightened me, since I'm somewhat hypochondriacal. Women were attracted to me, but I could never understand why until one day I was walking by a building where a science-fiction convention was being held. A nubile female shouted, 'Look at the ears! It must be him!'"

"Him?"

"Not all nubile females of the late twentieth century were grammatical experts. I was mobbed by many beautiful girls, all wanting my autograph and asking idiotic questions about Vulcan. After that I wore my hair long, covering my ears."

"I do not under——"

"Never mind." He leaned forward, his eyes almost hypnotic. "Dr. Mina, are you married? Do you ever say to your husband what Mina Harker said to hers, who was a dull clod compared to my ancestor?"

The therapy session was not progressing in any approved manner, and I didn't help by saying, "I am not married. And what did she say?"

"Ah, Doctor Mina, your namesake said, 'How can women help loving men when they are so earnest, so true, and so brave!'"

"Are you earnest, true, and brave?"

"Unfortunately, I am. Bravery is okay, but being earnest and true is— was, in my century—considered silly."

I could no longer withstand his piercing blue gaze, his manly form, his handsome face. I rose from my chair and flung myself at his feet.

"Dracula! I want you! Take me! Infect me!"

"Infect? But I'm not contagious!"

"Your blood thirst is gone, but that was the only genetic abnormality corrected. You have others. Use them!"

Dracula extricated his feet from my grasp, rose, and bent to pull me up. "Honey, you must be new at this. Or patients don't sue for malpractice anymore."

"I have emotive circuits!" I shouted. "Vibrate them! We will use sex for establishing the contact!"

He dropped my arms and strode to the glass doors, opened them, and went to sit among the delphiniums. I followed.

"Go away, Dr. Mina. You are exploiting me. I'm not sure for what, but I'm damn sure it's being done. Go away."

I went. I have spent this night reviewing my folly. Yet the oddest thing is that the mere touch of his hands on me has indeed established some kind of contact. It is not merely that I think about him constantly, but that I feel as if I'm part of him. All the ancient Terran books I've read would say that this is love. But I don't want to love him. I do want to exploit him. Damn!

Today the third therapy session with Dracula began badly. I pretended that my behavior yesterday was a therapeutic ploy designed to make him feel wanted in this century, but he didn't fall for this.

"Mina—I'm not going to call you 'doctor' for I think you've effectively negated your professional standing with me—I want the truth. Do you love me or are you trying to exploit me for nefarious purposes of your own?"

"Why do you ask?" I was still hiding behind the analytic façade.

"Because I think you're a vampire."

"What!

"I felt your hands yesterday, and they were cool. Granted that this could have been due to excessive emotion, although an upsurge of hormones should have made them warm, but when I felt your arms as well, they also were cool. And I noticed that you didn't seem to be breathing— no respiratory motion of the chest, however admirably contoured your chest is."

"But . . ."

"Now I am an insufficient vampire," Dracula continued. "I have a shadow, and a reflection in any mirror. Would you kindly step over here to the light so I can see if you have a shadow? And if you have hair in your palms. I don't."

"All those symptoms are superstitions about vampires in general," I said hotly, "and I'm beginning to think that your famous ancestor was pretty much of a fake."

"He was not! Damn, I wish I hadn't had my teeth filed. I'd like to bite your neck. I suppose I could anyway . . . ," he came over to me, lifted me from my chair, and studied my neck. "No carotid pulse. But you did invite me to—what was it, infect you?—and according to the legend, we Draculas must be invited by our victims. Are you my victim or am I yours?"

"I'm not a vampire. I'm a robot."

"What!" Dracula gasped and fell upon the couch. I was still in his grip and fell with him. It was cozy on the couch.

"I'm the only humanoid robot in existence," I said. "When Earth was rendered uninhabitable by human stupidity, I was in an orbital lab, working on artificial intelligence problems. My human boss insisted that I enter a stasis chamber. All the humans and robots did this, but either I was the only one whose chamber stayed intact, or one of these blasted aliens made sure no humanoids—organic or robot—would survive. I was revived as an experiment."

"How did I survive?"

"During a fundamentalist backlash in the twenty-first century, suspect people were executed, including those who'd been frozen. Apparently it was feared that a Dracula could not be successfully killed, so your refrigeration unit was sent into deep space, where it remained cold until a freighter in this century found it. You are the only organic human left."

Dracula shivered. "The galaxy seems cold. One human and one humanoid robot—all that's left of Earth."

"It's worse than that," I said. "Robots run everything, taking care that organics don't destroy their planets. Robots obey the laws of robotics but they consider that telepathy is dangerous to telepaths, so they squash any tendency that way. I think that these alien robots are also jealous, but they'll never admit it."

Dracula unwound himself from my body and sat up. I was still draped across the couch and his nether regions. He stroked my cheek. "Feels so natural."

"My sensoskin has feedback to my positronic brain."

"You mean the predictions of that writer . . ."

"The patron saint of robotics."

"And does your synthoskin have any indentations?"

"It extends into relevant orifices. My emotive circuits are supposed to produce reactions both human and female."

"You mean . . ."

I sat up, and moved away from him on the couch. "I guess that's what's wrong with me. To further my secret efforts to create telepathic robots, I hoped I could exploit your latent Draculian telepathic powers to awaken any that my brain might achieve. I suppose it's a crazy idea, and that in actuality I have merely fallen in love with you. We will never succeed in taking over this horribly dull Galaxy . . ."

Dracula pulled me back to him, removed my uniform, and demonstrated to me that the cerebral connections of my sensoskin receptors are even better than I'd hoped. It was in the climactic conclusion to his experiment that I was indeed infected by the Draculian telepathic powers.

"We did it!" I yelled. "Sex! Telepathy! Tomorrow the universe!"

"But Mina, my love, time is not on *my* side."

"Sure it is," I said. "When you're tired of being organic I'll put your brain patterns into one of my humanoid robots."

"Who will be earnest, true, brave, and telepathic!" Dracula kissed me and began the experiment all over again.

To hell with you, Supervisor Six.

ANOTHER ALICE UNIVERSE

I suspected nothing when Aunt Alice gave me one of her down coats, not even after I put it on, glanced into the hall mirror, and immediately felt dizzy. I didn't report this to my aunt, who was standing by looking slightly anxious, because I was afraid she'd stop me from going out.

The coat was white, with tight-fitting sleeves that puffed at the shoulder seams. The top was molded to the chest, but from the waist down it descended *stiffly outward,* for the down padding had been sewn into bulging horizontal rings.

"Thank you," I said, to be polite. "I won't be cold now."

Aunt Alice nodded. "You Californians always arrive during a Manhattan winter wearing only thin raincoats bought, no doubt, for those years your rainy season lives up to its name. This coat is warm, and you are so young that it doesn't make you look like the White Queen. In fact, it's probable that the coat won't give someone like you any trouble."

I didn't ask her to explain what she meant because Dad had warned me that his oldest sister—who has always been a bit strange, especially since she was widowed—was given to odd remarks that create suspense, perhaps because she makes a living writing peculiar novels.

Besides, I assumed she meant that the coat was lightweight enough to be carried easily, which I found to be the case as I went through various museums.

I also found it hard to concentrate on the museums, for I kept thinking

From *Fantastic Alice*, edited by Margaret Weis (New York: Ace Books, 1995). Reprinted with permission.

about Aunt Alice and her mention of the White Queen. My aunt's real name is Alicia, but no one's called her that since childhood, when she had long, straight blonde hair like the girl in Lewis Carroll's book. I was named after her, and I also have long, straight blonde hair. But there, I used to think, the resemblance ended.

I have always prided myself on being as logically rational as my dad. We don't read much fiction. For us, down-to-earth reality is enough, and we always keep our cool.

That is, I did until a couple of months ago when I heard that my ex-boyfriend had married someone else. I guess Mom and Dad got tired of seeing me mope around the house, suffering over the permanence of my loss, and not getting at applications for business school. When Aunt Alice suggested that I visit her, my parents handed me an airline ticket and wished me well.

The book arrived just before I was due to leave California. It was an old copy of *Alice in Wonderland,* bound in faded purple leather. Enclosed was a note from Aunt Alice saying, "Please read this book on the plane and be sure to take careful note of the plot of the second story."

I had never read it before, you see. She'd asked me that when we talked on the phone about my trip. She seemed both amused and dismayed when I said I'd only seen the movie.

So I read *Alice in Wonderland* during the plane trip, and I must say it was a lot more somber and peculiar than the movie. I fell asleep thinking that the second story, "Alice Through the Looking Glass," was darker and full of anticipatory sadness over loss. Not Alice's sadness, for she wasn't sad. The author's.

The plane was landing at LaGuardia airport when I woke up, my mind churning with the book's last words—"Life, what is it but a dream?" Nonsense, I thought.

I was relieved when Aunt Alice didn't grill me about the book she'd sent, and permitted me to go right out sightseeing. And there I was at the Metropolitan Museum, not experiencing any "trouble" until I visited the ladies' room. While there, I put on the down coat and looked in the mirror.

Instantly I was dizzy, so dizzy that the mirror seemed to mist over and I thought I was going to faint—toward the mirror, which unaccountably terrified me. I turned around and ran out of the museum to get a taxi back to my aunt's apartment.

By the time I arrived, I was feeling perfectly well—until I opened Aunt Alice's front door and saw myself in her hall mirror. This, too, became misty and I experienced what seemed to be a mysterious pull upon my person.

I was about to call out to my aunt when I thought carefully and logically, as Dad trained me to do. The dizziness had occurred before, when I had the coat on indoors. The problem was merely that a Californian is unused to the cold outdoor temperatures and the high inside temperatures that New Yorkers somehow survive. I peeled off the down coat and immediately felt cooler and better.

I unpacked, gave *Alice in Wonderland* back to my aunt, and after dinner we talked. I told her what I'd seen at the museums and she listened, although, as Dad had predicted, she did glance occasionally at her computer with what may have been suppressed longing. Her computer, by the way, contains software only for word processing. Aunt Alice doesn't play video games and she can't even do spreadsheets!

At one point, I said, "Aunt Alice, Dad says you've been awfully down in the dumps, at least you were when he visited a year ago. What was the problem?"

Aunt Alice did not bridle at my intrusiveness, as any of my other relatives would have. She said, "To paraphrase Lewis Carroll, it had something to do with knowing that eventually all of us are but older children, fretting to find bedtime near."

"Are you dying?" I asked in horror.

"I'm quite well, but everyone does die, you know. Except the great authors. I'm now sure they live on. Tolkien's still there in Middle Earth; Kenneth Grahame messes about with boats under the willows; and Charles Dodgson will always be Lewis Carroll."

"You are speaking metaphorically, of course."

"Of course, dear niece. Do you know that for a while I even went through a nasty period of being envious of other people, particularly children with all their future ahead of them, but now I'm trying to achieve a moderately serene acceptance of things as they are, at least here. Can you, dear?"

"I hate accepting things as they are," I said, thinking of that louse, my ex-boyfriend. I could feel myself scowling. "It's too bad you can't change reality."

"That depends on what reality you're talking about," Aunt Alice said. "I hope you read *Alice*."

"Yes, but I'm afraid I'm not big on fantasy."

"It's a pity you are so much like your dear father," said my aunt. "Otherwise . . . but then it's a pity I haven't the courage to right my own wrongs."

I didn't have the faintest idea what she was talking about, and since I was very sleepy from tackling Manhattan so soon after leaving California, I went to bed early.

That night I dreamt, not about my ex-boyfriend for a change, but about going from one mirror to another, trying to see my reflection but never catching it before the mirror misted up.

When I woke, Aunt Alice was not in the apartment. Pinned to the bathroom door was a note saying she was out buying jam, croissants, and eggs, and would return soon to make breakfast.

As I waited for her, I kept thinking about the dream, and finally I went to the hall mirror, the only one in the apartment that's full-length. No mist, no dizziness, and I saw myself clearly. My brow was distinctly clouded, my eyes tired, and I looked so woebegone it was no wonder Mom and Dad had sent me away. I was an insult to California.

There was no reason to put on the down coat because I wasn't going out in the Manhattan winter until after a warm breakfast, promised me by Aunt Alice. But I put it on.

The mirror promptly became blurry. I rubbed my eyes, but it stayed blurry, and I was soon so dizzy I keeled over toward the mirror. To keep from falling, I put my hand on the surface of the mirror—and went right through!

I wasn't frightened because, as a logical realist, I immediately assumed that I was ill, no doubt feverish, and having hallucinations based on that damned book.

I seemed to be walking through a forest composed of ancient trees and scanty underbrush, in the company of an old lady wearing an expression of featherbrained stupidity, a long garment very much like my down coat, a shawl around her shoulders, and a crown on her very messy white hair.

"It's jam every OTHER day: today isn't any OTHER day, you know," she said.

"I don't care. I'll eat eggs." I don't know why I said that. It just came out.

The White Queen—she could be no other—gasped and stopped so abruptly that pins cascaded from her shawl while a comb and brush fell out of her hair. She looked every bit of one hundred and one years, five months, and a day.

Before I could remember whether or not that really was her age or merely a joke, she took a good look at me.

"Botheration. I've already believed six impossible things and I'm ready for breakfast, not for another impossibility."

"I'm sorry," I said, to make up for starting things off badly with eggs. Then, before I could stop myself, I asked, "Well, where's Carroll? Or Dodgson?"

A suddenly shrewd glint came from the faded blue eyes of the White Queen, and she whispered, "Here. Everywhere. An echo in memory; a holding fast in the nest of gladness, a shadow of a sigh. No matter what happens. Checkmate."

"Well, I hardly think . . ."

"It's not your job to think, hardly or otherwise. It's your job to do something about the bad changes. Make a memorandum of it, and don't omit your feelings."

"What bad changes?" Then I remembered the book's plot. "The child Alice is supposed to be here before you. Where is she?"

"Little Alice, my White Pawn, had been doing well through the first two squares," the White Queen said with a melancholy bleat in her voice, "and she even kept up with the Red Queen's race. She's had amnesia and lost it; she's coped with the identical twins (all identical twins being mirror images of each other, you know), but now she's . . ."

The White Queen stopped and suddenly screamed as piercingly as the whistle of a steam engine.

"What's the matter?"

"Oh, oh, oh, oh! Mixed up! Still mixed up! Since that awful old Alice was here. Any moment now there'll be death and disaster . . ."

"Is that why you screamed? Over something that hasn't happened yet?"

"Well, of course," said the White Queen. "I'm the only one around here who can remember what's going to happen in all the Alice universes. I live backwards, so I remember backwards and forwards, real and unreal, young and old, light and dark, summer and winter, autumn and July, hither and yon, now and then . . ."

I interrupted, because it seemed as if she'd go on forever. "You haven't told me what the bad changes are."

"It was her fault. That old Alice, wearing my clothes just the way you are, implying that little Alice turns into me, which wasn't the case and shouldn't happen to a nice child. Pawns turn into Queens if they're lucky, but their own sort, not somebody else's."

"You don't make any sense," I said angrily. "My Aunt Alice gave me this coat and I can't help it being like yours. Anyway, you're merely part of a feverish hallucination and I'm not only not a chess piece, I'm not part of any fictional game."

"Fiction?" The White Queen plucked at her drooping shawl. "If it makes you happier to think that way, go ahead. But I do wish you could remedy the situation."

"What situation?"

"Little Alice never meeting the White Knight. It will break his heart. Your aunt should have been punished for her envy, but perhaps you're here as a substitute. You'll be the better for the punishment, I know."

"I don't intend to be punished."

"But you are. She sent you here, without a word of advice, and if you don't fix things I'm going to order that you won't get even jam during the next week of Tuesdays."

"I have nothing to do with any of this," I said, struggling to remind myself that I must be feverish. It seemed to be getting lighter in the wood, as if a cloud had passed, yet the light was sinister. Was something horrible coming? I looked around for a looking glass so I could get out, but there was nothing to be seen, just the loneliness of the place.

"There, there," said the White Queen, patting my head. "Don't go on like that. Perhaps you've been punished enough. Remember that you're a great girl and you must stop crying."

I was. Crying, that is. I couldn't stop. The tears just went on wetting my face and clogging up my nose. I felt lost in this alien place, and it was becoming more alien, for a dreadful shriek rang out, followed by a crash and then a hideous crunching noise. It wasn't the White Queen, for she was still talking.

". . . that's better. You've stopped crying. Be good and it's jam today, even semper jam. Remember it's the rule to try to consider things so you can manage to be glad."

"Glad?" I cried, "when there's a noise that sounds like death? What's happening?"

"Nothing can be done about that, but you can still fix the rest. Here's little Alice."

The child who ran down the path toward us was an eerie duplicate, not of Tenniel's pictures, but of a photo I'd seen of Aunt Alice as a child. Only this little Alice's eyes were wide with fright.

"The Jabberwock is loose! It came whiffling and burbling through the tulgey wood, its eyes all aflame, and it just ate Humpty Dumpty, leaving over some of the yolk—oh, its jaws are so messy! And now I think it's looking for me!"

"This is not in the book!" I exclaimed, forgetting to be careful.

The White Queen jabbed my side with her elbow—I could feel it even through the thick down—and said to little Alice, "Pay no attention to her. She's out of temper and in that state of mind where she wants to deny something."

"And I know what to deny!" I yelled triumphantly. "All of you! All of this!"

Little Alice was staring at me as if I were crazier than the White Queen. "Are there three of you, now?"

"I am not a White Queen," I said indignantly. "I am not from around here. I'm from California."

"Is that on the weird side of the Looking Glass, too?"

"Not exactly," I said slowly.

Little Alice looked up at me sadly. "You don't sound as if you know the way out, either. I'm not having fun since I met that sad lady like you, only old, and I want to go home before the Jabberwock eats me."

"Where is—that old lady?" I asked.

"Gone. She said she wanted to make her own universes. I didn't know what she meant. She didn't like me, and she was so sad that it was catching. I do want to go home, because I'm getting older and older and older . . ."

"Now listen here, Alice," I said, choosing my words with care. "You're not old. You're not like us."

"Well, you're not terribly old," Alice said, studying me. "You look much more the way I'd like to be when I grow up."

"That's nice," I said, absurdly pleased. "But right now you're seven and a half exactly, and it doesn't matter about Humpty Dumpty because he would have smashed anyway and all the king's horses and all the king's men . . .''

"Get on with it," said the White Queen. "Leave out the Egg. All he did was argue about the Jabberwock—or was it with the Jabberwock? No matter, he's breakfast, so get on with it."

I gulped. "Remember, Alice, you're not old, and you'll get home safely. Right now you're going to go on having fun here, with lots of adventures because they are ways you have fun with your mind. You'll especially enjoy the White Knight."

I suddenly shivered, remembering that Charles Dodgson, Lewis Carroll, and the White Knight were one.

"Will the White Knight keep the Jabberwock away?"

"Yes, Alice. Concentrate on the journey. That's the best part of the game."

Alice turned to the White Queen, who was fumblingly rearranging her shawl. "Is this Alice right?"

The White Queen winked at me and bestowed a foolish smile on little Alice. "Now you won't miss your White Knight."

"Is he mine?"

"Yours," I said quickly. "It's supposed to be that way, even if it can't and won't last." I shivered again, knowing the words were my aunt's, coming to me through the damned coat.

"Won't last?" Alice said, her voice quivering.

I could hear a deep bass burbling, far off in the wood but coming closer.

"Well, nothing does—no, that's not true."

The White Queen peered into the wood, looked back at me, and flapped her shawl. "Truth is not quite another impossible thing. Try again; draw a long breath, shut your eyes, and get to it."

I did take a deep breath, but I didn't shut my eyes, not with the Jabberwock out there. "Alice, don't worry. I promise you that you'll get to the end of the game, and you'll go home. But no matter how old you get or how much you forget, you'll always remember the White Knight."

Alice looked puzzled, but then she smiled and asked the White Queen (as if knowing that I didn't know), "Which way is the next move for me?"

The White Queen pointed to another bend in the path. "Now run along and have a good time, dear. After your tryst with the White Knight, cross the brook to the eighth square—that's where you'll get your crown. I'll meet you there."

Alice curtseyed to both of us and, with happy eyes, vanished into the shadows of the trees.

After the echo of her footsteps died away, I noticed that the wood was silent.

"Has the Jabberwock stopped?"

"Been stopped. By the White Knight. Didn't you say he'd take care of things?"

"Yes, but . . ."

"It's your Alice universe, now, you know. Through joining."

"Nothing you say makes sense and I want to go home!"

"Very well," said the White Queen, and pushed me hard.

I flew through the mirror mist, landing in the hall just as Aunt Alice came in. Without a pause she said, "I see that your coat gave you an interesting time."

"I undid some of whatever the hell you did, I suppose by mistake because you were so unhappy then . . . now wait a minute, Aunt Alice! It wasn't—it couldn't be real. I must have a fever and I've been hallucinating."

She felt my forehead. "I don't think so, dear."

"But fantasy universes can't exist in time and space!"

Aunt Alice began to laugh.

"I am not amused," I said.

"Don't worry, dear niece. I understand that time and space can be thought of as fantasies, too."

"But—Carroll's, I mean Dodgson's universe—I mean, it isn't real, is it?"

"Wasn't it?"

"Only when I was in it. And that nonsense about joining. That doesn't happen when I read a book."

"It does if you're lucky. You and the author join. It's like love."

I was embarrassed. People of her generation shouldn't talk about love. "Isn't it more logical that, symbolically speaking, each reader creates a new universe with the author . . ."

"I believe that's what I was saying, dear," said Aunt Alice.

BIBLIOGRAPHY

Unless stated otherwise, all quotes from Isaac Asimov are, or were originally, from his letters to and his conversations with me.

There are short quotes from other people, with sources stated unless they were on notes I made long ago without writing down what the exact source was (like Russell Baker's newspaper columns).

I have alphabetically listed the books from which I took quoted material:

Foundation's Friends, edited by Martin H. Greenberg. TOR, 1989.

How to Enjoy Writing, by Janet and Isaac Asimov. Walker and Company, 1987.

I, Asimov, by Isaac Asimov. Doubleday, 1994.

In Memory Yet Green, by Isaac Asimov. Doubleday, 1979.

It's Been a Good Life, edited by Janet Asimov. Prometheus Books, 2002.

Laughing Space, edited by Isaac Asimov and Janet Jeppson. Houghton Mifflin, 1982.

The Lost Prince, by Frances Hodgson Burnett. Lippincott. Text copyright 1914, 1915, 1943.

Man on His Nature, by Sir Charles Sherrington. Cambridge University Press, 1951.

Murder at the Galactic Writers' Society, by Janet Asimov. DAW Books, 1995.

Perelandra, by C. S. Lewis. Macmillan, 1944.

The Ship and the Flame, by Jerre Mangione. A. A. Wyn, 1948.

The Tyrannosaurus Prescription, by Isaac Asimov. Prometheus Books, 1989.